SIN LIKE FLYNN

A REGENCY ROMANCE DUET

ALEXA ASTON
&
KATHRYN LE VEQUE

ONE MAGIC NIGHT

A REGENCY HISTORICAL ROMANCE

BY ALEXA ASTON

A SIN LIKE FLYNN NOVELLA

CHAPTER ONE

London—June 1813

H E LOOKED LIKE his Flynn brothers. Moved like them. Spoke like them.

Yet Aidan Flynn felt nothing like a Sinning Flynn.

His family had descended from a long-ago Irish pirate who had fallen in love with a Cornish lass and settled in Cornwall. Flynns had continued the family tradition of smuggling for several generations, including his own father, Sean Flynn. Da had continued smuggling and apparently was involved in other mysterious activities, which the crown had decided to reward, much to the chagrin of the *ton*. King George III had bestowed upon the commoner from Cornwall an earldom and land. With the title Earl of Sinbrook, a large estate, and his own vast wealth behind him, Da had married a duke's daughter, who had jilted her betrothed for the darkly handsome Sean Flynn.

And thus was born the legend of the first Sinning Flynn.

Though Da had taken the Flynn family business to legitimacy in recent years and now owned a large shipping empire with a huge fleet that traveled the globe, his four sons' legacies had been to live down the unscrupulous Sinbrook reputation.

The *ton* had no idea why the king had bestowed an earldom upon Sean Flynn. Thanks to George's periodic bouts of madness, no one in Polite Society was quite sure if it had been the mad king who had presented the gift of an earldom—or the rational one who appeared from time to time.

That led to the vicious gossip throughout the *ton* as to the enigmatic circumstances surrounding the Earl of Sinbrook. That murkiness, coupled with Da's smuggling and Mama's rejection of her oh-so-suitable fiancé, led to the division in Polite Society, where half its members accepted the Flynns because of their ties to the crown and the powerful, influential Duke of Savernake, while the other half rudely ignoring them— although no one had ever been brave enough to give any Flynn the cut direct.

Yet.

Instead of trying to assimilate into the *ton* and show they were beyond reproach, Aidan's three older brothers had embraced the family's blackened reputation, showing Polite Society that they were even wilder and more reckless than Sean Flynn ever dreamed of being.

From a young age, Aidan had sensed he was different from his brothers, more like his mother's side of the family. His brothers were all intelligent men, yet they scoffed at book learning. Carmack and Kellen had refused to go to university altogether, though Rory had attended Oxford. Aidan had insisted upon going to Cambridge, which his beloved grandfather, the Duke of Savernake, had attended. Aidan was drawn from an early age to Doo, his nickname for his grandfather. Apparently, he had not been able to say *Duke* when he was learning to talk and it had come out *Doo*. The nickname had stuck and Aidan was the only one of the four Flynn brothers who called the duke such.

He had insisted upon spending a portion of his summers with Doo after he turned eight. Those times away from his family with his grandfather were treasured ones. Doo took him out on his various estates and taught Aidan the lessons needed on how to run one successfully. Not that Aidan would ever inherit such an estate. As the youngest of four brothers, he would not inherit the title Earl of Sinbrook or receive any of the entailed lands belonging to the earldom. Any land he got, he would have to purchase himself. That had been a goal he'd set from an early age.

Because of it, he had also worked in his father's shipping business. Aidan had a head for figures, the same as Doo, and he worked closely with the manager who kept the ledgers for Flynn Fleet. By the time Aidan finished university and came to work fulltime in his father's shipping enterprise, Da had told Aidan he was the best prepared of all his Flynn sons to run a business. Any kind of business.

The gleam in his father's eyes let Aidan know that Da approved of him stepping out on his own. So while he maintained an office at Flynn Fleet in Falmouth, most of his time was spent managing his own private business.

Smuggling.

He supposed it was in his blood to be a smuggler as his ancestors had been. While his three older brothers often took risks in real life, Aidan was willing to take them as he smuggled goods. And smuggling was very, very profitable with the war with Bonaparte going on. His ships had increased in size and number and now, at twenty-eight, Aidan was wealthy in his own right, independent of his family's wealth. Mostly, he smuggled French luxury goods, keeping Doo and his *ton* friends in French brandy, silks, and perfumes. The war had gone on for what seemed to be forever but with the new allied coalition formed, consisting of England and six other powerful countries, Aidan knew the day was coming when the Little Corporal would taste defeat. The English were notoriously stubborn people and felt their naval superiority, coupled with the officers among their ranks, would defeat Bonaparte in the end, no matter how long it took.

Until then, Aidan planned to make as much money as possible. When the war was finally over, he would be able to retire with a massive fortune.

He supposed he would start some kind of legitimate business after that, most likely in shipping since it was what he knew. A part of him, though, longed for the life a country gentleman. He was interested in crops and breeding animals, especially horses. Doo had taught him quite a bit about horse breeding and encouraged his grandson in his endeavor. Because of it, Aidan actually had bought a few racehorses and kept a small stable. Instead of living near the sea, he might move further inland, closer to Doo, who's ducal country seat at Summerwood was twenty miles northeast of Dorchester.

All this led him to the idea that he would need to take a wife. Especially if he wanted to pass on his wealth and property to someone other than his brothers or their children.

That would be hard to do, though, thanks to the reputation he held as a Sinning Flynn. Carmack and Kellen, the two oldest Flynns, had been outrageous rakehells, cutting a large swath through the *ton* with their sexual escapades. Rory was now following in their footsteps. He was a womanizer, gambler, and known card sharp. The few times Aidan had bothered to attend events during the Season over the past few years, his brothers' reputations had preceded him. Though he was the grandson of a duke and the son of an earl, many in Polite Society viewed him with suspicion, mainly because of the Sinning Flynns' reputations and labeled him thus.

Because he wanted to fit into his family, Aidan had tried to live up to his brothers' roguish reputations, figuring he would never take a bride who came from the ranks of Polite Society and might as well enjoy his time whenever he came to town. When in London, he frequented gaming hells and found himself winning more often than not. He had one of the finest pairs of matched bays and would race anyone in his phaeton through Hyde Park, the higher the stakes, the better.

He had never lost a race.

He also had had a string of mistresses over the years when he came to town, keeping away from the houses of ill repute. He found he preferred getting his satisfaction from a mistress. He knew what to expect from them and the understanding was reciprocated on their part. Usually, their affair would last a few weeks, no longer than a month or so, and then he would end it amicably, awarding his mistress with some pretty bauble for her time.

He was back in London now for the Season, arriving late last night. He had not come in the spring when it began because his smuggling operations had needed his full attention. Recently, however, Doo had sent him a letter, asking him to come by summer solstice, when Doo's famous Stag Ball would be held. The ball achieved its nickname because the Duke of Savernake's standard was a stag. Aidan and his brothers always tried to attend the Stag Ball, which had a reputation of wild and wonderful things occurring during it. In fact, both Carmack and Kellen had found their brides during this very ball. Even

Aidan had heard the old saying that a reformed rogue made for the best husband—and he had witnessed this with his two older brothers. Both Carmack and Kellen had been tamed by strong women and now they stayed happily in Cornwall, not bothering to attend the Season, much as his parents did.

Aidan knew, however, that Rory would be at the Stag Ball, too. He had said as much before he left Cornwall. His hot-headed, brilliant brother had bragged, telling Aidan that he planned to land a bride at the Stag Ball—one taken for revenge.

Without being told, he knew exactly what that would entail—ensnaring one of the daughters of the Earl of Exford. Exford was the man their mother had tossed aside decades ago when she had fallen in love with the new Earl of Sinbrook. Lord Exford had never forgiven his former fiancée for that particular sin. While Exford had married well and had two daughters, he continually badmouthed the Flynns to anyone willing to listen. In fact, Aidan wouldn't be surprised if had been Lord Exford who had hung the albatross moniker about their necks.

"Sinning Flynns," he muttered to himself, disgusted by it.

His family was a good one. Hardworking. Loyal to a fault. If only his brothers hadn't raised so much holy hell when they were in town, leaving him with a reputation already in tatters before he ever stepped into Polite Society.

Aidan rose from his bed and rang for hot water so he could shave himself. He didn't employ a valet, another breech the *ton* would never forgive. He thought the idea ridiculous, one man dressing another, as if he weren't capable of doing so himself. In fact, he thought most of the unwritten rules of Polite Society to be completely absurd. He was only here because Doo had asked him to come. He had no plan to attend any *ton* events beyond his grandfather's Stag Ball. He would visit his banker and solicitor while in town. Aidan had men in the same positions back in Falmouth but he also employed ones here in town. He wanted to discuss some of his investments with them because he had plans of adding another ship to his smuggling operations. Since he believed the war would come to an end in the next year or two, Aidan wanted to get as many black market goods out of France as he could, making as much profit as possible.

Then he would see about turning his small enterprise legitimate. Perhaps Da would wish for Flynn Fleet to buy Aidan's ships. If not, he had made connections in London and could sell off what he owned, making a tidy profit from the sale. Or he might even do what Da had done and become a true, law-abiding citizen and simply operate a small shipping company. He might need to relocate, however, because he wouldn't want to be in direct competition with Flynn Fleet. And there was still the thought of buying land and breeding racehorses. He was young and still had time before he needed to finalize the plans for his life, including settling down.

A servant appeared with the hot water. "Anything else for you, Mr. Aidan?"

Having arrived at Doo's London townhouse late last night, Aidan wondered if Rory was already in residence.

"Has my brother arrived by any chance?" he asked.

The servant nodded. "Mr. Rory came four days ago. I haven't seen him in the last day or two."

That meant Rory was on a winning streak and had probably stayed at one of the gaming hells he frequented.

"Will His Grace be downstairs for breakfast?"

"His Grace is always at breakfast, come rain or shine, Mr. Aidan."

The servant left and he washed and shaved before dressing, making his way downstairs to the breakfast room. As he did, he saw the flurry of activity as servants scurried back and forth. With the Stag Ball happening tonight, the household would be a busy one today, reason enough to get out and see to some of his business interests.

He passed Simms, Doo's longtime butler, and nodded a greeting. Doo thought so much of Simms that he took the butler with him to whichever of the five households he traveled to. Doo once said Simms was brighter and wiser than any man in the House of Lords.

Entering the breakfast room, he saw Doo already present and went to hug his grandfather. Though they regularly exchanged letters, Aidan had not seen his grandfather since last autumn. It surprised him how thin Doo had grown in that span of time. Though eighty, the old man still had a headful of hair, which had finally grayed a decade ago and then turned white during the last two years. As always, his posture was that of a duke, as he sat ramrod straight in his chair.

As Aidan approached, worry filled him. Doo had never appeared old to him yet he seemed so now, prominent lines about his eyes and mouth.

"Good morning, Doo," he said, embracing his grandfather and inhaling the familiar bergamot scent he always associated with Doo. It alarmed him just how thin Doo was beneath his tailored coat.

"Grandson. How are you?"

"I am well. Business is booming."

Aidan took a seat to Doo's right and they spoke of inconsequential things after that, neither man being one to openly speak in front of servants regarding anything of consequence, though many of the *ton* did so, spilling their secrets as servants waited upon them hand and foot. Doo had emphasized to Aidan from a young age to keep his mouth shut until behind closed doors—and even then speak very softly—because servants listened behind every door.

"What will you do while in town?"

"I plan to see my solicitor and banker and also stop at Tattersall's. I was hoping you might wish to go with me."

Doo's eyes gleamed. "I do love a trip to Tattersall's. What are you interested in purchasing?"

"This is more of a browsing trip. Unless a particular horse catches my eye."

"I read in the newspapers how Dandy won his last two races."

Doo referred to the best racehorse Aidan owned. "Yes, and Galahad will soon be running in his first race."

"I believe that horse has immense potential."

They discussed both horses and racing in general and then Doo asked, "Would you care to come to my study? I have a few matters to discuss with you."

"Of course."

He rose and saw Doo was having a bit of trouble doing the same so he helped move the chair out and assisted his grandfather to his feet. This troubled him. Doo had always been physically fit and of sound mind, even at his advanced age.

"Take my arm," he urged quietly and Doo did so as they left the breakfast room and moved at a much slower than usual pace to the study.

This room held wonderful memories for Aidan. He and Doo had spent countless hours in it, discussing everything from history to horses to crop rotation. The room smelled faintly of the pipe tobacco Doo frequently used.

He helped seat his grandfather by the window and took a chair opposite him.

"I have things to say to you, Aidan," Doo began.

"I thought as much when I received your summons to come to town."

"I know you aren't much for the Season and its many events."

"Can you blame me?" he asked, honest as always when in his grandfather's presence. "Polite Society has never welcomed the Sinning Flynns into their fold. Oh, we are invited to affairs, mainly to allow the *ton* to be entertained by their gossip regarding us. At least my brothers' antics have entertained the masses up until now."

Doo studied him a long moment. "You always have been different from your brothers. Yes, you resemble them physically. I know you have acted in a manner to fit in with them, wenching and gambling and racing. But you have always been more like your mother. Like me."

It was true. Aidan's nature was quieter than his boisterous brothers. When he had gone off to university, he had been in his element, studying the classics and history and architecture. Around his family, though, he always tried to fit in—and that meant acting like a Sinning Flynn.

"The *ton* thinks I am exactly like my brothers. I love them, Doo, you know that. I am as loyal to the Flynns as I can be. But am I one for madcap adventures as they are? No. Oh, I have gone along with them countless times, simply to show them that I am one of them. But my nature is different."

"I know that, Aidan. And I have a request of you now. You have been such a blessing to me all these years. I am closer to you than my own son."

Aidan had never liked Uncle Martin, who was the Marquess of Martindale. His mother's older brother had been bitterly disappointed when she flouted Polite Society and jilted Lord Exford to marry the Earl of Sinbrook. Uncle Martin avoided the Sinning Flynns whenever any of them came to town. Aidan knew he regarded them all as inferior upstarts. The few times Aidan had been in Uncle Martin's presence, the marquess had displayed such an air of superiority that it sickened him. Aidan was just as embarrassed to be related to Uncle Martin as his uncle apparently felt about the familial connection with all his Flynn nephews.

"I have always enjoyed time spent with you, Doo. You know that."

Doo's gaze penetrated to Aidan's soul. "I have already arranged matters with my solicitors and now I am sharing this information with you. Larkhaven is to be yours. With conditions."

Shock rippled through him. "What?"

Larkhaven was Doo's favorite estate, small when compared to Summerwood, the ducal country seat located ten miles northeast of Dorchester in Dorset. Many times when Aidan had come to Doo during the summers, they would wind up journeying to Larkhaven, which was twenty-five miles east of Dorchester and only three miles outside Swanage, a coastal village in southeast Dorset. They both enjoyed being close to the sea and enjoyed hours of sailing and fishing together.

He shook his head vigorously. "You cannot do that, Doo. When you are gone, Uncle Martin will inherit Larkhaven."

"No, he won't," his grandfather said, steel in his voice. "Two of my estates are unentailed, which means I do not have to pass them along to my heir apparent. I know how much you love Larkhaven, Aidan. I want the property to be yours. You love the land. You could continue to have tenants farm it. A portion of it could be used to raise your horses. And you could even settle down and bring up your family there."

His head swirled with thoughts. It was true. Larkhaven was embedded in his soul. Living there would always bring sweet memories of his times with Doo. Then he recalled what his grandfather had said.

"You mentioned conditions. What exactly would those be?"

"Ah, we get to the heart of the matter now," Doo said. "You will inherit Larkhaven *if* you wed in the next two weeks. In fact, that is why I wanted you present this evening. I would prefer that you find your bride at my Stag Ball."

"Are you joking?" Confusion filled him. "Why would I need to wed within two weeks?"

"Because I am dying."

Aidan felt as if he'd been punched in the gut. "No," he said hoarsely.

Doo gazed at him in sympathy. "I am sure you noticed I have lost weight since we last saw one another. I have also grown weak and frail."

"I don't believe it," he said stubbornly, ignoring everything he had seen this morning.

"You must, my boy. I lost my appetite around Christmastime. The doctors—and I have consulted several—all say there is something eating me up inside. This will be my last Stag Ball, though I do hope Martindale will continue the tradition."

He heard Doo's words but his mind refused to comprehend a world without Doo in it.

"My brothers would object if you give me land," he said. "It would anger them that you favored me in such a fashion. I don't wish to create animosity between us."

Doo shook his head slowly. "They know how close we are. None of them would care. They have never been interested in land. They are tied to the sea, as Flynns always have been. Besides, they are wealthy in their own rights—and I will bequeath something to each of them, as well. They will not be neglected.

"But you, Aidan, have always seen me for who I am. Not a duke, but a man. The bond between us is unbreakable. I wish for you to realize your own dream. To own land. Land you love. You could move your smuggling operation to Swanage if you must. Frankly, I hope you will decide to step away from it altogether. Being an earl's son will not protect you if you are caught by the authorities."

"Why should I retreat? The war is still going on. My profits are skyrocketing. Many of the *ton*, including your closest friends, greedily look forward to what I provide for them."

"My advice to you—and I hope you will take it—is to quit while you are ahead. That has been my philosophy when playing cards and I have found it to be useful in other areas of life, as well."

Doo looked at him sternly. "You are to find a bride at my ball or there will be no Larkhaven for you. I want a wedding no longer than two weeks from today, Aidan. Because I want to see you wed while I still can."

CHAPTER TWO

LADY LARISSA WARREN tossed aside the bedclothes and rose. Strong sunlight streamed into her bedchamber. Excitement filled her, knowing tonight was the Stag Ball, the annual event held by the Duke of Savernake, one of the most powerful men in all of England. The ball was known for being a place where strange and wonderful things occurred each year, with several couples coming away from it engaged.

She wished with all her soul that she might be one of them.

Not that she had any particular suitors this Season. In fact, she knew of no one who would be calling upon her this afternoon. No bouquets of sweet-smelling flowers would be delivered. It would be another thing Mama chose to berate her about. Being in her second Season, Mama had already thought Larissa would be wed and off her hands after the first one. Not that her mother ever truly had much to do with her. She hadn't cared for any of her children and made that obvious. Mama ascribed to the adage that children should be seen and not heard.

While she had friends whose mothers were their confidantes and friends, Larissa's mother had kept her distance from the time Larissa was in the nursery. She had with all her children. Mama was not the nurturing kind and while friendly and polite to others, her acerbic tongue often lashed out at her children.

Peter didn't care. Her older brother was thoughtless and selfish and had never listened to Mama. He was a rogue of the worst sort, following in the footsteps of their father, who had had countless affairs with women in the *ton* and a string of mistresses which he was frequently seen in public with, from the opera to the theatre. Perhaps that was why her mother was the way she was. Larissa had learned through gossip that Mama had been in love with a young man but was forced by her parents to wed the Earl of Campton. She had produced the requisite heir but failed twice in adding a spare, having two females instead. Her parents rarely spent time in the same room and when they found themselves face-to-face with one another, simply turned and both left. The *ton*, who gossiped ferociously, said the earl and countess loathed one another with a deadly calm.

Larissa wondered if they hated her, as well.

Peter, as the heir, had always had their father's ear. The Earl of Campton was a man's man, one who had little use for a female unless she was spreading her legs for him. He had ignored both his daughters but did save cruel barbs for Larissa. She hadn't understood as a child why he would single her out in such a manner. When she grew older, she began to understand.

She doubted she was his daughter.

Her brother took after Father, with his height and dark hair and brown eyes. Cressida, her younger sister, also had the Warren height and coloring. Larissa, however, possessed a head of auburn hair and sky blue eyes and had a dimple in her right cheek that appeared whenever she smiled. Since Mama was blond and had brown eyes, Larissa was the misfit in her family.

While Father was open and flaunted his affairs, Mama was more discreet, as Polite Society expected of women who strayed from their marital vows. Larissa supposed she was the result of one of Mama's affairs and had been passed off as a Warren. When she met Lord Silverton during her come-out last Season, she knew she had found the man who had sired her. The viscount had her eyes. Her smile. The same dimple in his right cheek. And though he was going white at his temples and bits of white were woven through his hair, it was the same shade of auburn as hers. Lord Silverton had been most polite to her when Mama had introduced them and Larissa had found him studying her from a distance on more than one occasion.

Though her parents and brother had little to do with her, at least Larissa had had Cressida. Her sister was the sweetest soul, always thoughtful and with a kind word for all. Unfortunately, she had been frail from birth and was frequently ill. Mama, selfish woman that she was, had claimed she could not be around anyone who was ill, not even her own flesh and blood. For that reason, it had been Larissa who nursed her sister during the last three years of her life. Cressida had been diagnosed with consumption and it had taken that long for her to waste away. A bit of Larissa had died every day, watching Cressida fade into nothingness.

Because of her sister's lingering illness, Larissa had not made her come-out when other girls did. She had kept watch over Cressida at their country estate until her sister passed two years ago. After a year in mourning, which neither her father nor brother observed, Larissa made her come-out at two and twenty last Season. It had been underwhelming. She had felt out of step at *ton* affairs. Her friends, all whom had made their own come-outs on schedule, were now wed and mothers themselves. The new crop of debutantes didn't really care to make friends with someone Larissa's age. In fact, one rude young lady had told Larissa that her time had passed and she was already on the shelf.

The girl was probably right.

While fairly pretty, Larissa had what was considered only an adequate dowry, Polite Society's way of saying it was rather small. Most men sought a substantial dowry and good political connections. With her father—and now Peter—being notorious womanizers, no gentleman had stepped up and shown much interest in her. Mama lamented Larissa's lack of callers, even telling her that outfitting her for the Season was expensive and that if she did not land a husband this second time around, there would not be a third one.

She didn't know if this would mean she would be banished to the country or languish in town while she watched her parents leave to go to events.

That was why she needed to find a husband at tonight's Stag Ball. It had a reputation for bringing lovers together. She had prayed she would find a husband at it. If she didn't, she hated to think what her future might hold, as the Season wound down and she returned to the country once again.

The problem was that any of the men who had come around had either been friends of Peter's from university or other rakehells, assuming that because her entire family was loose in their morals that she also would be the same. More than anything, Larissa was bound and determined not to wed a rogue. She wanted a kind, faithful man, one who was steadfast and would be a good husband and father to their children. She desperately wanted children. She had been a mother to Cressida for all those years and had so much love in her heart to give to little ones.

How could she let the *ton* know she didn't run in a fast crowd? That she yearned for a faithful man? She wasn't so foolish as to believe in love, much less that it would find her. All she needed was a gentleman who would treat her with kindness and respect.

Her maid appeared with a pitcher of hot water. "Good morning, my lady."

"Good morning, Lizzy," she replied.

The servant's eyes sparkled. "Tonight is the night, isn't it? The Stag Ball."

"It is," Larissa confirmed. "We need to go this morning for the final fitting of my ball gown."

She hated that the modiste had dragged her feet with this particular dress. All her wardrobe had been completed a good two months ago except for this special gown, meant for the Stag Ball. If it did not fit perfectly when she tried it on, she and Lizzy would have to put their heads together and figure out what she could wear in its stead.

"We will go to the modiste's shop after I breakfast," she told Lizzy.

The maid helped Larissa to dress and then she went downstairs, hoping no one would be in the breakfast room. It was late for her father to still be there and much too early for Peter to make an appearance if he were at home. He rarely was, usually staying at his mistress' house or club. Fortunately, Mama always took a tray in her room so Larissa never had to face her before noon.

Unfortunately, her father lingered over his coffee and the

newspapers. She said a crisp good morning as a footman seated her.

The earl never acknowledged her presence.

A footman brought her tea and a few minutes later, the kitchen sent breakfast in for her. She never was hungry when she awoke in the morning during the Season. The lavish midnight buffets had her belly still full. She would eat a light breakfast and then wait for tea in the afternoon for something more substantial. Actually, she might buy something from one of the street vendors while she and Lizzy were out to collect her gown. Somehow, street food always tasted the best to her.

Her father folded his paper and took a final sip of his coffee. Rising, he actually looked at her. She couldn't remember the last time that had occurred. Her nerves began to fray at the stare.

"Find a husband tonight," he snapped. "I won't pay for another Season's wardrobe for . . . the likes of . . . *you*."

The last word was spoken with so much contempt that she flinched.

"If you don't," he continued, "then I will find one for you. I hear Lord Langdon is in the market for a bride."

Horror filled her. Lord Langdon was sixty if a day and had already outlived four wives. The thought of coupling with the fat, beady-eyed earl caused a shudder to run through her.

Her father left his spot and came to stand beside her. Larissa met his gaze with trepidation.

"I mean it, Girl. I want you off my hands. If you want it to be your choice, then you have until the ball ends to find yourself a mate. If you come up emptyhanded?" His eyes narrowed. "Then it will be my pick."

He strolled from the room as if he hadn't a care in the world, leaving her sick to her stomach.

Today was the summer solstice, the longest day of the year. Sunset would not occur until almost ten o'clock tonight. The Duke of Savernake's Stag Ball lasted all night as his guests celebrated the midsummer day as their ancestors did in ancient cultures centuries ago. After the midnight buffet, guests would take to the square in front of His Grace's townhouse, where a large bonfire would be lit as in days of yore. She had read where bonfires were associated with magic and people thought they could banish evil spirts that roamed the earth, as well as lead young women to their future husbands. Last year's display, the first she had ever seen, had been most impressive.

After the bonfire, the duke's guests would return to the ballroom and dance until dawn, when the sun rose around a quarter to five this time of year.

Could she possibly convince someone to marry her in the next eighteen hours?

If she didn't, then her fate would be sealed and she would become another doomed bride of Lord Langdon. Two had died in childbirth. One had fallen from their terrace and broken her neck. The last one had died of childbed fever and the babe only lasted a day longer than his mother.

Larissa did not plan on dying anytime soon.

That meant she would have to do whatever it took to persuade some eligible bachelor to marry her.

Determination filled her. She would not go quietly into Lord Langdon's arms. Somehow, some way, she would coax, entice, urge—or even tempt—some gentleman of the *ton* to offer for her. She hadn't a deceitful bone in her body so she didn't believe she could trap a man into ruining her.

If she didn't, though, she would spend the rest of her life miserable.

Larissa vowed to do whatever it took to find a husband tonight.

Even if it meant selling her soul.

CHAPTER THREE

Doo's fatalistic tone shook Aidan to his core. While he had always thought of Da as being larger than life, his grandfather had been the steadying influence on Aidan for his entire twenty-eight years. To think this time next year that the Stag Ball would be opened by Uncle Martin cut him to his core.

"Give me more details of your illness, Doo," he demanded. "I want you to see another doctor—another dozen if we have to. Medicine has advanced so much in the last several years. This is the nineteenth century, after all. We aren't living in the Dark Ages when superstition ruled and illness was thought to be payment for your sins."

His grandfather shook his head. "I am done with all that, Aidan. I accept my fate. I wish for you to do the same. My time is up. I have walked this earth for eighty years and am happy, for the most part, with how my life turned out." He frowned. "I am not quite happy leaving my title and the bulk of my lands in Martindale's hands. It is why I want to give you something all your own."

"I don't want Larkhaven," he said stubbornly. "It means nothing to me without you here."

Doo snorted. "Oh, so you want your uncle to sell it? It is unentailed. If anything, Martindale is a skinflint. He wants money by any means possible. Because Larkhaven is unentailed, I fully expect my son to sell it off before I turn cold in my grave." Doo paused. "He'll do it. You know he will. And I would hate for it to leave the family. It is the place I love best."

Larkhaven was special. The times he and Doo had spent there provided Aidan with many wonderful, lasting memories. His grandfather was right. Uncle Martin was tightfisted with money and always wanting to amass more. The fact he was close to sixty and had waited all his life to inherit the dukedom had stuck in his craw. Aidan smiled at the reaction his uncle would have, knowing he had no control over Larkhaven.

"No, I don't want it to leave the family." He gazed steadily at his grandfather. "I want Larkhaven and will do whatever it takes to get it. But you knew that, didn't you?"

Doo chuckled. "I did. Then you'll find a bride tonight?"

He shrugged. "I will try my very best, Doo, but you know what the *ton* thinks of the Sinning Flynns. Even if my parents hadn't caused such a tremendous scandal years ago, Carmack and Kellen spent a decade titillating Polite Society with their outlandish behavior and antics. You know what the gossip columns said of them—that the Sinning Flynns were wicked, carnal, amorous rakehells, bent on bedding every female in sight."

"But they found women to wed," Doo pointed out. "Look at those boys now. They are fine, upstanding, law-abiding citizens who are faithful to their wives."

Aidan raked a hand through his thick hair. "I haven't even mentioned Rory."

Doo nodded. "Yes, Rory is a wild one."

"Wild doesn't even begin to describe his reputation. He pushes the boundaries even more than Carmack and Kellen ever did, making their antics look like child's play. Rory is a libertine of the worst sort. His risqué conduct has cemented the Sinning Flynns' reputation in everyone's mind. His drinking and gaming are out of hand, not to mention the women. How am I supposed to live down the reputation of the Sinning Flynns and find a respectable woman who might take a chance and wed me? Not to mention, I only have one night to convince her before I purchase a special license and drag her to the altar." He shook his head in despair.

Doo smiled indulgently. "You have always been a clever lad, Aidan. You will find a way. I have no doubt. If you want Larkhaven badly enough, you will use your persuasive skills to convince an attractive, intelligent woman to wed you."

"Why tonight, Doo? Can't you give me a little longer? I haven't even attended a single event this Season. I am going into this blind, not knowing anything about the women who have made their come-outs this year."

His grandfather frowned sternly. "I have told you. I don't have a little longer," he said flatly. "In another two weeks, I will be bedridden—or dead."

Doo sucked in a breath, pain flashing across his face.

Immediately, Aidan fell to his knees before his grandfather. "What can I do?"

Grimacing, Doo said, "I want to see you wed, Aidan. I wish to meet the woman who will be the mother of your children."

He moaned suddenly and Aidan knew the pain growing inside him must be great because Doo was the most stoic man he knew.

"I know you think I am forcing your hand, Grandson. Perhaps I selfishly am. But I want what I want—and I am a duke."

"And a duke always gets what he wants," finished Aidan.

He had heard Doo say the phrase enough times. But to find a bride in a single night? Especially when Polite Society looked down its nose upon the Sinning Flynns so much? What woman would be foolish enough to risk her entire future in order to take a chance on him? Better yet, what father would be willing to hand over his daughter to a Sinning Flynn?

What if Doo was wrong about his diagnosis and he actually had longer to live?

Aidan determined to go at once and see Dr. Lawford now. Hear the truth. Just to make certain Doo was not playing him.

"I have much to think about," he said. "I need some time alone to sort through things."

Doo bit back a groan. "And I need to go to bed to rest for tonight's festivities. I plan to spend most of my day there so I can make a series of appearances tonight. It is important that I be seen. Dance the opening number. That kind of thing."

"You won't be present the entire time?"

"It is doubtful I could manage that, Aidan. I tire easily. After the receiving line ends, I will open the ball and then disappear for a few hours. I won't be missed. There will be too many guests here, doing God only knows what." He grinned. "After all, it *is* the Stag Ball. You know what they say— remarkable things happen at my ball each year."

His grandfather sighed. "I will appear again for the midnight buffet and make the rounds of a few tables before I leave and rest again. Then I will be the one to light the bonfire. Perhaps you and Rory will want to do so with me."

"If you wish," Aidan said reluctantly, knowing how that would irk Uncle Martin.

"I will announce that I am making myself scarce for the rest of the night. After all, I am an old man and will tell the others my dancing days are done. That they are to dance until dawn— but this man needs his beauty sleep."

Aidan couldn't help but chuckle. Doo had always had a keen sense of humor.

He rose and kissed his grandfather's cheek. "Let me get you upstairs to your bedchamber. I will come and see you before the Stag Ball starts."

Doo rose shakily and Aidan swept the old man up in his arms, fully realizing now how gaunt and light Doo was.

Carrying him from the study into the hall, he found Simms lingering there. The butler followed them upstairs. Aidan placed his grandfather on the bed.

"I will see that His Grace gets settled," Simms said, walking Aidan to the door.

"Is he still seeing Dr. Lawford?" he asked quietly.

"Yes, Mr. Aidan."

"Then I am going to see Lawford now."

Sadness filled the butler's eyes. "It won't change the situation, my lord."

"I want answers, Simms. Hopefully, Dr. Lawford will provide them."

Leaving the house, he hailed a hansom cab, giving the driver the address. He hadn't wanted to use the ducal carriage. It simply wasn't his way.

Aidan wondered if Rory had seen Doo and what he thought. If he knew the old man was dying. Knowing Rory, he was so wrapped up in himself and his plans for revenge that he hadn't truly seen what was before him. Rory's vices were many and he usually became caught up in them anytime he came to town.

The cabdriver slowed and Aidan climbed out, paying and then dismissing him. He didn't know how long he would have to wait to see Dr. Lawford or how much time he would spend with the physician.

Entering the offices, he used the one card he rarely did.

"I am the grandson of the Duke of Savernake. I wish to see Dr. Lawford as soon as possible," he told the clerk.

The man's eyes widened considerably. "I see. Please wait here a moment, my lord."

The clerk quickly vanished without Aidan correcting him. Yes, in most every case a duke's grandson would hold a title. As the youngest son of an earl, however, Aidan was the Honorable Mr. Flynn in correspondence and simply Mr. Flynn in public. The only exceptions were their servants and Doo's addressing each son by his first name, since having that many Mr. Flynns in the household became too confusing.

The clerk reappeared. "Dr. Lawford will see you now, my lord. If you will follow me."

Aidan did so, moving through what he assumed was a waiting room since several people sat in chairs, all meanly dressed. Several of them hacked away, while others looked feverish or jaundiced. He didn't know Lawford saw members of the public, assuming he would restrict his services to the *ton*. Guilt filled him for jumping ahead of people who were suffering but it was too late. They were already in a corridor and the clerk knocked upon on a door.

"Come," a deep voice said.

"Go in, my lord."

Aidan did so, finding Dr. Lawford sitting behind a large mahogany desk, stacks of papers in neat piles all across it.

He rose, offering his hand, which Aidan shook. "Mr. Flynn. I am guessing you are here to discuss His Grace's case."

"I am. My grandfather says he is dying."

"Have a seat, please."

They sat and the physician said, "His Grace is being eaten up on the inside by something we call cancer. We know little about it—other than it is fatal."

Aidan swallowed, trying to get his emotions under control. "Tell me about this disease."

Dr. Lawford shook his head sadly. "It is a tumor—a malignant one—which grows inside a person. Why, we have yet to determine. Once it invades the body, it expands and spreads destructively throughout. My suspicion is that it even can metastasize into the brain. Fortunately, His Grace does not seem to be exhibiting any symptoms of that. He is still coherent and maintains all his faculties."

"His Grace said he only has a few weeks."

"I believe a couple of weeks in which to move about freely. Or as best as he can. When I saw him yesterday, I noticed he is already having trouble walking. His balance will continue to erode." Dr. Lawford met Aidan's gaze. "Once ten days—or possibly two weeks pass—His Grace will be completely bedridden. The pain he is experiencing now will grow exponentially."

Aidan flinched. "Will you be able to give him something to ease it?"

"We can. Laudanum is the most effective. But once we do that, Mr. Flynn, His Grace will not be conscious except for brief periods of time. The laudanum not only dulls his pain but his mind. He will have trouble forming thoughts, much less words."

Dr. Lawford paused. "His Grace has asked that I give him as long as possible before I administer the laudanum to him. But I will share with you that once he is too frail to leave his bed, the pain will be substantial and I will give him the opiate with speed. Because of that, I hope that you will make the time to stay in town with him. He loves you a great deal, Mr. Flynn. He loves all his grandchildren—but his relationship with you is quite special."

Tears stung Aidan's eyes. He now understood the gravity of the situation and that the Doo he knew wouldn't be here for long. That once Dr. Lawford began giving Doo doses of laudanum, his grandfather would have difficulty in conversing and lapse into death.

"I am sorry to share this with you, Mr. Flynn, but I believe it is important for you to know these details."

"I appreciate you taking the time to see me, Doctor, and your honesty regarding my grandfather's condition." Aidan rose. "I assure you that I will remain with His Grace until the end."

The physician smiled gently. "That will mean a great deal to him, Mr. Flynn." He paused. "Has His Grace discussed you taking a wife?"

The words took him aback. "He shared that with you?"

"His Grace is, shall we say, a very determined man," Dr. Lawford said. "He cares a great deal for you and wants to see you happy and settled before he departs this life."

"He has instructed me to find a woman to wed at tonight's Stag Ball." Aidan said. "Do you, in all honesty, believe a Sinning Flynn can do so?"

The physician nodded. "From what I hear—and read about in the newspapers—I believe a Sinning Flynn is capable of almost anything. Even if it is finding a bride in one night." Dr. Lawford smiled. "After all, aren't extraordinary things said to occur each year at the Stag Ball?"

Aidan thought he was being given far too much credit. In fact, he worried that everywhere he turned, he would have an invisible door slammed in his face.

"Thank you for your time, Dr. Lawford. I apologize for butting ahead of your other patients."

The physician smiled. "They are my charity cases, Mr. Flynn. While I do spend a great deal of my time catering to the ailments of Polite Society, I also wish to put my medical knowledge to good use for all."

"That is most admirable, Doctor. Good day."

As Aidan left, he made a mental note to instruct his banker to send a hefty donation to Lawford's medical practice. Very few men in his position would care about the poor and their illnesses.

He exited the building and began roaming the streets, wondering what magic he might concoct to fool Polite Society for a single night.

And convince them—and one still unknown single, eligible lady—that it was worth it to take a chance on a Sinning Flynn.

CHAPTER FOUR

L ARISSA EAGERLY WAITED as the carriage was brought around. She wished Mama would have wanted to go with her to her dress fitting but she had told Larissa that she had a headache and wanted to lie down and rest in order to be fresh for the Stag Ball. In truth, her mother had only gone with Larissa on the very first visit to Madame Floseau this season, back in late February. Mama and the dressmaker had discussed patterns and materials and, after that, Lizzy served as Larissa's chaperone to the dress shop each time.

She had noticed she didn't have nearly as many gowns made up this year as for her come-out Season. Because of that, she and Lizzy had put their heads together and remade a few of her dresses from the previous year so that no one would be able to tell they had been worn last Season. Lizzy was so talented with a needle and thread. Larissa hoped that if she managed to find her betrothed this evening that Papa would allow Lizzy to accompany Larissa to her new household.

Hopefully, a household of her choice—and not that of Lord Langdon.

She had no doubt that if she could not convince a gentleman to wed her this evening that Papa would choose someone horrible for her, possibly even worse than Lord Langdon, just to punish her for not being his own flesh and blood. She believed that was why her dowry was so small when compared to other girls making their come-outs. She had overheard several of them speaking of the amount of their dowries in the retiring room one evening early in the Season and was horrified at how miniscule hers was in comparison.

The pressure was now on her to find a decent man who would be good to her, one who wasn't in search of a huge dowry to prop up his ailing estate. To do that, she must look her best.

The gown she was about to try on would help.

It was a pale ice blue, set off her shoulders, and showing a discreet but ample amount of her bosom. When she had first tried it on, she felt like she was royalty. This gown must help her find her betrothed tonight. It simply had to.

The butler informed her that the carriage was waiting and she and Lizzy made their way outside. The June day had a few clouds with the sun peeking through them and no visible wind.

In the carriage, she said to her maid, "I must look my absolute best tonight, Lizzy," trying to keep her worry from her tone.

"You will look beautiful, my lady. After all, this is the best of all the ball gowns you have ever worn. I am glad you saved it for the Stag Ball. I'm able to read the newspapers sometimes, after his lordship and then then the butler and valet. They put them in the rubbish bin—and I take them out."

"I did not know you enjoyed reading them, Lizzy."

The servant's nose crinkled. "Oh, I don't like anything about politics or people getting robbed or murdered. But I do enjoy reading the gossip columns. They say fantastic things happen every year at the Stag Ball. Why, you might even find a husband tonight, my lady. Wouldn't that be grand?"

It would be if it did happen. But how should she even begin? Larissa did not know how to flirt and would feel foolish trying to do so. If she didn't, though, how was she to lure a gentleman in? Oh, dear, that sounded as if she were fishing for a husband, casting a line and slowly reeling it in, hoping to hook just the right man.

She would ask her friends tonight about flirting, though her three closest ones were all wed and their flirting days were far behind them. All had made good matches, according to Polite Society. Secretly, Larissa thought none of them were happy with the husbands they had. Ann and Ellen had been strongly urged by their parents to wed men they approved of. Betsy had wed the first gentleman who offered for her. Unfortunately, despite the fact he already had two children with Betsy, the viscount was already being unfaithful to her, if discreetly.

Was it too much to ask for a man who wouldn't betray her as her father did her mother over and over, even as Mama retaliated in kind?

Peter was no better. He bragged about not wishing to be leg-shackled until he was at least forty years of age. Larissa had even overheard him say to his friends on more than one occasion that he hoped his father would be dead by the time he decided to wed. He wanted to be the Earl of Campton in his own right and not on a quarterly allowance. At least he received money from their father's estate. Mama also got her pin money. Larissa got nothing. She had to beg her mother just to be able to purchase a book.

The carriage arrived at the dress shop and Lizzy asked, "Do

you mind if I stay here and take a nap, my lady? I will be up late tonight waiting for you. Besides, you know I get so bored standing around during your fittings."

"Of course, Lizzy. I know if I need anything that you will be right outside."

The footman handed her down and she entered the modiste's shop, spying Madame Floseau and greeting her. The modiste was very cool in her response and summoned an assistant to help fit Larissa. She found that odd. Usually, Madame did all final fittings herself.

A very bad feeling crept through her.

The assistant, however, was nice if a bit shy. She took her time and Larissa was pleased to see the gown fit perfectly.

"You have a lovely figure, Lady Larissa. Do you have a sweetheart?"

Blushing, she said, "No. In fact, I don't really have any suitors at all."

Frustration filled her. How was she to land a husband tonight when no one at all even seemed interested in her?

Of course, the one sure way to guarantee a marriage was to be found in a compromising position with a gentleman. Larissa had no idea how to get into one of those with a man and decided it would be impossible for her to do so. It would have to be the gentleman who would lead her into one. If she tried to get any of Peter's friends to walk her through the gardens or encourage them to kiss her during the bonfire, she feared they wouldn't be honorable and offer for her if they were caught together. In that case, she would be totally ruined. Not even Lord Langdon would want her and her measly dowry in those circumstances.

The assistant started to ease Larissa out of the gown when

Madame Floseau appeared.

"Wait," the modiste commanded, looking with her critical eye. "Turn. Slowly."

Larissa did as asked, feeling the modiste's eyes drilling into her.

Finally, Madame nodded. "I wish to speak to you when you are dressed again, my lady."

"Of course."

Her belly began churning as she wondered what the modiste might wish to discuss with her. She composed herself as she left the dressing area and returned to the main shop. Madame nodded brusquely and Larissa followed her into the back again. This time, they entered a private office.

"Have a seat, my lady," the modiste said, frowning as she took a seat behind the desk.

She decided to speak first, hoping to take control of a situation she feared might spiral out of control.

"I am disappointed it took so long for this gown to be fitted, Madame. Fortunately, no alterations will need to be made to it as it fit perfectly and you have done your usual, beautiful job. It will be perfect for tonight's Stag Ball."

"You will not be wearing it, Lady Larissa, unless I receive payment for it."

She felt the color draining from her face. "What do you mean? My father should have taken care of that, as he did payment for the rest of my wardrobe this Season."

Madame Floseau snorted. "Getting any coin from Lord Campton has been like wringing blood from a turnip. He has yet to pay for any of the outfits I have created for you this Season. In fact, I have sent the earl numerous bills, to no avail. I am afraid I cannot let this gown leave my shop unless I receive my full compensation."

The modiste stood. "I hope you will convey my message directly to his lordship, my lady. If payment can be sent this afternoon, I am more than happy to release the gown to you. In the meantime, good day."

Larissa rose shakily. She could feel her cheeks burning with embarrassment. "I will see to it, Madame. I am so sorry for this misunderstanding."

She left the office, feeling hollow, tears forming in her eyes. When she reached the main shop and caught the pitying look from the assistant who had fitted her, she lowered her head. Tears now began streaming down her cheeks.

She would have nothing to wear to the Stag Ball tonight. Her gut told her that her father wouldn't pay for anything else for her. Larissa felt like a fool. He might as well announce to the *ton* that she wasn't of his blood.

When she had first suspected he wasn't her sire, she had actually looked into what that might mean. In a bookshop she frequented, she found some used legal books for sale, perusing them for the information she sought. She learned by English law, any issue in a marriage is legally the husband's. That meant she would never be labeled as a bastard. At least in the eyes of the law, she was legally Lady Larissa Warren, daughter of the Earl and Countess of Campton.

That still didn't solve her current problem. Every suitable ball gown she possessed had already been seen by others this Season. While men probably didn't notice, the vipers of the *ton* certainly did. The gossip would begin tonight and continue at a ferocious pace. How was she to attend the Stag Ball in old clothes, much less win the attention of a gentleman who would be so besotted with her that he proposed marriage this very night?

She could never go to the earl and beg for him to pay the bill. Larissa could hear his biting remarks now and refused to lower herself.

Stepping out of the dressmaker's shop, she kept her head down, tears blinding her.

Then, unexpectedly, she collided with someone and felt herself falling before strong hands steadied her.

She glanced up, not able to see through her tears and began apologizing. "I am so sorry. I did not see you."

"I ran into you, my lady," a deep voice answered. "I am afraid I wasn't watching where I was going. I have a lot on my mind. I walk when I need to think."

Blinking furiously, Larissa's vision cleared enough for her to see the man who still grasped her elbows. He looked familiar. Had she seen him at a *ton* event before? If so, it had not been this Season because she would certainly remember one so handsome and striking as this gentleman. Perhaps he had come to a few affairs last Season.

He was tall. Very tall, as she looked up. At least a few inches over six feet. His coal-black hair was thick and slightly wavy. Striking emerald green eyes gazed back at her. His cheekbones were high and looked as if they could cut glass. His mouth was . . . sensual. Funny how she had never even thought of that word before yet it most certainly applied to this handsome man and his lips.

While some men of the *ton* padded their clothes to appear larger and broader, Larissa knew this man would never accept such a practice. He already was broad-shouldered, his coat and breeches fitted tightly to show off his muscular frame. She didn't believe fencing or riding would create this outstanding a physique. Something told her this man labored hard. Perhaps on his estate, where he might work side-by-side with his tenants, yet she had never heard of any gentleman doing such a thing.

He released her elbows and quickly handed her a handkerchief. She thanked him and wiped away her tears, embarrassment flooding her.

"What is wrong, my lady? Can I be of any help to you?"

The kindness in his eyes and tone caused a fresh flood of tears. "No one can help," she said, hopelessness escaping in her words.

"Tell me what ails you," he urged.

Having nothing to lose, she said, "I went for a final fitting for a gown to wear to the Duke of Savernake's ball tonight. It is the highlight of each Season and all of Polite Society will be there." She swallowed. "It was the dress of my dreams. I have never owned a gown lovelier than this one."

"Was there a problem with its fit? Had the modiste made a terrible mistake and ruined it?"

"No, my lord," Larissa said. "It actually fit beautifully. But Madame Floseau will not hand it over." She gave him a rueful smile through her tears. "It seems my father has not paid my modiste in quite some time."

Understanding filled those green eyes and she saw a flash of anger in them.

"So, the woman is holding your gown for ransom until she receives payment."

Larissa nodded. "I am afraid so." Knowing she had shared far too much than she should have, she added, "If you will excuse me, I must return home. I will work with my maid on trying to find something to wear so as not to embarrass myself."

He took her hand, surprising her, and bent over it, pressing a kiss against her knuckles. The gesture was kind—and yet the most marvelous tingle rippled along her spine.

"Whatever you decide to wear, you will look lovely in it," he declared.

Larissa blushed at his compliment.

"May I walk you to your carriage?" he asked.

"Yes, please. It is over here."

They approached it and she hesitated a moment before asking, "Will you be at the Stag Ball tonight?"

"Yes. It will be the first event I have come to this Season. I only arrived in town late last night." He smiled at her. "Perhaps you might even grant me a dance. Or perhaps we could watch the bonfire being lit together?"

"I would like that," she said shyly.

Lizzy popped her head out the window. "Lady Larissa, get in this carriage at once! You can't be talking to the likes of him."

The man chuckled. "I will see you tonight then, my lady."

He handed her up and she entered the carriage, feeling flushed as those wonderful tingles raced through her.

The carriage started up and he raised a hand. She waved back as they passed him.

And realized she had never learned his name.

CHAPTER FIVE

A IDAN WATCHED LADY Larissa's carriage as it moved down
the street. His heart went out to the beauty, knowing she
must be very sheltered. To have learned she would not be able
to receive the dress she yearned to wear to the most important
ball of the Season would be heartbreaking for most women. She
most likely wanted her favorite suitor to see her in it and offer
marriage to her. Aidan had heard how many gentlemen of the
ton proposed on summer solstice each year against the
backdrop of the Stag Ball.

It did more than irk him that Lady Larissa's modiste was
holding out on her, simply because the lady's father was a
bloody arse.

He decided he wanted to see her in her dream gown. Fortunately, he was in a position to be able to make than happen.

Aidan strode toward the dress shop and entered, seeing
three women within. An older one, obviously the Madame
Floseau whom Lady Larissa had referred to, hurried toward
him.

"*Bonjour, mon Seigneur.* Are you looking for something for
someone special?"

The way she said it, Aidan knew she meant for a mistress and not a wife.

"I am looking to see Lady Larissa's gown."

The modiste's mouth dropped as her two assistants twittered. "What? *Je ne comprends pas.*"

"You heard me," he said, gazing levelly at the Frenchwoman. "And I know you understand me. I wish to see Lady Larissa's gown. The one she left behind at your dress shop because you refused to give it to her."

The modiste's mouth set in a hard line. "I am a businesswoman, *mon Seigneur.* I cannot give away my clothes for free. Lord Campton would need to pay his bill before I would be able to release the gown to Lady Larissa."

"Bring the gown to me now," he commanded, giving her no choice.

"Of course," she said brusquely, leaving the room and heading through a set of curtains.

He browsed the shop for a few minutes until she returned, the gown draped over her arm.

"*Voilà!*" she said, holding it out.

Yes, the gown was lovely—and Lady Larissa would look ravishing in it. The shade would suit her coloring, especially the rich auburn hair that was so unique.

Could she possibly be the one?

"What is owed?" he asked, controlling his tone because he wished to punch Lord Campton and slice this modiste with his words.

Madame Floseau named a staggering figure.

His eyes narrowed. "I am a businessman myself, Madame. I know you are lying. How much was this gown?"

She placed a hand over her heart. "Oh, you mean only this

gown? I thought you meant the entire amount owed to me."

"*This* gown," he said succinctly.

The modiste told him and Aidan withdrew the notes in his pocket, counting out what the modiste claimed the gown costs and handing it over to her.

"Have the gown delivered to Lady Larissa's house at once. Is that understood?

Madame's head bobbed up and down. "Of course, Monsieur."

"*If* you do, I will see tomorrow that you receive the full payment owed to you."

Her eyes lit with understanding. Yet Aidan did not trust this woman, whom he even doubted had a drop of French blood in her.

"I will know if you do because I will be attending the Stag Ball tonight. If I do not see Lady Larissa in this gown, I will be back tomorrow. It won't go well," he warned.

The modiste's eyes now gleamed with greed, as she realized she would be paid in full for her work. "I understand." She smiled seductively at him. "Might I ask whom will be paying the bill?"

"You may not," he barked at her.

She flinched and nodded in understanding, moving away from him and issuing orders to her two assistants.

Aidan left the dress shop. He had a purpose now.

He intended to find Lady Larissa tonight. It was important to see if he noticed another suitor paying particular attention to her. Despite the tremendous pressure he was under to find a bride before the ball ended, he was an honorable man. He would not wish to infringe where another man had already planted his flag, so to speak. If he determined that the lady favored no gentleman in particular and none some to be possessive toward her, he would seek her out. He only hoped her maid hadn't poisoned her against him. By the servant chastising her mistress and telling Lady Larissa she shouldn't talk to the likes of him, Aidan worried that the maid knew he was a Sinning Flynn.

Because of the time constraint placed upon him, Aidan would have to be blunter than usual if he did seek out Lady Larissa, something he tried to avoid with the fairer sex.

It boiled down to how open-minded she could be. He would need to see if she could set aside the gossip surrounding the Sinning Flynns long enough to get to know him before passing judgment.

And if she could?

Aidan would ask for her hand in marriage by the end of the Stag Ball—because he wanted Larkhaven badly enough to wed a stranger in order to possess it.

❧

"WHAT WERE YOU thinking, my lady?" berated Lizzy. "You were in public, talking to a gentleman without a chaperone in sight. I only hope no one saw you. Why, I—"

Larissa had raised her face to her maid, causing the servant to stop mid-sentence.

"My lady," Lizzy said, her tone now softened. "Whatever ails you?" She took Larissa's hand. "Your eyes are red and swollen from crying. Did your gown not fit properly? Did you have to leave it at Madame Floseau's? Are we to go back for it later this afternoon?"

She sighed. "The gown fit most beautifully, Lizzy. Nothing has ever made me feel so attractive."

Puzzled, Lizzy asked, "Then where is it?"

Biting her lip, she felt the tears welling in her eyes again and noticed she still gripped the handkerchief from the stranger. Quickly, she dabbed her eyes before they could spill down her cheeks.

"Madame Floseau refused to let me leave her shop with it in hand." She swallowed, knowing she had to speak the truth. "My father has not paid her in some time, you see. Not merely for this particular gown—but for the rest of my wardrobe this Season. Unless she receives payment, I cannot have it. For the Stag Ball or any other ball."

Anger darkened the servant's eyes. "Why, that is just plain wrong, my lady. You have no say over the bills Lord Campton pays or doesn't pay. There are noblemen all over London who run up bills, sometimes for years before they take the time to pay them. I've even heard tale of merchants having to wait for a peer to die before they try to collect from his heir."

Larissa dabbed at the corners of her eyes again. "Regardless, Madame was quite adamant that I would not be wearing the gown unless her bills had been paid." Glumly, she added, "I have no funds of my own, Lizzy. You probably possess more coins than I do."

Lizzy's mouth tightened. She remained silent a moment and then she swore softly under her breath.

"The servants will help you, my lady," she proclaimed. "I will speak to them when we return. You are well thought of throughout the household, always with a kind word to everyone and never asking for anything special."

"You . . . think to take up a collection from the servants to pay for my ball gown?" She shook her head furiously. "No, I will never allow that, Lizzy. I am already embarrassed enough by the situation. To take charity from my own servants is beyond the pale. I cannot allow you to do something such as this."

She grimaced. "Besides, if my parents—or even Peter—got wind of what you were doing, you would be dismissed on the spot."

"I could do it quietly, my lady. I know everyone would pitch in."

"No," she said firmly. "I forbid you from doing so." Seeing the hurt spring up on Lizzy's face, she said, "I am grateful to you for even having such a thought. You are quite dear to me. If I do wed, I am hoping Father will allow me to take you with me."

The maid sniffed. "His lordship won't have to allow anything, my lady. If you are wed, then your husband would pay my salary. Let Lord Campton fire me without references. I wouldn't need them if I were to go with you."

Larissa hugged Lizzy tightly. "Oh, you are so very loyal. I do appreciate you more than words can say." She wiped her eyes again with the stranger's handkerchief, wondering who he might be.

"Well, if you won't let me gather the funds to claim your gown, then you and I will have to put our heads together and come up with something for you to wear this evening."

She smiled through watery eyes. "That is exactly what I was hoping that you would say."

They began talking over gowns she had worn previously, ones she looked particularly good in, and discussed how to disguise one enough so that it would not be recognized by the fiercest gossips of the *ton*. They hit upon a gown from last Season which had been a favorite of hers and discussed how to remake it in a single afternoon.

"What we could use," Lizzy began, her gaze avoiding Larissa's, "is some of that lace from Lady Cressida's dress that you kept."

Upon her sister's death, Larissa had saved a dress Cressida adored, a lock of her sister's hair saved inside a locket, and a poem Cressida had written in which she had spoken of how sisters made the best of friends. Though she hated to pull the lace from the gown, she believed drastic times called for drastic measures. Given her father's ultimatum that she find a husband tonight—else he would do it for her—Larissa was desperate enough to agree to Lizzy's suggestion.

"All right. But once the Stag Ball is over, you must help me right Cressida's dress so that it looks as it did before."

"I will do my best, my lady. I'm no miracle worker, though."

Larissa hugged her again. "You are my miracle worker this day, Lizzy. I appreciate every kindness you give me and I do love you for that."

The maid sniffed. "Well, someone's got to love you, my lady. Your family is blind to how truly wonderful you are. Selfish is what they are, to the very end. They don't deserve to have you in their ranks."

She understood what her maid was saying without voicing it. "I know that I am not the earl's daughter, Lizzy," she said quietly.

The servant's eyes grew large. "You do?"

Shrugging, she said, "How could I not? I look nothing like either Mama or Father. You and I—and everyone in our household—turns a blind eye to their tomfoolery. Father may have been the first to step out but Mama has done her fair share of breaking her marital vows for years now. I know I am the result of one of those affairs. I even think I know who my real father is. Lord Silverton."

Lizzy sucked in a quick breath. "Did you hear the servants gossiping about this, my lady?"

"No. The *ton*. I also was introduced to Lord Silverton during last Season by Mama herself. I favor him too much for the situation surrounding my birth to be a secret." She sighed. "I fear it is why Father is punishing me now by not paying for my gowns."

What Larissa left unsaid was the earl wanted her gone from his household and would see to a husband for her if she couldn't produce one herself after tonight.

The carriage pulled up in front of the Campton townhouse and the door opened. A footman handed her and Lizzy down and they entered the foyer.

Immediately, the butler said, "Lady Campton wishes to see you, my lady."

What would Mama want with her? They spoke so little as it was.

"Where is her ladyship?"

"In her rooms," the butler replied. "I am to take you there since you have returned."

"I can go myself," she said, raising her chin a notch. Then looking to her maid, Larissa said, "Lizzy, if you will begin work on that gown?"

"Of course, my lady."

With trepidation, she ascended the staircase and went to her mother's suite of rooms and knocked at the door. A muffled response sounded, so she hoped Mama was bidding her to enter.

"There you are," her mother said when she slipped inside the room. "I have spoken to your father. Or rather, *he* spoke to me."

"Oh, dear," she said, knowing her parents could go weeks—even months—without a word passing between them since they were rarely in the same room together. The only time they were ever in close proximity was in the carriage when they made their way to Season events. Even then, they would refuse to speak to one another and oftentimes their coachman had to make two trips, first driving Larissa and her mother and then returning to pick up the earl and convey him to the very same place.

"Campton has told me that he has ordered you to find a husband at tonight's Stag Ball. Why, you haven't had but a handful of callers this Season or last. I truly don't understand that. You are quite pretty."

"But my dowry is not as attractive," Larissa pointed out, deciding to boldly speak the truth for once in this household of lies. "And thanks to your behavior and Father's over the years—not to mention Peter's reputation of being a rakehell of the worst kind—no gentleman of any good name wishes to bring me home to his family. Peter's friends have said horrid, lewd things to me. They think I possess the morals of an alley cat simply because I am a member of this family."

She paused. "Or as much a member of this family as I can be."

Mama gasped. "What on earth do you mean?"

"Oh, Mama, let's have no more dithering about, shall we? You and Father have been engaged in a war ever since your wedding day. He has been unfaithful to you countless numbers of times and hasn't bothered to hide his infidelity. You, in return, retaliated by doing the same. You both have made a mockery of your wedding vows. Everyone in this household—

and I daresay most of Polite Society—knows that I am the daughter of Lord Silverton."

Mama swayed. "No," she said in a hoarse whisper.

Larissa went to her and steadied her, leading her to a chair and pushing her into it.

"Yes, Mama. I resemble Lord Silverton. I do not look like Father or you. Legally, I am his issue since I was born during your marriage and you have spent no significant time apart. He has decided to take out the sins you and Lord Silverton engaged in on *me*. Did you know he has not paid the modiste for my wardrobe this Season? I have just come from Madame Floseau's shop and she is holding my gown for the Stag Ball hostage because she has not been paid. If you will excuse me, I need to go to my bedchamber and help Lizzy in sewing something for me to wear this evening. Especially if I am supposed to land a husband on my own tonight and not allow Father to burden me with Lord Langdon for a husband."

Mama turned pale. "He told you that?"

"He did," she confirmed.

Her mother shuddered. "He told me the same thing." She took Larissa's hand, shocking her, since she couldn't recall the last time her mother had touched her. "Campton is as evil as my own father was. I was forced by Papa to wed Campton when I loved another. It all came down to money. I will not see that happen to you, Larissa."

"I don't see what you can do about it, Mama."

Determination filled her mother's eyes. "You will not wed Lord Langdon. I cannot see what happened to me be repeated with you. I will send a note to Silverton at once. *He* can help."

"How?" she asked, baffled. "Even if Lord Silverton claimed to be my father, Campton holds the legal rights over me. In the eyes of the law, I am his daughter. End of story."

Mama began wringing her hands. "Well, then Silverton can do something. Surely, he knows of some nice young man who would be willing to wed you." She paused. "And if I ask him, he would secretly add to your dowry. We parted on good terms and have remained friendly over the years. He would do this for me. For you."

How did her life become such a genteel mess?

Larissa cleared her throat. "Do what you think you must. I am going to help Lizzy in finding a way to make me not just presentable tonight—but spectacular."

With that, she left the room, shaking from head to toe.

Would Lord Silverton actually step in and provide the largest portion of her dowry? Might he know a gentleman who could be persuaded to offer for her?

Larissa's head spun with everything in it. She reached her bedchamber and waited a moment before entering, trying to calm herself.

The handkerchief was still in her hands. The one loaned to her by the handsome, green-eyed stranger. Was there the slimmest of chances that *he* might be interested in her and if so, could she expect him to take a leap of faith and offer for her tonight?

She sensed someone passing by and turned, spying a maid.

"This needs to be laundered and pressed at once," she said, handing the handkerchief over. "I want it returned to me as soon as possible."

"Yes, my lady," said the maid, obviously puzzled as she continued on her way.

"Please, God. Let him be the one," Larissa prayed fervently.

If the stranger was already attached to someone, then she

would have to do something completely out of character. Larissa would pack her things and leave this household. Where she would go, she couldn't say. But she refused to wed a man old enough to be her grandfather.

It all came down to what might happen at tonight's Stag Ball.

CHAPTER SIX

L ARISSA RETURNED TO her bedchamber and saw Lizzy sitting by the window, Cressida's gown in her lap. Another gown was spread across the bed, the one she had favored last year, which they would try to remake now.

"Do you think this is truly going to work, Lizzy?" she asked, trying to keep the doubts from her voice.

Determination filled the maid's eyes. "It must work, my lady. I will not let you down."

She went to sit in the chair opposite the servant, who was carefully removing the lace from Cressida's dress. Larissa saw Lizzy frown as she worked.

"Is there anything I can do to help?"

"Not now, my lady. This is simply slow going. The lace is delicate and difficult to extract. I have to make sure I do not damage it as I do so."

As Larissa watched Lizzy's fingers work, her spirits sank. They only had this afternoon to turn an old, recognizable dress into a new creation.

She feared it could not be accomplished.

Nevertheless, she knew Lizzy would give her best effort and

so Larissa sat quietly, brooding.

A knock sounded at the door and she held out a hand. "Let me get it. Keep doing what you are doing."

Larissa moved to the door and opened it, surprised to see a footman standing there with a large box.

A dress box . . .

"This just arrived for you, my lady. The messenger said you were to get it at once. That it is very important you see it."

"Thank you," she said absently as she took the box in her hands and closed the door. Turning, she saw Lizzy staring at her in confusion.

Larissa brought the dress box to the bed as Lizzy set aside Cressida's gown and joined her. Her heart pounded as she opened it.

Inside lay the pale blue gown, the color of winter's ice on a day when the sun struck the ice, catching the slight hint of color within it.

Lizzy gasped. "It is your ball gown, my lady. Why would it be delivered now?"

Why, indeed. Mama had told her she was going to write to Lord Silverton and ask for his help. Had she already done so and the viscount paid for the gown and demanded its immediate delivery? Surely, not. Not enough time had passed for that to occur. Still, she would not look a gift horse in the mouth. Perhaps Madame Floseau had a change of heart and felt guilty keeping the gown from Larissa on such an important night. Whatever had happened, the gown was now in her possession and she could wear it this evening. She leaned down and lifted it from the box, staring at it in wonder.

"Hold it up to you, my lady," Lizzy requested.

Larissa did so, one arm draped across the top of the gown,

her other at the waist, holding it to her snuggly. She glanced down and knew her chance of finding a husband tonight had improved simply because she would be wearing this lovely creation.

"Please try it on, my lady," her maid said. "I want to see how it fits and then I must press it because I do see a few wrinkles with it having sat in the box a short while."

Larissa placed the gown on the bed and allowed Lizzy to undress her. Then her servant lifted the gown over Larissa's head and arranged it. Lizzy stepped back and Larissa couldn't help but see admiration in the maid's eyes.

"You are a sight, my lady. If the gentlemen at tonight's Stag Ball don't notice you, it is because they are blind. Here, let's remove it and I will take care of it for you."

Once Larissa was out of the dress and back into her day gown, she embraced her maid. "Lizzy, I thank you for what you were willing to do to help me prepare for this evening."

Lizzy chuckled. "Well, after I press this gown, I will be reattaching the lace to Lady Cressida's gown. I don't want to rush it, though. I may finish today or it may take another day."

"Take all the time you require," Larissa told the servant.

Yet the idea of time frightened her. In a little more than twelve hours, the Duke of Savernake's ball would be coming to a close. She would either have convinced some bachelor it was worth taking a chance and wedding her or she would be making plans to run away and leave behind the life she knew.

"I will leave you to your work then," she said. "I think I will go to the library and read."

Reading had always been a comfort to her, as well as Cressida. Larissa had spent hours at her sister's bedside, reading the classics to her. Because of it, she was most likely better read than most men who had attended university. She pulled a volume of Shakespeare's plays from the shelf and soon became engrossed in *Julius Caesar*.

A light knock sounded and their butler entered the room and came toward her.

"Yes?" she asked.

"I have a note for you, my lady." He handed it over and said, "I must wait for a reply."

She found it odd to be receiving a note because she rarely did so. She would see her three friends at tonight's ball, unless perhaps one of them—or their child—was ill. She hoped that wasn't the case as she broke the seal. Before reading the message, she glanced at the bottom, surprised by the signature.

Lord Silverton.

Quickly, she read the note.

My dear Lady Larissa –

It is of utmost importance that I speak with you at once. My carriage is waiting outside at the end of the block and I ask that you come and grant me a few minutes with you. Bring your maid as your chaperone. However, we will drop her a few blocks away so that we may converse in private. I will make certain once we have discussed certain matters that we return and claim her again.

Please come, my lady.

Lord Silverton

Larissa closed the note and looked to the butler. "I will be going out for an hour," she told him. "I must retrieve my bonnet and reticule. That is your reply."

"Very well, my lady." He left the library, seemingly satisfied with a verbal reply.

She replaced the book on its shelf and hurried upstairs to her bedchamber, flinging her door open and entering quickly.

Lizzy looked up. "Your gown is ready for this evening, my lady, and—"

"We are going out at once," she said. "Get my things."

The maid frowned slightly but did as told, bringing Larissa a bonnet and tying the ribbons beneath her chin. She retrieved Larissa's reticule and handed it to her.

"Are you going to tell me where we are going? I thought you might wish to nap in order to be fresh for the ball this evening."

"Lord Silverton wishes to speak with me immediately. You will serve as my chaperone."

Lizzy's eyes widened and she nodded. "Of course, my lady."

They descended the stairs and, in the foyer, the butler greeted them. "His lordship's carriage is to your right, my lady." He gave her a smile. "Good luck."

His words surprised her. Lizzy led her to the front door and a footman opened it. He, too, wore a sympathetic smile. Larissa supposed the entire household knew she was the daughter of Lord Silverton and wondered how many times the viscount had called here as he and Mama conducted their affair years before.

Outside, she spotted Lord Silverton's gleaming, black carriage, stairs already placed at the door's entry. They hurried down the block to it. Immediately, a footman opened the door and helped her and then Lizzy up.

Inside the carriage sat Lord Silverton. Larissa and Lizzy took a seat opposite him as the door to the vehicle closed. The viscount merely nodded and tapped his cane on the roof. The carriage began rolling along the street and stopped after a few blocks.

Lord Silverton looked directly at Lizzy and said, "You are to wait at this corner. It may be five minutes or an hour but I will return your mistress safely to you. Is that understood?"

"Yes, my lord," Lizzy replied.

The door opened and her maid exited the vehicle. Once again, the door closed and the carriage started up, this time with no signal.

"I received a distressing message from your mother," Lord Silverton began. "She wrote that Campton had issued you an ultimatum."

She might never have a chance alone with this man again and decided she would be forthright with him. "Yes, the earl insists that I become engaged tonight else he will choose a husband for me. Most likely, Lord Langdon."

Lord Silverton grimaced. "I must ask this, though I believe I know your answer. Would you be willing to wed Lord Langdon?"

"Never!" she said vehemently. "I would rather leave the Earl of Camden's household than accept a betrothal with Lord Langdon."

"I thought as much. Your mother seems to think you do not have any suitors who might step forward tonight. Is this correct?"

Heat filled her cheeks. "Yes, my lord. That is true. No eligible men seem to be interested in me this Season."

Sympathy filled his eyes and she saw a question there, as well.

"You are quite comely, Lady Larissa. I find it hard to believe that no gentlemen in the *ton* have shown an interest in you. Do you have any idea why?"

"May I be frank, my lord?" she asked.

Lord Silverton nodded and she said, "I have two problems dogging me, my lord. One is that my dowry is quite small compared to that of most other girls on the Marriage Mart."

He waved a hand. "That will not be a problem, my lady. As a favor to an old friend, I would gladly supplement it."

She heard something in his tone and asked, "How long have you known my mother?" She paused and added, "I have guessed that you are my sire, Lord Silverton."

He sighed. "Your mother told me you were a clever girl," he revealed, surprising her because Mama never complimented her in any fashion. "She knew the moment we were introduced that you would deduce who I was to you."

"Please answer my question, my lord. Who were you to Mama?" she pressed, believing she already knew the truth.

"Your mother and I grew up on adjoining estates and our parents were friends. We were childhood companions who fell deeply in love. We assumed our parents knew of our feelings and our desire to wed. During her come-out Season, I courted her to show my good intentions."

He hesitated, a faraway look in his eyes, and Larissa knew he was reliving a part of his past.

"Though our parents were friendly, apparently your grand-father had higher aspirations for his daughter. He sought a higher title and a wealthier gentleman to become her husband. Separately, our parents told us of this decision. That she was to wed Lord Campton." He smiled ruefully. "We went against their wishes and set out for Gretna Green."

Larissa could not believe her mother had been so bold as to elope to Scotland. "But . . . you did not wed. What happened?"

"A servant betrayed us and our two fathers raced after us.

We were caught and forced to return to London. Campton had already purchased a special license and he made your mother his countess the very next morning."

Strong emotions thickened her throat and she reached over and took his hand, squeezing and then releasing it. "I am so sorry, my lord."

"I was, too. I became deeply depressed and withdrew from Polite Society for several years. When I emerged, I heard the gossip of how Lord Campton stepped out frequently on his wife and made no secret of it. I sent word to your mama and we began meeting in secret. You were the result of those precious times together. I have always loved your mother but when we found she was with child, I told her the affair must end. That she must try again with her husband to make a go of her marriage. I myself wed soon after your birth and have been faithful to Lady Silverton." He paused and added. "I still love your mother and will until my dying day. I would not make a mockery of my marriage vows, though, and have had little to do with your mother ever since then. We speak politely when we come across each other at events.

"But I want to help you now, Larissa. Your mother and I don't wish for you to suffer and be forced to wed as she was. I will add to your dowry if that will make a difference. If no one of your choosing offers for you this evening and you wish to leave the earl's household, you would be welcomed in mine."

She was touched by his offer but asked, "How would Lady Silverton feel about my presence there?"

"She knows of my feelings—and you. We have become great friends over the years and have two children of our own. If you wish, you could go to my country estate instead. I merely wanted to let you know that you have options—and that I have always loved you, too."

Tears streamed down her cheeks and she whispered, "Thank you. I have been so alone. The earl, while never raising a hand to me, has been verbally abusive for years. Peter is an embarrassment to me. I believe that is the second reason why no one is interested in me, Lord Silverton. It is because my parents have conducted numerous, public affairs throughout the years and my brother is a scoundrel of the worst kind. What gentleman would care to wed a girl form such a family, especially with a miniscule dowry?"

"You have me, Larissa. I know you were close to your sister and her death greatly affected you. Whatever you think, I want you to know that you are not alone."

"Thank you, my lord. Your support means a great deal to me. If I do not become engaged by the end of tonight's ball, then I will need to come to you. I want to avoid a scandal of any kind, however, and would prefer to go to your country estate, wherever that might be. I would hope then I might possibly ask you to use your connections in finding me a post. I believe I would make for an excellent governess. I am well-educated and spent the majority of my childhood caring for Cressida. I have a nurturing spirit and would be good with children."

"I hate for you to go into service, Larissa, but I do understand why. We will see how tonight progresses and then make the necessary decisions come tomorrow. I have a few friends with sons who are looking to wed and I may try to put a word in for you with them. Though my son married last year, he also has friends still perusing the Marriage Mart."

"Do your children know of me, my lord?"

He smiled sadly. "They do, Larissa. I think most of Polite Society does. We favor one another far too much, especially with the shade of our hair."

She sighed. "Merely another reason I am not wanted by any man."

At least the viscount had given her a way out of her miserable situation. In her heart, she doubted anyone would sweep her off her feet and wish to become her fiancé this night, no matter how beautiful her gown might be. Now, though, she had a place of refuge and would most likely turn to her real father tomorrow.

"If I do not receive a marriage offer at the Stag Ball, I fear the earl will want to move quickly," she said. "Even though I am of legal age, I am under his care."

"I don't want you trapped in his household as he summons Lord Langdon." Lord Silverton took her hands in his. "When the ball ends, go home with your parents—but do not go to bed. Have your maid pack a few things for you. Go to your room and come down with your valise as soon as you can. My carriage will be waiting for you where it was today. We will take you home with us and then send you to the country at first light."

Tears filled her eyes. "You are being so very kind to me, my lord."

"It is the least I can do for the daughter I have never been able to acknowledge publicly." He released her hands. "Have your maid come along, as well, if she is willing to do so. Campton will likely toss her from the household without references."

"Thank you. For everything. I am sorry you and Mama were torn apart. She would have been a much different woman had she been able to wed you."

He nodded. "I think so, too. Make certain as you leave the

ball that you give me a sign so I know whether or not to be waiting for you. After all, you are a beautiful young woman— and it *is* the Stag Ball. Wondrous things seem to occur at it. A handsome gentleman might fall under your spell and want to whisk you away."

"You are kind to think so, my lord, but I expect no offers of marriage this night." Larissa thought a moment. "If I plan to come to you, I will tug on my right ear."

"Then I will look for that sign. And I hope you won't have to use the gesture."

The viscount lifted his cane and rapped on the ceiling. A few minutes later, they stopped and she saw Lizzy standing on the pavement.

"Let me get out here, Lord Silverton. We are only a few blocks from home. I would rather Lizzy and I walk those together. I would not want the earl to see us together and guess at our scheme."

He leaned forward and took her by the shoulders. Kissing her cheek, he said, "I will see you this evening."

She nodded. "This evening."

The footman opened the door and Larissa held out her hand, surprising Lizzy, who thought to enter the carriage.

"It is a nice day. We are walking home, Lizzy."

"Of course, my lady," the maid replied.

They started down the pavement and she listened and heard Lord Silverton's carriage pull away.

Slipping her arm through Lizzy's, Larissa said, "He is the one Mama loved before she was made to wed Lord Campton."

"I suspected as much."

"I have been told by the earl I must find a husband tonight or he will select one for me," she finally revealed to her maid. "It would be Lord Langdon."

"That old goat?" Lizzy cried.

"Yes. Lord Silverton wishes to prevent me from a lifetime of unhappiness."

Quickly, she explained the plan to Lizzy, who promised to pack a small bag for her.

"Slip some of your things in it, as well," she said. "Lord Silverton said I can also bring you with me."

Tears filled the servant's eyes. "Oh, that is so kind, my lady. I figured his lordship would sack me."

"Lord Silverton thought the same and is happy for you to come with me to the country. You don't mind?"

"I will follow you anywhere, my lady."

They entered the townhouse and Larissa told the butler, "I believe I will nap now. Please have a tray sent to my room. I will have my dinner there." She paused. "And thank you. You have always been so kind to me."

She knew it sounded like a goodbye—and it was. After tonight, she would leave this household and embark upon a new life. A much different one but at least one of her own choosing.

Larissa went to her bedchamber and despite her swirling thoughts, fell fast asleep.

CHAPTER SEVEN

AIDAN LEFT THE dress shop and decided to head over and see Franklin, his London banker. Their appointment wasn't until tomorrow but the bank held a good deal of Aidan's funds and he thought Franklin would make the time to see him.

Entering the white, stone structure, he went directly to the desk of the man who served as Franklin's clerk and right-hand man.

"Mr. Flynn," the startled clerk said, rising to his feet. "I have you on tomorrow's diary."

"I realize my appointment is not until then. I will be back for it. I just need to have a brief word with Mr. Franklin. Would that be possible?"

"Let me check with him. One moment, please."

As expected, Aidan was quickly shown into Franklin's office. He turned down the offer of tea and the clerk left them alone.

"My man says you only needed a few minutes, Mr. Flynn. What might I do for you?"

"I still plan to discuss several business ventures with you tomorrow, Franklin. For now, I have a few monetary requests that I would like seen to in the meantime. One is to go to a Dr. Lawford."

The banker brightened. "Ah, I actually know Dr. Lawford. I am on the board of trustees at my church and he serves on it, as well. A brilliant man. Kind and compassionate."

"He is my grandfather's physician. I have recently learned of Dr. Lawford's charitable efforts in tending to illnesses of the poor. I would like to make a contribution to his efforts. It might help him in purchasing new equipment or needed medicines. Possibly even hire new staff."

Franklin nodded. "Dr. Lawford does take on charity cases when he is not attending to the aches and pains of Polite Society. How much would you like to donate, Mr. Flynn?"

Aidan named an amount and the banker's eyes widened.

"Very well. I can see to that, Mr. Flynn."

"I would request that you not share with him the source of this donation."

"You want no credit for it?" Franklin asked, clearly puzzled.

He had long ago decided to do good for others and regularly donated to charities in Falmouth and the surrounding area, all anonymously.

"That is my wish. Can you manage it?"

"Of course, Mr. Flynn. We enjoy doing business with you and want to keep you happy."

"I have a second request. You may immediately send the monies to Dr. Lawford but this is to be held until mid-afternoon tomorrow."

Aidan shared the figure that Madame Floseau had given him, the total of what Lady Larissa's wardrobe had cost for the Season. He still thought the modiste padded the number but hadn't wanted to haggle with her over it. He assumed Lord

Campton wasn't the only nobleman who delayed in a payment to a tradesman. Or welched on it altogether. Doo had emphasized to Aidan to always pay for any goods and services he engaged. When he went to university, he heard talk among the students there how oftentimes their fathers reneged on payment to all kinds of people, including the very tutors who were helping their sons along at Cambridge.

He resented that about the *ton*, thinking they were better than everyone else. Simply by chance, they had been born into families with a title and were brought up to believe they were superior because of it. He looked at his own father. Da had been a hard worker before being awarded his earldom and he continued to put in long hours, both on the docks and in his offices even after he became Earl of Sinbrook. Da had always told his sons that being gifted with a title did not mean he was better than the next man and Aidan held that belief to this day. He also knew there were good men in Polite Society, such as Doo, but far too many of them were liars, cheats, or fools. Or gossips like the Earl of Exford. He supposed he wouldn't mind seeing that man humiliated when Rory wed one of Lord Exford's homely daughters and the earl's grandchildren would be born Flynns. That would be a bitter pill for his mother's former fiancé to swallow.

Franklin made a note. "Mid-afternoon tomorrow then, my lord. I will see that my clerk delivers the fee to Madame Floseau in person." He hesitated. "Do you wish Madame to know who is sending this payment and for which mistress' account is to be credited?"

Aidan stared daggers at the banker, who shrank before him. "I currently have no mistress, Franklin. If I did, it would be none of your business. I spoke directly with Madame Floseau today and she already knows the payment is coming to her tomorrow. There is no need to mention any names. Do you understand? I want this modiste paid without mention of my name."

The color had drained from the banker's face. "Yes, Mr. Flynn. No names will be mentioned. Madame will not know the payment came from you. I guarantee that."

Well, the modiste *would* know the payment came from Aidan. Just not his name. For some reason, he wanted the matter to remain private. If Lady Larissa wished to believe her cruel father, who had withheld payment up until now, was responsible for the release of the ball gown, so be it.

Aidan still looked forward to seeing her in the creation tonight, whether she was spoken for or not.

He rose, offering his hand to show Franklin there were no hard feelings. "Thank you again for seeing me briefly. I will return tomorrow for our official appointment."

Franklin pumped Aidan's hand enthusiastically. "Thank you, Mr. Flynn. I will take care of everything now."

He left the bank, nodding to the nervous clerk, hoping he would be able to make the delivery of payment to the dress shop without accidentally revealing the name of Lady Larissa's benefactor. If it leaked that a man unrelated to her had paid for an entire Season's wardrobe, she would be utterly ruined. Perhaps he might have to pay a call on Madame Floseau, after all, just to make certain the modiste knew to keep her mouth closed regarding the payment she received.

His step was lighter as he continued down the pavement, having arranged for Dr. Lawford to receive funds for his clinic and seeing that Lady Larissa had an appropriate gown to wear to the Stag Ball.

Then he spied the sign for a jeweler up ahead. Suddenly, his feet took him to the door and he found himself entering the establishment. Several long cases of glass ran the length of both sides of the shop. The man he supposed was the owner sat behind one of them. He glanced up at Aidan and removed the loupe from his eye.

Rising, he said, "Good day, my lord. Are you looking for a special piece for a certain occasion? Or do merely wish to browse?"

"I will browse for now," he replied, wondering why he had even obeyed the impulse to come inside. He had no one to buy jewelry for.

Or at least not yet.

Visions of Lady Larissa danced before him, those sky-blue eyes and abundant auburn hair calling out to him. He would enjoy taking the pins from her hair and seeing it fall about her shoulders. Running his fingers through the fiery locks of silk. Wrapping her in an embrace and pressing his lips to her soft, pink ones.

Once again, he wondered if she might be the one.

He told himself that was nonsense. That a woman of her beauty—and figure—would already have a bevy of suitors at her fingertips. But as he thought of the weeping beauty, he wondered why she wasn't already wed. She wasn't fresh from the schoolroom, the usual type who made her come-out. She seemed a bit older, possibly in her early twenties. Had she been wed before and was now a young widow? Or had she neglected to make her come-out because she cared for a dying parent? There could be several reasons why the lovely Lady Larissa had yet to have a wedding ring slipped onto her finger.

That led him to look at the case that held a variety of rings.

If he was going to wed in order to claim Larkhaven, he would need a wedding ring for the ceremony, which must be held sooner rather than later. If he could find a fiancée tonight, he would prefer they wed in a week's time, just to make certain Doo was able to attend and enjoy the day. The memory of his grandfather in pain seared his soul. There was no need for Doo to delay taking something for that pain.

That meant Aidan needed to press for the wedding to take place as quickly as possible.

None of these rings spoke to him, though. He continued past them and found himself looking at earrings. Sapphires, rubies, aquamarines, topazes. The jewels sparkled in the case, longing for someone to purchase them. Not that he wanted to bribe his bride-to-be, but it might be a nice gesture to have an engagement present for her. Or at least a wedding present. Perhaps both might help convince an eligible young woman to wed him.

Aidan peered through the case and found a set of diamond earrings beside a matching necklace.

"Sir, may I look at these?" he asked. "The diamond earrings and necklace. They seem to belong together."

The jeweler came toward him and unlocked the case from behind the counter. "It is a lovely set. You have a good eye, my lord."

Lifting the jewels, which sat nestled against black velvet, the jeweler set it on top of the counter.

"Do you know anything about diamonds, my lord?"

"It's Mr. Flynn," he told the man. "And no, I don't. Other than they are expensive."

The old man chuckled. "They are if of good quality. This set certainly is."

The jeweler proceeded to tell Aidan about what he called the four Cs, which he said impacted a diamond's appearance and structure.

"The cut of a gem involves the quality of its angles. Its facets and proportions. It shows off the diamond's brilliance and fire. To the naked eye, it is the cut that allows a diamond to sparkle and engage. The color—or lack of color—is also important. A more colorless diamond is worth more."

Aidan was fascinated. "Tell me more."

The jeweler shrugged. "Clarity involves how flawless a diamond is, versus whether it has blemishes or not. And carat refers to its weight, not necessarily the diamond's size. The cut of the gem and its shape can mean two diamonds each weighing one carat might be very different in size. All four of these components interact with one another and decide the quality of the diamond you purchase. Sometimes, all four properties work together."

"How so?"

The jeweler retrieved his loupe and had Aidan place it against his eye. Then he removed one of the earrings from the velvet and had Aidan study it a moment.

"Look carefully, Mr. Flynn. Turn the diamond. Its ability to reflect light back to your eye depends mostly on the quality of its cut—but it also is a part of the jewel's color and clarity."

He turned it slowly as the jeweler moved away, soon returning with a diamond ring.

"This is three carats." He handed the ring to Aidan. "Note the facets. The reflection of light. Its almost colorless state."

Aidan examined it carefully. "I see what you mean. This is fascinating."

He returned the loupe and ring to the shop's owner, who

placed the ring back in the case and joined him again.

"Not many are interested in such small details, whether a man or a woman. They see a pretty gem and like its flash and brilliance."

"I like the story behind things," Aidan admitted. "I am in shipping. My father owns Flynn Fleets."

"Ah, I have heard of them." The jeweler studied him a moment. "You wouldn't happen to be one of those Sinning Flynns the papers are enraptured with."

He felt the flush creep up his neck. "I am one of four brothers who sometimes answer to that nickname. But I can tell you that we all have an excellent work ethic and spend time both on the docks and in the shipping offices."

The jeweler shrugged. "I like reading gossip the same as the next person. But I take it all with a grain of salt."

"I will take the necklace and earrings," he said, making a swift decision. "I can tell they are of good quality."

"A wise decision, Mr. Flynn."

The shop's owner named a hefty price but after having examined the pieces and learning about the four Cs, Aidan knew his purchase was a wise one.

"Are they a gift for your wife?"

"I am not wed. My oldest two brothers are. I am the youngest. But," he added, "the set is to be a gift for my future wife."

The old man's eyes gleamed. "Have you decided who this wife is to be, Mr. Flynn?"

Determination filled him. Aidan knew he had been lying to himself all along.

He wanted Lady Larissa as his bride.

"Yes, as a matter of fact, I have. I plan to offer for her this evening."

"At the Stag Ball?" the old man asked eagerly. "The newspapers are always full of things after the Duke of Savernake's annual ball takes place. It seems a good number of couples become engaged at it each year."

"Let us hope that I am part of the couples who will celebrate tonight. I will have my banker send payment to you tomorrow if that is satisfactory."

"It is." The jeweler finished wrapping up Aidan's purchase and handed the package over. "I hope your young lady enjoys wearing these."

He hoped so, too.

Taking the package, he bid the jeweler farewell and stepped outside, ready to return to his grandfather's townhouse. When he reached it, he found Simms.

"Is His Grace still resting?"

"I took him some tea and cakes a few minutes ago, Mr. Aidan. If you wish to speak with him a few moments, I am certain he would be happy to see you." The butler paused. "Did you get a chance to speak with Dr. Lawford?"

"I did. I know now what to expect. Thank you, Simms."

Aidan bounded up the stairs and knocked on Doo's door before slipping in. He found his grandfather sipping tea, a half-eaten slice of cake on his plate.

"Hello, Aidan." Doo indicated his plate. "I did better than I usually do. I got down half a piece of cake. Cook will be pleased with me. What's that you've got?"

"A gift for my bride."

He unwrapped the parcel and showed Doo the necklace and earrings, explaining about cut, clarity, color, and carat and why this purchase had been such a good investment.

"My, you have learned an awful lot about gems in a short

amount of time," Doo exclaimed.

"I thought to purchase a wedding ring, which is why I went inside the jeweler's shop in the first place."

"So, where is it?" Doo asked.

"None pleased me. But this set did. I will gift my fiancée with the earrings upon our betrothal and the necklace on our wedding day."

His grandfather chuckled. "Your good looks aren't enough? You intend to bribe her with diamonds?"

"If I have to."

Doo set his saucer down. "I think I have something you might like. Look in the snuff box beside my bed."

Elaborate snuff boxes were the rage in the *ton*. Aidan had tried snuff once and swore off doing so ever again, the experience unpleasant.

As he went to the bedside table, he said, "I have never seen you using snuff, Doo. Only smoking your cigar after dinner."

"That is because I don't use the nasty stuff. Makes me sneeze—and then sweat."

He didn't feel right about opening the snuff box and picked it up, returning it to his grandfather. Doo opened it and removed something, handing it to Aidan.

Opening his palm, he saw a ring lying there.

His grandmother's wedding ring . . .

"She died just before your tenth birthday," Doo said, reminiscing. "She was a lovely woman. I wish you had been able to get to know her better." He gazed at the ring, a trace of a smile playing about his lips. "I have kept it close all these years. I believe she would want you to have this."

Aidan stared at the gold band, a row of five diamonds twinkling back at him.

"Are you sure, Doo? You might rather be buried with it."

"No, that would be a waste. I would rather your wife enjoy wearing it on her hand. Perhaps when you catch a glimpse of it, you will think of Her Grace and me—and how happy we were together."

He closed his fist, the ring inside his hand. "Thank you, Doo. You have provided the wedding ring and the place for us to live." He chuckled. "I only wish you could also pick out my bride."

Doo shook his head. "You wouldn't want that, Aidan. Your heart will tell you who the right choice is. However, I will let you stand with me in tonight's receiving line. I have asked Rory to do the same. It will be a way for you to meet every eligible woman who attends the Stag Ball. I may, however, whisper in your ear which ones I like the best."

Aidan roared with laughter.

CHAPTER EIGHT

LARISSA WATCHED LIZZY arrange the final strands of hair. "I look the best I ever have," she said softly, gazing at her image in the mirror.

Lizzy placed her hands on Larissa's shoulders. "You look beautiful, my lady." Squeezing her gently, Lizzy added, "No one will outshine you tonight."

The maid moved away and then answered the knock at Larissa's door. To her surprise, Mama entered the bedchamber and flicked her hand, dismissing Lizzy. The servant looked to Larissa, who nodded, and Lizzy slipped out the door.

Rising, she said, "Good evening, Mama. What brings you here?"

Her mother came closer and Larissa saw tears brimming in her eyes. Her mother never cried. Ever.

She took Larissa's hands in hers. "Lord Silverton sent me a note. He told me that the two of you discussed . . . the past. That you know you are his natural daughter and not Campton's."

"We did. He is a lovely man, Mama. One who still loves you very much."

"I made a mess of things," her mother admitted. "After I

had Peter, I was so lonely. Your father—that is, Campton—had his heir and didn't care much for me or my feelings. My father, who had been so keen on the marriage, died the year Peter was born. He didn't live long enough to enjoy the match made between our families."

Mama sighed and seated herself at Larissa's dressing table, picking up things absently as she spoke.

"When Silverton came back to town after being gone several years, I had already engaged in a few illicit affairs. I begged him to come to me. The passion between us still existed."

Mama put down the hairbrush. "But when I discovered I was with child and had not been with Campton in many months, Silverton told me I must go to my husband and do whatever it took to have him bed me. That I must make my husband believe you were his child. I did so but he wasn't fooled for long. Once I began to show, he berated me, knowing the child I carried was not his. The only thing he said to me after your birth was that he was thankful you were a female and not his spare."

Mama rose and embraced Larissa. "Silverton wed shortly after and he let me know we could never be close again. That he wanted to honor the vows he had spoken with his wife. He has watched you over the years, though, Larissa. Gone to the park when your nanny took you so that he could see you from afar. Sat at a table at Gunter's a few feet away from us so he could admire what a beauty you have become. He is very sorry he cannot acknowledge you in public."

"He told me as much," she said, stepping away from her mother, needing a bit of space. "Did he say . . . anything else?"

"He told me you would not be wedding Lord Langdon. I know nothing beyond that. Silverton is clever, as you are. You take after him in that respect. He would never write to me of something he did not want Campton to know." Mama paused. "Do you have some plan?"

Larissa hugged her mother. "Nothing you need to worry about."

Though she knew her mother hated her husband, Larissa didn't quite trust her enough to reveal the escape which she and her father had plotted. Perhaps after she was in the country, she might send a letter to Mama through Lord Silverton. Somehow, he would see that Mama received it.

"This gown is lovely on you," Mama commented. "No wonder you were so eager to wear it. I suppose Silverton paid to have the modiste send it over."

She didn't think so but she merely nodded, letting Mama think that was the case.

"We should get downstairs. You know how put out Campton is if anyone is late."

That meant they would be riding in the carriage together as a threesome. She supposed since the crowd would be the largest of the Season tonight that the earl did not want their coachman to have to make two trips and become clogged in traffic.

Larissa claimed her reticule, which contained the laundered and pressed handkerchief the mysterious stranger had lent to her. She did hope she would see him at tonight's Stag Ball, if only to thank him for being so kind to her at such a low point. A man that handsome had to be attached to someone else, however, so she squelched any fantasies that might stir within her, knowing he was not the answer to her fervent prayers. Besides, if no one offered for her this evening, which she fully expected, she had an escape plan. She didn't need a husband.

She was going to build a new life on her own.

Following her mother down the staircase, they arrived in the foyer.

"We are ready, Campton," her mother said haughtily.

Without a word, the earl turned and walked out the front door, which the footman managed to open in time for him to do so.

The two women followed and sat opposite him in the carriage. Not a word was spoken until just before they arrived.

"You remember what you are to do tonight?" Campton asked her.

"Find a husband," she said neutrally. "And if I don't, you will select one for me."

He snorted. "Since I doubt you will be able to do so, I have arranged for Lord Langdon and his solicitor to come to the house tomorrow morning at eleven. My solicitor will also be in attendance. We will hammer out the marriage settlements. Once that has occurred, I will send for you." He paused, his smile evil. "The earl is most anxious to make you his bride."

A chill rushed through her. At least Larissa knew now exactly what was planned. Campton required little sleep and would go straight to bed when they arrived back at their townhouse. She would give a quarter-hour to make certain he was asleep and then she and Lizzy could slip from the house. Since a footman would be on duty at the front door and Larissa would not want him fired for letting her escape, she had told Lizzy they would leave through the French doors in her mother's sitting room. They led out to the terrace. She and Lizzy could cut through the back garden and go out the back gate and head straight for Lord Silverton's waiting carriage all while the earl slept.

He would not send for her once he arose. He would breakfast and then wait for Lord Langdon and the solicitors to arrive. He would not discover her missing until she was already on her way to the country.

The carriage stopped and Larissa looked out the window. The Duke of Savernake's footmen were directing traffic. Since large quantities of cut wood had been brought in for the bonfire and placed in the square directly across from the ducal townhouse, carriages had to travel beside the townhouse. As they got out, she saw occupants were being dropped off and the carriages hustled away, while the duke's guests moved along the pavement in front of the townhouse.

She looked at the impressive pile of wood which had been laid in three tiers in the square. Fortunately, Savernake's neighbors' residences were set back far enough from the square so would not be damaged by the burning pile of wood when it finally collapsed. It still amazed her that London officials allowed the duke to hold a bonfire in a public place. Then again, he was the Duke of Savernake. Dukes, it seemed from her limited experience, were a law unto themselves.

They reached the front doors of the vast townhouse, reported to be the largest private residence in London, and stepped inside, joining a long receiving line that snaked about the massive foyer, up the stairs, and down the hall to where the duke's ballroom was to be found. Last year, her first Season, she hadn't minded waiting in the lengthy line because she had been fascinated by all those who had turned out for the Stag Ball.

Tonight was much the same. Larissa admired the various gowns of the women in line and listened to snippets of conversations around them. Naturally, her parents spoke nary a word to one another, each finding people in front and back of them whom they chose to converse with. Normally, Campton skipped receiving lines altogether, making straight for the cardroom at these affairs. He knew better than to do so at the Duke of Savernake's residence.

She saw Ann standing next to her baron and waved. Her friend whispered something to her husband and came back to join Larissa for a few minutes.

"This gown is amazing," Ann exclaimed. "Madame Floseau outdid herself."

"I do like it," she said, keeping to herself that she almost didn't get to be seen in the wonderful creation tonight.

Leaning close, she said in her friend's ear, "I am in desperate need of your help. Ellen and Betsy can help, as well. We all need to meet once we are inside the ballroom."

"What is troubling you, Larissa?"

"I need to learn how to flirt," she blurted out, though thankfully she said it quietly. Though she still didn't expect a marriage proposal tonight, she would do her best to try and wring one from someone.

Ann's brows arched. "Flirt? What brought this on?"

Not wanting to burden her friend with her plight, Larissa said, "I have never done so. Perhaps that is why I haven't been able to get any gentlemen interested in me. You know, however, that the Stag Ball has a reputation for marvelous things occurring during it. If I can flirt a bit tonight, who knows?"

"You might find a handsome suitor," Ann agreed. "Very well. I will go find the others now and tell them what you wish to discuss. We will all have clever ideas for you by the time we meet. *If* any of us can even recall how to flirt. After all, you are talking about three married ladies, Larissa," she teased.

Ann said her goodbyes and returned to her husband.

Mama leaned over. "I heard the word flirting in your conversation. Do you plan to do so this evening?"

"I am going to try, Mama," she promised. "I would rather have a husband of my own choosing than one chosen for me."

"Bat your eyelashes a bit," her mother advised. "Then glance down and back up with them still lowered." Mama demonstrated.

"Oh, that is interesting," she said. "May I try it?"

She did and Mama corrected her until Larissa had the gesture down.

"Use that tonight. It has worked for me on many occasions," her mother bragged.

By now, they had reached the staircase and were halfway up it. Being at such a height, it was easier for her to gaze down at those in the foyer and up to those still ahead.

The handsome stranger was nowhere in sight.

She sighed, thinking she might never spy him in such a crush of people. He could have already made his way through the receiving line an hour ago or still be outside since the line now ran out the door. She passed the time continuing to look for him and eavesdropping on the conversations around her, learning nothing new, other than rumors as to what might be served on tonight's midnight buffet.

They reached the top of the staircase and turned down the corridor. Larissa stood on tiptoes.

"I see the duke," she told her mother.

And then she saw him. The man who had given up his handkerchief to her. The one who had asked what was wrong with her as she wept.

He was standing next to the Duke of Savernake.

CHAPTER NINE

A IDAN CONTINUALLY PEERED down the line, on the lookout for Lady Larissa.

At one point, Doo asked, "Is there someone in particular you are searching for?"

"No," he mumbled and then pasted on another social smile, greeting the next guests in line.

Then he saw her. Or rather, he saw the ice blue gown in the distance—and knew it was her.

She was here.

His heart banged against his ribs. He leaned to the side in order to get a glimpse of her. She was talking to an older woman, whom he assumed to be her mother. An older gentleman with a head of graying hair and a hawklike nose stood behind them, his arms crossed. Aidan recognized the look of disdain on his face even from this distance.

He had to be the Earl of Campton.

Aidan wanted nothing better than to break the man's nose. Anger simmered through him.

Doo claimed his attention, introducing him to the next set of guests, who had their daughter with them. Aidan smiled brightly and promptly forget the chit's name the moment she passed through the line. The girl had been pretty—but not nearly as pretty as Lady Larissa. Actually, Lady Larissa was more than pretty. She was beautiful. Even through her swollen eyes, he had seen her beauty. Soon, she would be before him.

He eagerly awaited her.

Returning his attention fully now, he welcomed Doo's guests with gusto. At one point, his grandfather leaned in and asked why he was suddenly happy.

"Oh, I know now," Doo said knowingly as he caught Aidan glancing at Lady Larissa. "She is quite attractive. Too bad she is Campton's daughter. Now there is a scoundrel. His reputation is far blacker than that of the Sinning Flynns. The wife is almost as indiscreet as her husband. And the son raises holy hell."

"But you would not hold that against Lady Larissa?" he asked worriedly.

Doo turned to him, his back to the next group of guests. "You know her?"

"We met today. Briefly. We weren't properly introduced."

Light filled Doo's eyes. "You think she is the one."

Aidan swallowed. "I am hoping so."

His grandfather shook his head. "We will see." Doo then coughed. Turning around again, he apologized. "I am sorry. Felt a bit of a cough coming on. My throat is parched after greeting all these guests."

He continued to watch as Lady Larissa and her parents drew closer. Just before they reached him, a man rushed along the corridor and joined them. Aidan suspected it was her brother.

Finally, she stood near him. Her father had brushed against her, stepping to the front. Her brother did the same. Aidan's simmering anger flared.

Doo turned. "Ah, Campton. How good of you to come. My grandson, Aidan Flynn." He then turned to his other side and said, "And another grandson, Rory Flynn."

"Good of you to have us, Your Grace," Lord Campton replied, ignoring Aidan. "My son, Peter."

Then the two men walked off, leaving the female members of their family behind.

"Lady Campton," Doo said smoothly. "How pleasant to have you at my Stag Ball. And who might this lovely young lady be?"

Aidan saw Lady Larissa's eyes were large, cutting from him to Doo.

"This is my daughter, Your Grace. Lady Larissa."

Doo graciously took Lady Larissa's hand and kissed it. "It is indeed a pleasure to have you at the Stag Ball, my lady. This is my grandson, Aidan Flynn. He has only come to town yesterday and isn't much for *ton* affairs. Perhaps you would be kind enough to grant him a dance with you this evening?"

Doo smiled at her and she swallowed, mustering a smile in return, yet looking like a hare about to be ensnared in a trap.

"I would be happy to, Your Grace," she said, her voice shaking a bit.

Aidan took her gloved hand in his. "I didn't think I would have to resort to my grandfather claiming dance partners for me but I would enjoy your company in a dance this evening, Lady Larissa. Might you wish to dance the opening number with me?"

He raised her hand and kissed her knuckles, his gaze never leaving hers. He could see her pulse beating wildly in her throat.

"Yes, Mr. Flynn. I will dance it with you," she said, her voice soft and low.

"Then we will speak soon," he replied, squeezing her fingers before releasing them.

As he watched her and Lady Campton retreat, Doo said, "She is lovely. I'll grant you that. But have a care, Aidan. Her family is more notorious than the Sinning Flynns." Doo leaned in, his lips grazing Aidan's ear. "And rumor has it she is not even Campton's daughter, if you know what I mean."

Doo stepped away and welcomed the next guests. Aidan understood immediately what his grandfather meant.

Lady Larissa's mother had had an affair—and her daughter was the child of another man. It explained in part why Lord Campton had been so cruel to her. With her auburn hair and blue eyes, Lady Larissa favored neither parent. Aidan wondered if she knew the circumstances of her birth. Naturally, she would be Campton's offspring in the eyes of the law but if Doo knew Lady Campton had strayed from her marital vows, then most of Polite Society did, as well.

Pity filled him for the young, beautiful woman who most likely had been mistreated or ignored by Lord Campton.

Yet learning this didn't change his mind in the slightest. Where Doo questioned him, Aidan knew the gossip didn't matter to him. After all, he was a Sinning Flynn. The *ton* regularly raked him and his family over the coals. They must do the same to the Camptons, only Aidan never listened to gossip and hadn't heard of Lady Campton's infidelity. Obviously, her husband also engaged in extramarital affairs, based upon what Doo had said. The brother looked like a rakehell of the worst kind.

He wanted to rescue Lady Larissa from her family. Something told him she might be willing to entertain an offer of marriage from him if only to escape her troublesome family and their reputations.

Aidan smiled broadly—and greeted the next guest in line.

Cʒ

LARISSA COULD HARDLY catch her breath as she and Mama moved away from the Duke of Savernake.

And his grandson.

While everyone in Polite Society had a healthy respect for His Grace, his family was another matter. Everyone in the *ton* knew the story of Lady Amy, Savernake's only daughter, who had spurned the Earl of Exford. Lady Amy broke her engagement for a man rumored to be a smuggler at best and according to some, a criminal. A Cornish commoner who had been elevated by the Mad King to become the Earl of Sinbrook. While that scandal was over three decades old, it was still talked about—mainly because of the offspring produced by Sinbrook and his countess. They were parents to four of the wildest libertines to walk among Polite Society.

The Sinning Flynns.

The Sinning Flynns weren't truly welcomed anywhere although they occasionally showed up at *ton* events. No one had the courage to tell them they were not wanted in Polite Society, mainly because they were favored by the crown and because of their strong family connection to the esteemed Duke of Savernake. Years ago, Larissa used to read the gossip columns in the newspapers to Cressida, where tales of the exploits of the oldest two Sinning Flynns were reported for a good decade. Those two had wed a few years back, close to when Cressida passed, and their names no longer appeared anywhere in the newspapers. In fact, Larissa did not recall seeing them or their parents during her come-out Season last year and supposed they had settled into their marriages and remained in Cornwall.

But she had seen Rory Flynn a few times during her come-out, a man branded unscrupulous and disreputable by the *ton* and gossip columns alike, due to his womanizing and gambling. Ellen had pointed out Rory to her, warning Larissa to avoid him like the plague. She was never to be introduced to him, much less dance with him. Until tonight, when she was briefly introduced in the receiving line.

Betsy had been the one to tell her of the other Sinning Flynn, the youngest of the four brothers. Though Larissa had only seen Aidan from a distance once at a ball last year, she read about his various exploits in the newspapers. He owned several racehorses and raced his phaeton in Hyde Park when in town. It was rumored that Aidan Flynn had never lost a race. The newspapers alluded that he might cheat to maintain that winning record. While Rory was constantly gossiped about in the ballrooms of the *ton*, Aidan had not been mentioned much.

Still, he was a member of the Sinning Flynns, which meant he was the last man she wished to be around tonight. She still clung to the miniscule chance that she might convince someone to wed her tonight. If she went into service, she would never have children of her own but instead care for the children of others. She supposed being a governess would be rewarding and lonely at the same time, not quite a part of the life of a downstairs servant and yet certain not on equal footing with the family above stairs.

As Mama moved them toward the ballroom, she said, "That was quite a coup, my dear."

"What?" she asked, her thoughts still spinning.

"Why, having Savernake's grandson ask you to dance with

him," Mama said. "Actually, it was the duke himself who arranged the dance. But his grandson is most handsome, don't you think? You will be the envy of every woman in the ballroom."

She steered her mother to a corner. "Are you mad?" she hissed. "I will be the envy of no one. Mama, he is a Flynn. A Sinning Flynn."

Mama smiled. "He is handsome and charming, my girl. More importantly, I have heard that the Earl of Sinbrook's shipping empire has made him and his four sons quite wealthy."

"Don't you understand?" she pressed. "If I dance with a Sinning Flynn, everyone will think I am some trollop. Enough of Polite Society already lumps me together with my amoral family as it is."

"Larissa!" her mother chastised.

"Well, it is true and you know it, Mama. Your friends over-look your casual affairs but a good portion of the *ton* disapproves of your behavior. Men can get away with more but even then, Papa has never been discreet in his many affairs. Peter takes after him, cut from the same cloth. The pair of them are known reprobates. What little chance I have of obtaining a husband will be utterly lost when the duke's guests see me dancing with a Sinning Flynn."

Mama stared hard at her. "You could do worse, Larissa. You could marry Lord Langdon and go to his bed. If I had the choice, I would choose a young, handsome, wealthy Sinning Flynn over an old codger such as Langdon. Besides, you already promised Mr. Flynn a dance—and in front of the duke. There is no graceful way to back out of it, dear." Mama patted her shoulder. "You must soldier on."

Unhappiness filled her. Her social life was already ruined. She might as well leave the Stag Ball and go home and help Lizzy pack their things because she certainly wasn't landing a husband at tonight's affair. After the first dance, Lady Larissa Warren would be a laughingstock. Any gentleman who had signed her dance card before the ball started would surely stand her up afterward.

The die was cast. She would march to her own personal guillotine and become a social outcast.

Her mother steered her toward the ballroom and, once inside, they parted ways. Mama went to the right and her close circle of friends she had possessed since childhood. Larissa looked to the left and saw Betsy wave at her. Glumly, she headed toward her friends. Thank goodness none of their husbands were in sight.

Joining them, she tried to smile and failed miserably.

"Ann told us you wish to learn how to flirt," Ellen said. "My earl will tell you that it was my flirting with him that caught his eye. It is all in how you use your fan, you see."

"There are other ways that are not nearly as complicated," Betsy told Larissa. "The viscount caught me looking at him. I *wanted* him to catch me gazing at him, you see. You don't stare. You mere look and wait for a gentleman to look at you. Then you look away. Briefly."

"Betsy is right," Ann said. "Then you look back and hope he is gazing at you. Hold his gaze for a moment and smile before you look away again. You see, flirtation is all a game."

She knew her friends meant well. She wasn't about to explain the mess she had gotten herself into. Larissa decided she might as well play along for the moment.

"Mama tried to teach me a bit." She explained about lowering her gaze and then looking up through her lowered lashes.

"Oh, your mother is right," Ann gushed. "I have done that myself."

Larissa demonstrated, looking demurely at Betsy and then down before glancing up slightly.

"You should have been doing this all along, Larissa," Ellen said. "And you are blushing slightly. Men love when they get a woman to blush."

"They do?" She felt so ignorant now.

And so hopeless.

Their advice kept coming. Smile with her eyes as well as her mouth. Keep the conversation light. Casually place her hand briefly on a gentleman's sleeve and then remove it.

"I know," Betsy said brightly. "You must compliment him. Men love it when you compliment them, even more so than women do."

Puzzled, she asked, "Why have none of you ever told me any of this before?"

Ann shrugged. "I suppose these were things we talked about five years ago when we made our come-outs. We are all old married ladies now, with children and sagging breasts and bellies. Our flirting days are over."

Betsy sniffed. "Well, mine certainly aren't. I am quite put out with my husband. He is at it again, you know."

"He is seeing someone?" Larissa asked.

"Yes. I have given him his heir and spare and think it is about time I found a lover of my own."

Ellen and Ann tittered, while Larissa bit her lip. She did not approve of extramarital affairs, even though she adored Betsy.

"I speak from personal experience," she said quietly. "Having watched my parents for years. Taking a lover for revenge will only hurt you in the end, Betsy."

Her friend was nonplussed. "But . . . your parents have despised each other from the beginning. My husband and I at least get along most of the time. I simply want a man who will put me first." Betsy sighed. "Perhaps I will even find love."

A passing footman handed Larissa a dance programme. Her friends declined. They usually danced the supper dance with their husbands, who left the card room long enough to claim their wives for that dance and the midnight buffet.

They continued to talk. Three gentlemen did come and ask to sign her dance card. One was a rather shy baron Ann had introduced her to but he had never asked for a dance before. She handed it to him, watching him scribble his name, knowing he would not return for their dance. Two others were friends of Peter's, both plying her with false compliments. She allowed them to sign as well.

No other dances were claimed.

"It is almost time for the Stag Ball to begin," Ellen said. "The orchestra is tuning their instruments." She kissed Larissa's cheek. "Do your best tonight. Be lighthearted. Take our flirting lessons to heart."

She nodded and waved to her friends as they departed, watching them retreat to where the matrons sat and watched the dancing.

"It looks as if I have just missed meeting your friends," a deep voice said near her ear.

Larissa whirled and found Aidan Flynn standing there.

"Are they good friends of yours? You seemed quite animated talking to them."

"We have been friends since we were girls," she said stiffly. "They made their come-outs five years ago, however, and all have wed and birthed children. Unfortunately, that means we have little in common these days."

"You have been out five years?" he asked.

"No. I . . . remained in the country. My sister, Cressida, was quite ill. I nursed her for several years. When she passed, I observed the mourning period for a year. That made last year my come-out Season."

Her throat thickened with tears.

Mr. Flynn moved closer to her. "I am sorry to hear your sister passed. It seems you were close."

"Quite close," she said, thinking he was too close to her because she caught a whiff of his cologne. "We were the best of friends."

"Did your mother stay behind in the country with you?"

"No," she said, baffled by his question, then realizing that was what most every other mother would have done. "I suppose your mother would have nursed her sick children."

He chuckled, the sound low and quite seductive. "Mama wouldn't have allowed anyone else near us if we had been sick. Not even Da."

"Da?"

"It is the Irish word for father. A tradition in my family. You see, we are descended from an Irish pirate. Scandalous, I know. I shouldn't even be talking about it while I am trying to impress you."

His words took her by surprise. "You wish to impress me, Mr. Flynn?"

"Very much, Lady Larissa." He paused and slowly looked her up and down. "You look divine in your dream gown."

A hot blushed heated her cheeks. "I . . . should not have told you that. I am afraid I was quite indiscreet regarding our conversation outside the dress shop, Mr. Flynn. I should never have mentioned my . . . situation to you. You caught me off-guard, I am afraid. I have never spoken ill of the earl, you see."

"You call him the earl."

Her face now flamed and she thought it as red as her hair. "Well, he is one."

"He also is not your father."

"What?" She stared at him. "You did not just say that. You couldn't have. No one speaks so outrageously in Polite Society."

"Even if Polite Society is saying that very thing behind your back?"

She raised her hand to strike him. He caught her wrist and lowered it.

"Calm down, my lady," he advised. "You do not want to bring unwanted attention."

"That will already happen when I dance with the likes of you," she snapped.

"I see. You have learned that I am not merely Mr. Flynn—but that I am a Sinning Flynn."

He gazed into her eyes a long moment. Larissa was spellbound, unable to look away. His fingers tightened slightly around her wrist. Something ran through her, like an electrical current, bringing heat, warming her blood.

"There is more to me than that shameful moniker, my lady. I apologize for my indiscretion."

"You mean for calling me a bastard?" she hissed.

"You aren't one. By law, you are Campton's daughter." He studied her a moment. "But you already knew that, didn't you?"

"I searched through legal books until I found the answer," she replied through gritted teeth. "Yes, I am a Warren by name. Campton has always had a cruel streak, though. It took me a long time to realize how much he hated me. And why."

She saw Mr. Flynn's eyes darken in anger. "He has hurt you?"

"Only with words. More harsh ones recently. If I hadn't known I was another man's child before then, I would have swiftly come to that conclusion." She sniffed. "You pointing that out, however, is the antithesis of gentlemanly behavior, however. And here I had your handkerchief laundered and pressed, ready to give back to you."

"You did?" he asked, his eyes lighting up, a pleased smile turning up the corners of his sensual lips.

Larissa opened her reticule, shrugging off his hand from her wrist. She reached inside and retrieved the handkerchief.

Handing it to him, she said, "I owe you nothing more, Mr. Flynn."

He caught her elbow as she started to turn away. "You owe me a dance, Lady Larissa. I aim to claim it now."

With that, Aidan Flynn led her to the center of the ballroom.

CHAPTER TEN

A S AIDAN ESCORTED Lady Larissa to the middle of the
ballroom floor, he could feel the eyes of the *ton* upon
them. He had gambled, taking a calculated risk in acknowledging her parentage. He wanted to be candid about this because
when he offered marriage to her later this evening, he did not
want that to be a barrier between them. She might have actually
said no because of it or even thought it an obstacle that could
not be overcome. By acknowledging that he knew of the
circumstances of her birth, Aidan hoped to lay those fears to
rest.

Because he wanted this woman. Nothing would stand in his
way of having her.

They reached the center of the room, where he had known
they would be the focus of attention. What surprised him was
seeing Doo coming to join them, Lady Campton on his arm.
Doo rarely danced anymore and that in itself would make
enough of a statement. But with Aidan partnering with Lady
Campton's daughter and his grandfather, the Duke of
Savernake, to be dancing with the countess herself, their actions
would speak volumes to Polite Society.

Lady Larissa looked about and he saw panic fill her eyes. "This is a waltz!"

"Yes, it is, my lady. Do you not know how to waltz?"

She gave him a withering look. "Another ungentlemanly statement, I see."

"I suppose you believe the Sinning Flynns have no manners at all."

"Well, you would certainly have to change my mind about that," she retorted, "but . . ."

Then Aidan saw determination fill her eyes, and she said, "If I am to go down in flames, so be it."

"You believe dancing with a Sinning Flynn will result in your ruin? It is merely a dance, my lady, albeit a waltz."

The music began and he swept her away, noting she moved with grace and ease.

"Being seen with you in front of the entire *ton* will definitely ruin any chance I have of ever securing a husband," she said flatly. "I might as well enjoy this dance—since it will be the last of my life."

He wondered about such an odd statement and asked, "Have you no other dance partners this evening?"

"I have a few but after they see me with the likes of you, I doubt they will claim the dance they signed up for."

He smiled. "In that case, would you grant me the supper dance?" Pressing further, he added, "And the final dance of the evening? I would request it as well."

"You obviously don't know or care about the unwritten rules of Polite Society, Mr. Flynn," she told him. "To dance twice with a lady shows your interest in her. Thrice simply isn't done. Tongues will wag."

"You have already told me those tongues will be wagging

merely because we danced this opening number together," he pointed out.

"You are correct, I suppose."

He saw her come to a quick decision. "All right, Mr. Flynn. You may have all three of those dances if you choose. As I said, these will be my last dances at any *ton* event."

It was hard for him to believe that merely dancing with a Sinning Flynn would make her an outcast in Polite Society but he realized how vile his family's reputation was. Her family's wasn't much better but he didn't think now was the time to point that out.

Especially because he was enjoying this dance with her. Both the verbal and physical one.

"You waltz beautifully, Lady Larissa," he complimented. "I have danced upon occasion and I would say you are by far the most graceful woman to partner with me."

Color rose in her cheeks and she primly said, "Thank you, Mr. Flynn."

The rest of the waltz they dance in silence. Aidan was aware of everything about her. The subtle scent of vanilla which wafted toward him. The feel of her, warm in his arms. His lips itched to kiss her and he wondered what that would be like. As the dance came to its conclusion and the music ended, he held her in his arms a moment longer, reluctant to let her go. Knowing they had already drawn more than their fair share of attention, however, he released her and placed her hand upon his forearm, escorting her from the floor.

"You remember, my lady, that you have promised both the supper dance and the final one to me."

"I will be easy to find. Look for me sitting with the other wallflowers who won't dance at all."

She turned from him and Aidan walked away, biting back a smile. Lady Larissa was sweet but she also could be quite feisty. He believed, because of that, a passion lay deep within her—and he was the one ready to awaken it.

He wondered if she had ever been kissed and decided most likely not. He went and joined Doo, who looked across the ballroom floor as the dancers began a Scotch reel.

"Thank you," he said, his voice filled with gratitude.

"For what?" Doo asked, feigning ignorance.

"You know what. Actions speak louder than words. By my partnering with Lady Larissa Warren, I have already spoken volumes to Polite Society this evening. You, by asking her mother to dance, put your seal of approval on our union."

Doo's eyes lit with amusement. "And is there to be a union, Grandson? The girl is quite comely. Despite her family's tattered reputation, I believe hers to be pure."

"I do also, Doo. I like her quite a bit."

"Do you think it could grow beyond like?"

"Only time will tell," he told his grandfather. "But I believe the potential is there."

"Her Grace and I were not a love match in the beginning," Doo revealed, surprising Aidan. "We did have quite a bit in common, however. It wasn't long before passion ignited between us, followed by a lasting friendship—and love. I hope the same for you, Aidan."

He saw Doo grimace and said, "You need to lie down now. I'll take you."

"No, stay and enjoy yourself with your young lady. She seems to be enjoying herself out on the dance floor. I will see you later."

As his grandfather moved slowly away, Aidan turned his

attention to the dancers, his eyes searching for Lady Larissa. Despite the mass of people, he spotted her with ease. Doo was right. She had a smile on her face and the color bloomed in her cheeks. She had told him she didn't think she would dance again but here she was, out on the floor, having the time of her life. A frisson of jealousy rippled through him. He would not let it overwhelm him as his eyes followed her across the dance floor.

Rory came up to him, the first he had seen of his brother since the receiving line.

"My, you have certainly caused a stir at the Stag Ball," his brother observed. "Do you know of the lady's reputation?"

"The lady has a name," Aidan snapped. "Lady Larissa. And her reputation is spotless."

"Not her family's," Rory said. "I would say their reputation rivals that of the Sinning Flynns." Rory grew serious, the teasing gone. "You like this woman, don't you, Aidan?"

He nodded. "I do. I want to marry her."

His words surprised him but it was true. He had come into this evening seeking a bride in order to be able to inherit Larkhaven. Something had changed, though. Lady Larissa had sparked something within him. He wanted to get to know her. Laugh with her. Make love to her. Possess her.

He pushed aside the strong rush of emotion and asked, "And what of your search for a bride tonight, Rory?"

His brother smiled enigmatically. "I will let you know after the Stag Ball concludes," and he moved away.

The Scotch reel finished and Aidan watched as Lady Larissa's partner returned her, where she was claimed by a second gentlemen. Ire rose within him and he tamped it down. He already had danced with her once and had claimed two more.

By asking her for the supper dance, it would ensure they spent more time together. He would make certain they shared a table meant only for two. He wanted to get to know his bride-to-be better.

Summoning a footman, he requested that a table for two in a far corner be reserved for him.

"Of course, Mr. Aidan," the footman responded. "I will see to it at once."

Aidan spoke to a few friends from his university days between sets though his eyes never strayed far from Lady Larissa. She had danced every number.

Finally, the supper dance arrived and he made his way through the throng in order to claim her.

When he stood before her, he saw her eyes were bright and her cheeks flushed with color, making her simply irresistible. He didn't know how much longer he could hold out without kissing her.

"I believe this is the supper dance which you promised me, Lady Larissa. Shall we?"

He offered his arm to her and she placed her fingers upon his sleeve. Once more, he escorted her to the center of the ballroom.

"Another waltz, I believe," he commented. "I am particularly fond of waltzes. Especially now," he added, his gaze pinning hers.

She licked her lips and his gaze fell to them, even as the music began and he took her in his arms.

"You were wrong," he told her.

"Wrong? About what?" she asked testily.

"About having no dance partners. In fact, it has been the opposite of what you led me to believe, my lady. Instead of sitting on the sidelines with the wallflowers, you have danced every single number."

"You noticed?" she asked, wonder in her voice as her gaze dropped. Then she glanced up at him through lowered lashes and the blood pounded in his ears.

She was flirting with him.

"I did notice. How could I not when you have become the belle of the Stag Ball?"

She laughed, low and throaty, and the vibration of her laugh seemed to echo within his chest.

"I should know because I have seen the line of men form in front of you."

"I will admit I am very surprised by that fact, Mr. Flynn," she admitted. "I thought dancing with you would leave my reputation in shreds. Instead, it seems to have enhanced it substantially. I still don't believe I will find a husband tonight as the earl has ordered. It is nice to go out on such a high note."

Her words confused him. "I do not understand, my lady. What do you mean about finding a husband tonight, in particular?"

She bit her full, lower lip and Aidan wished he were the one biting into it.

"I seem to continually be indiscreet around you, Mr. Flynn. I assure you that it is very unlike me."

He chuckled. "Perhaps I inspire confidences, my lady. Please explain to me what you mean?"

"I might as well tell you. It is not as if we will ever speak again after this night."

Little did she know . . .

"Lord Campton is tired of me being a presence in his household. I was given strict instructions at breakfast this morning—and he reminded me again just before we left the carriage tonight—that he wishes to be rid of me. He said if I did not become engaged tonight with a man of my choosing, then he will arrange a marriage for me. Lord Langdon is to be at our townhouse tomorrow morning to draw up the marriage settlements. I have an idea the marriage will take place soon after that."

"What?" he gasped. "Langdon? Why, that old goat has been wed multiple times, each wife younger and younger."

"Four to be exact, Mr. Flynn. I would be wife number five. It seems Lord Langdon is still in need of an heir and thinks to get one off me."

"I will not allow that to happen, Larissa," Aidan said.

"Ah, more ungentlemanly behavior from you," she noted.

Anger surged through him at her flippancy when the situation was so serious. "You are being forced to wed a man who is beyond ancient—and you call *me* uncivilized?"

"You used my Christian name, Mr. Flynn," she reminded. "I did not give you leave to do so. Why, even betrothed couples rarely refer to one another by their given names."

Then she gazed directly into his eyes. "Oh, why not? After all, this is the Stag Ball, where unusual things occur each year. I suppose I would like to break a few rules myself before this evening ends. What do you think, Aidan?" she asked.

Hearing his name come from her lips was all he needed to spur him into action.

He had to kiss her. Now.

But not in front of the entire *ton*. It would force her into a marriage with him and he wanted it to be her choice. Her answer to a new life. With him.

He continued turning, whirling her away from the center of

the room, until they reached the edge of the ballroom, where the entire wall of French doors was open to allow in the breeze.

Aidan waltzed Larissa out those doors and onto the terrace. He continued dancing with her, his heart hammering, the strains of the music fading the further he moved them away and into the darkness. They reached the far end of the terrace and he stopped moving his feet—but did not release her from his grasp.

"You think me ungentlemanly," he said. "You think me to be a Sinning Flynn."

"Aren't you?" she asked breathlessly, gazing up at him. "I have read of some of your exploits in the newspapers. About you racing your phaeton in Hyde Park, often cheating to win."

His hands moved to her shoulders, his fingers tightening. "I have never cheated a single time in my life," he said harshly. "It is the losers who plant those rumors, which the newspapers then pick up and print. Have you read anything else unseemly about me, Larissa?"

She licked her lips again nervously and said, "Not really. I do know you own several successful racehorses."

"There is nothing unseemly or ungentlemanly about owning racehorses. What else?"

"Nothing, I suppose. Although I have read terribly nasty things about your three brothers. Now, they are certainly Sinning Flynns. Your two older brothers cut a wide swath through Polite Society for a good ten years or more. And your brother, Rory, who is here tonight . . . he seems the wickedest Flynn of all."

"I will agree with you that my family has a terrible reputation, beginning with my parents' marriage. But Da and Mama are a love match. Mama never wished to wed Lord Exford.

When she met Da and fell instantly in love, they both knew it could be no other for them. As for my brothers, Carmack and Kellen were scoundrels of the worst kind, until they met their wives. Here, at a Stag Ball, in fact. Now, they are as tame as can be, very much in love with their wives, faithful and hardworking men.

"As for Rory? I cannot defend his actions. At his core, he is a good man but he does have a wild streak within him. I may physically resemble Da and my three brothers but I am no Sinning Flynn, Larissa. I am more like my mother and Doo."

Her brows knit together. "Doo?"

Aidan chuckled. "Apparently, I could not say the word duke when I was young and toddling about. What came out was Doo—and the nickname stuck."

"That is so sweet, Aidan," she said softly. "A lovely nickname for your grandfather."

"Not as sweet as our kiss will be," he replied, lowering his lips to hers.

CHAPTER ELEVEN

L ARISSA KNEW THE kiss was coming and could have stopped it.

But why would she want to?

She had never been kissed—and would never have an opportunity like this come her way again. As a governess, she would lead a chaste life. Why not take advantage of what Aidan Flynn offered?

The moment his lips met hers, a delicious warmth spread through her, starting in her belly and reaching outward, rippling along her limbs and along her spine. Softly, he brushed his lips against hers. Larissa smiled at the marvelous feelings it brought.

Aidan's hands slipped from her shoulders. One inched up to her nape, holding her in place, his thumb stroking her neck. The other moved to her back, roaming up and down it. The kiss, which was tender and sweet, changed then. He pressed his lips more firmly to hers. His hand flattened against the small of her back and brought her closer, her breasts brushing against the hard wall of his muscular chest, which felt as solid as granite.

Her heartbeat quickened. Butterflies exploded in her belly. The blood raced to her ears.

Then the pressure eased and his tongue touched her mouth, outlining it in a slow, sensual gesture. She swallowed, unsure of what was to come. Then he ran it along the seam of her mouth, teasing it open.

"Oh!" she managed to say just before his tongue plunged inside. Immediately, currents of electricity raced through her body and she grabbed on to his shoulders as her knees grew weak. His tongue glided along, thoroughly exploring her, bringing frissons of delight. Her nails dug into his shoulders and she clung to him, tasting him, reveling in these new sensations.

As his tongue massaged hers, she found herself answering some ancient call and her tongue also begin to move. He groaned, tightening his grip on her, holding her so close their bodies were now flush against each other. She could feel his thundering heartbeat against her breast and knew he could also feel hers.

Suddenly, he broke the kiss, his mouth hovering just above hers. Need crashed through, wanting his lips on hers again, his tongue stroking hers.

"The music has stopped. We must go in to supper."

"Supper?" she asked dully.

"Yes. The midnight buffet."

Aidan took her by the shoulders again. "We dare not tarry else your reputation will be in tatters."

She snorted. "It would merely make me a true Warren."

"Come inside," he urged, slipping her hand through the crook of his arm as he guided her toward the ballroom doors.

Larissa clung to him, afraid her legs would give out and she would crumple to the ground. She throbbed everywhere.

Especially the place between her legs.

She never touched there, other than to wash quickly. But now she wanted to touch it.

No, she wanted *Aidan* to touch her there.

What a wicked, delicious thought. His fingers stroking her as he kissed her. Using his tongue, of course. Why had none of her friends told her kissing involved tongues?

The ballroom was emptying, guests proceeding to the Duke of Savernake's famous buffet. It was said each year the spread of food was more lavish and expensive than the year before. When she had gone through it last June, she had thought it a veritable feast that might feed the citizens of London for a week.

Aidan didn't lead them to the buffet, however. Instead, he escorted her to a small table with only seats for two and seated her there. Larissa could feel hundreds of eyes upon them and sensed her cheeks heating. She could also still feel Aidan's mouth on hers. Even smell his cologne lingering on her skin. What on earth would her next dance partner think?

She chuckled. She didn't care. She never wanted another partner again, other than this Sinning Flynn. He might not have the atrocious reputation of his brothers, but he certainly knew how to kiss. His kiss tasted of sin and dark pleasures that she could only imagine.

"What do you wish to eat? Anything you name is available on the buffet."

"We aren't going through it yet?"

He captured her hand and brought it to his lips, his gaze penetrating. A warm flush rippled through her, heating her blood.

"I don't wish to waste time doing so. I refuse to be parted

from you."

Signaling a footman, he asked, "What would you have him bring us?"

Larissa named a few items and Aidan did, too.

"Right away, Mr. Aidan," the footman said and retreated.

He still held her hand. Even though the corner they sat in was dimly lit, she didn't think he should continue to do so and tried to ease away. His grip tightened.

"You should not hold my hand in public," she chided.

He slipped their joined hands from the table so that they could not be seen by a casual observer.

"Why are you paying such attention to me?" she asked, curious. "You obviously know I am not Lord Campton's daughter since you made no secret of that. Campton is known for conducting open affairs. Mama pursues lovers of her own in retaliation, not that her husband cares. My brother is the most promiscuous of all the Warrens, bedding women left and right."

"Is that why you have no serious suitors?" he asked. "Because of your family?"

She nodded. "It is only a guess but I believe that to be the case. The few who have paid me any attention are friends of Peter's and reprobates as he is. I had to slap a few when they became fresh with me. They were sorely disappointed to retreat without stealing a single kiss."

"You did not slap me when I kissed you."

"No, I didn't." She hesitated and then said, "I figured it was about time I was kissed. Who better to show me what a kiss is than a Sinning Flynn?" she said flippantly, trying to hide emotions that threatened to bubble to the surface.

"I thought we had established I was not truly a Sinning Flynn. That there was more to me than that ridiculous nickname."

"Have you kissed a lot of women?" she demanded. "I would think a Sinning Flynn would have."

"I have kissed my fair share. Nothing was ever serious, though."

"Then why did you kiss me?"

The footman returned with their plates, piled high with delectable wonders, allowing Aidan to avoid her question. Once the footman left, they began sampling different dishes, each one better than the previous one.

"Doo does have a marvelous cook. Both in town and at Summerwood, his ducal estate in Dorchester. I visited him there every summer when I was growing up. We would stay there a bit and often go to Larkhaven, another of his Dorchester holdings."

"Did your brothers also come with you?"

"No. They love Doo but they are Cornishmen, through and through. They preferred staying in Falmouth, where Da owns land. He also has a shipping company, where we all work."

"What do you do?"

He laughed. "A little of everything. Actually, since I graduated from Cambridge, I have worked mostly in the company offices, poring over ledgers. I have always had a talent for numbers. But I have put in my fair share of time on the docks, loading and unloading merchandise."

"I can tell. It is obvious."

"It is?" he asked, his gazing piercing hers.

Larissa sensed the blush creeping up her neck. "Well, you are rather . . . firm. Your chest. Your arms. And as tight as your breeches are, anyone can see how muscular your legs are," she said primly, heat now flooding her face.

"You are beautiful when you blush, Larissa," he said tenderly.

For a moment, she wished she could have this man. Marry him. Bear his children. Sleep with him. Laugh with him. Grow old with him.

But he was a Flynn at heart. She believed he was only toying with her now.

"Why did you kiss me? You never answered my question."

He slipped his hand around hers again, out of sight. "Because I wanted to. You have wonderfully plump lips which called out to me. You are an exceptionally beautiful woman, Larissa. I desired you. I wanted to kiss you more than anything. Taste you. Touch you."

Her earlier thoughts of where she wanted him to touch her caused her face to flame.

"Did you want to kiss *me*?" he countered.

"Well, I suppose . . . yes. I did. I thought it would be nice to finally experience a kiss."

Aidan smiled at her lazily. "Did you enjoy it?"

She lowered her gaze to their joined hands. "Yes," she whispered.

"Would you like to do it again?" he asked, his voice husky.

Her head snapped up. "No."

"No?" he questioned, his thumb slowly brushing against her palm.

"There are no more opportunities for that," she said.

"I think there are—if you wish to explore them."

Oh, she wanted to. With him. Very much.

"When?" she asked, almost dizzy now as his thumb continued to arouse her.

"Did you attend the Stag Ball last year?"

"Yes."

Aidan smiled. "Then you know after supper, I am to escort you out to the bonfire. We can slip away as others watch it burn."

"And kiss again?" she asked eagerly.

His smile turned devilish, as did the glint in his eyes. "Oh, I think we might even do more than kiss, Larissa."

He released her hand and picked up a tiny tart, popping it into his mouth. "Mmm. Lemon."

"How can you eat at a time like this?" she demanded.

"Men can always eat. If we could in our sleep, we would do so."

He quickly ate another miniature tart, licking his lips. She watched his tongue and wished it brushed against hers.

"Soon," he promised, reading her thoughts, causing her to blush again.

She had done nothing but blush around this handsome man. She still didn't understand why he had singled her out but, at this point, she didn't care. She was getting to live a little before she removed herself from Polite Society. It would be nice to have a few lovely memories of him. Of this ball. Of his kiss.

She glanced up and saw the Duke of Savernake coming toward them. He moved unsteadily and his face appeared ashen.

"Is His Grace ill?" she asked Aidan.

"You are observant. Yes, he is. This will be his last Stag Ball."

The duke reached them and Aidan released her hand, both of them standing to greet him.

"Are you enjoying my Stag Ball, Lady Larissa?" Savernake asked.

"Very much, Your Grace. I have danced more tonight than at any other ball I have attended."

"And my grandson is treating you well?" His Grace gave her a knowing look.

"He has been a perfect gentleman. No Sinning Flynn in sight," she declared, though something told her the duke might have guessed she had been thoroughly kissed by Aidan.

"Excellent. It is almost time to light the bonfire to celebrate summer solstice. Would you care to join me?"

"We would be happy to, Doo," Aidan spoke up for both of them. "After, we can help you inside." He took his grandfather's arm. "Get on his other side, Larissa."

She did so, knowing the old man had caught Aidan calling her by her first name.

His Grace turned to her and smiled. "He is a good man, my lady. Despite the ghastly albatross of a nickname hung about his neck."

"I am learning that, Your Grace."

They assisted the duke from the house, moving toward the unlit bonfire in the center of the square. Though no announcement had been made, Savernake's guests magically followed and, soon, the square teemed with people. Excitement filled the air as the crowd buzzed.

Then the duke held up a hand and the crowd grew quiet.

"Thank you for once again coming to my annual Stag Ball. It is the nineteenth one held without my beloved duchess by my side. I miss her more with each passing day."

Larissa saw tears misting His Grace's eyes and envied him for having loved a woman so much that almost two decades later, the thought of her still brought tears to his eyes.

"Enjoy the bonfire tonight. I hope you will continue the

celebration once it has fallen and dance until dawn. I will retire to my bedchamber—and dream of my duchess."

His Grace turned and Larissa saw a servant hand Aidan a lit torch. She stepped away as His Grace placed his hand atop Aidan's and they touched the torch to the wood. It took a moment to catch and then the wood began to crackle and burn. Suddenly, a bevy of servants appeared, all carrying torches, and they fanned out, touching them to the base of the bonfire. Within seconds, she felt the heat of the blaze and saw the entire base of the structure was now afire.

Aidan returned the torch to the servant and took his grandfather's arm. "We will escort you inside." He nodded to Larissa and she took the duke's other arm.

The smell of burning wood filled the air as they moved away from the bonfire and the crowd gathered around it. Once inside the vast foyer, a servant stepped forward. She assumed he was the butler.

"Simms, will you see His Grace to his rooms?" Aidan asked.

"Of course, Mr. Aidan," Simms replied, taking the duke in hand. "Come along, Your Grace. It has been a busy day for you."

"Goodnight, Your Grace," she called.

The duke turned. "Goodnight, Lady Larissa. I hope to see more of you in the near future."

Aidan slipped an arm around her waist as they watched the butler help the duke up the stairs. When they were out of sight, he turned to her.

"Are you ready to do a little kissing—and possibly more?"

"How much more?" she asked, worried about what he had in mind.

Then she realized it didn't matter. She wouldn't have a

husband by the end of the Stag Ball. There would be no marriage. No family or babies.

There was only now. With this man. No promises. No commitments.

He started to speak and Larissa placed a finger against his lips. "It doesn't matter," she told him. "I want as much as you can give me tonight."

Aidan wrapped his large hand around hers and lowered her fingers so he could speak. "Then come with me."

CHAPTER TWELVE

AIDAN HAD NEVER wanted a woman as much as he did Larissa Warren.

And he wanted to show her how much he desired her.

He couldn't rush things, though. She had only experienced her first kiss an hour ago. As much as he wanted to plunge deep inside her, he would not take her virginity this night.

That would be something to save for their wedding night.

He was certain now, more than he had been about anything in his life. Doo had been right—his heart was now leading him. A chance encounter this afternoon had led to a dance, kissing, and a shared supper with this stunning woman. It would lead to a lifetime together.

And hopefully, love.

The house was almost eerily quiet now with only a few servants inside it. Aidan led Larissa up the stairs to his bed-chamber, his fingers entwined with hers. He couldn't wait to get these damned gloves off her and feel her skin.

Leading her down the corridor, he paused before his closed door.

"I wish I had time to romance you," he said. "Stroll in the

moonlight through the garden with you. Take you on a picnic and feed you sweets."

She shook her head. "I know our time together is limited. I suppose this is your room?"

He opened the door and saw her inside, closing it behind them. "It is the one I stay in when I come to London. Eventually, people will return to the house. The Stag Ball is known for couples arranging a rendezvous, from the library to darkened alcoves. I knew we could find privacy here."

She glanced to the bed. He saw her pulse beating in her throat. "Will you . . . will we . . ."

His brave little dove couldn't finish her sentence.

"We will lie on the bed together. Kiss. Touch. You will leave this room a virgin, Larissa. I swear it on my family." He smiled ruefully. "Sinners that we are."

"I know you value your family. You love your parents and your brothers."

"Do you feel anything for yours?" he asked.

"Not for Peter or the earl. They have no regard for me and have overlooked and neglected me for years. Mama? She has always kept her distance. I believe I remind her too much of Lord Silverton for us to grow close."

"Lord Silverton is your sire?"

Larissa nodded. "He was Mama's first and only love. They grew up together on neighboring estates. He courted her during her first Season. Unfortunately, as many daughters of the *ton* learn, parents have different plans for them than the ones they have for themselves. Mama and the viscount ran away, hoping to wed at Gretna Green. They didn't make it and their fathers forced them to return to London. Mama wed Lord Campton the next day."

"They stayed in touch, though?" he asked, one palm cupping her cheek, his thumb brushing her bottom lip.

"Lord Silverton left Polite Society for a number of years. When he returned, he learned of how Campton took lovers left and right. The viscount's comforting of Mama turned physical. I was the result."

"How do you know all this?"

"Lord Silverton shared it with me. It upsets him that he cannot claim me as his blood. He urged Mama to work on her marriage and the viscount also wed. He is faithful to his viscountess. He and Mama are still friends, after a fashion."

Aidan kissed her softly. "You are upset speaking about this. I don't want you to think about your family now. I want you to think about us."

"There is no us, Aidan," she said, her hand circling his wrist. "There is now. Kiss me."

His heart ached because hers did. He wanted to explain to her that he would take her away from all this hurt but, for now, he would allow his actions to speak for him and show her how much he truly cared for her.

He brought his other hand to her face and framed it. "You are so beautiful, both inside and out."

Passion filled him and his mouth came crashing down on hers. Aidan kissed Larissa, trying to make her forget all that had come before. She was right. There was only now.

And he would take advantage of the time he had with her.

Larissa wrapped her arms about Aidan's neck, drawing him closer to her. His drugging kisses brought a sweet rush of what could only be desire. Her blood and body heated and she toyed with the hair at his nape, tugging on it playfully. She felt so unlike herself when she was kissing him—free, alive, lighthearted.

Her body ignited as the bonfire in the street below had, burning only for him. He deepened his kiss, causing her bones to melt away. Suddenly, she was caught up in his arms and lowered to the large bed. She trusted him when he said she would leave here a virgin. Not that she cared. No one was here. No one would see what they did by the light of the candle that glowed at his bedside.

He hovered over her and then his body rested against hers, driving her into the mattress. He kissed her and she returned his kisses with abandon, parts of her coming alive that she never knew existed.

Aidan kissed his way down her neck and even lower, reaching her breasts. His tongue playfully ran along the curves of her breasts, causing them to grow heavy with need. The ache between her legs thumped almost painfully.

"I must see you," he said, his breathing ragged as he pushed up to his knees and then climbed from the bed.

Before she could protest, he captured her waist and lifted her from the bed to her feet, taking her hem and lifting the gown from her. He placed it neatly across a chair and she knew, even now, he was thinking of her reputation. Returning to the Stag Ball with a wrinkled gown would be a dead giveaway for what they had been up to.

"May I remove the rest?" he asked and she nodded.

Soon, everything was gone and she stood bare before him. Larissa felt no shame, which surprised her.

"You are magnificent," he said, awe in his voice.

"May I see you?" she countered. "It seems only fair."

"Help me with my coat. It is tight."

"Not as tight as those breeches," she said, laughing.

She helped him from his coat and waistcoat, then untied his cravat and dropped it to the floor. He removed his shirt and she swallowed, amazed at the hard planes of his chest, lightly dusted with hair.

"That's enough for now," he said and then backed her up to the bed and pushed her down, falling atop her.

Larissa laughed. She couldn't remember when she had laughed so much.

Aidan's hands cupped and kneaded her breasts, making her feel womanly. Then he lowered his mouth to one and feasted upon it. The sensations that ran through her were indescribably delicious. His teeth nipped at her nipple and his tongue circled it, causing the pounding between her legs to rage out of control.

He turned his attention to her other breast, kissing and teasing and tormenting her further as his hands roamed her curves. If this is what men and women did in their marriage bed, why were so many husbands and wives unhappy?

Gathering her wrists, he lifted them above her head and pinned them to the pillow. She wriggled a bit but found he held her fast. His free hand started at her shoulder and gradually slid down her body, lower and lower, until he reached her core. Then he ran a finger along the seam of her sex and Larissa bucked against him, trying to free her hands.

"No. Your hands will only get in the way of my pleasuring you," he said.

She felt her eyes grow large as he slid his finger along her again, pushing it inside her.

"Oh! That feels . . . so . . . good," she said.

He grinned. "It will feel better in a moment."

He was right.

Aidan's fingers moved within her, caressing and stroking

her into a frenzy. Then the dam broke and she was laughing and crying and calling out his name as her hips moved and her body shuddered and it felt as if sunlight poured from her body.

Finally, she stilled and he kissed her deeply.

"What was that?" she asked when he finally broke the kiss.

"An orgasm. The French call it *le petite mort*."

"The little death."

"Yes. It is intense."

Larissa grinned. "It is incredible."

"Shall we try it again?"

This time, he released her wrists and massaged them a moment. Then his hands stroked her body, running down her hips to her legs and back up again. He lowered his mouth to her belly and began kissing her there.

"That tickles," she told him, giggling.

"Good," he said, his smile mischievous.

When he moved lower, she tensed.

"What are you doing?"

"Giving you the pleasure of your life. Trust me."

She did trust him. She couldn't understand why. They had only known each other this one day. Yet there was something about this Sinning Flynn that spoke to her heart.

"I do," she told him. "Probably more than I should."

He gripped her hips and placed his head between her legs. Larissa instinctively knew what was coming and yet had a hard time believing it.

Slowly, his tongue caressed her, causing her to whimper softly. Then his tongue plunged into her core and she gasped. Just as he had with her breasts, Aidan feasted upon her. Using his teeth, tongue, and fingers, he worked her into a frenzy, until she writhed on the bed, mindless.

His intimate caresses sent her over the edge again and she was falling deep into the abyss. Her fingers tightened in his hair and she heard sounds coming from her that were unfamiliar. Her body trembled and shook and then she collapsed, spent.

Aidan's tongue moved back up her body slowly, returning to her mouth, kissing her deeply. She tasted herself on his tongue and found it incredibly erotic.

He broke the kiss and smiled down at her. She returned his smile.

"I adore that dimple in your cheek," he said, his tongue swirling around it. "You taste sweet everywhere I sample."

He moved to lie on his side and she turned, facing him.

"You are a Sinning Flynn, after all. Anyone who kisses the way you do—the places you do—is naughty, through and through."

"As long as I am your Sinning Flynn, I don't care," he told her, cupping her cheek and leaning in for a slow kiss.

Larissa knew this was only pillow talk, a man enjoying being with a woman and saying things he truly didn't mean.

"We should dress and return to the ball. I don't want to miss my final dance with you." He grinned. "It's another waltz."

She giggled. "You haven't danced anything but the waltz tonight. I suspect you don't know how to dance any other dance, Mr. Flynn."

He kissed her hard and fast. "You should see me when a country dance comes up."

He rose from the bed and swept his shirt over his head. Larissa rose and began piecing herself back together. Aidan stopped and assisted her in lacing her corset and insisted on slipping her stockings back up her legs. His every touch made her sigh.

He lifted the ball gown over her head and she tied his cravat and helped him back into his coat.

Touching a hand to her hair, she asked, "How does it look?"

"For all we did, not a hair out of place. That fierce maid of yours who nearly came after me today certainly knows her way around pins." He caressed her cheek. "I wish I could have removed every last one of them. I have fantasized about running my fingers through that auburn mane of yours."

She frowned. "It is this auburn hair that marks me as a Silverton and not a Campton. Do you know how hard it is to know how much Polite Society gossips about you?' She paused. "Of course, you do. You, of all people, would understand what I mean because you have been labeled a Sinning Flynn. The gossip never ceases about you and your family."

When she saw his face fall, she touched his arm. "I am sorry. I did not mean to hurt you as the gossips do."

"I have developed a hard skin over the years."

"I understand. Their opinions shouldn't matter—but they do. At least I have had a few close friends who have been true to me and seen me for what I am." She smoothed her skirts. "We should return downstairs. Is there a way we can do so without being seen together?"

"There are two ladies' retiring rooms set up, one on the ground floor and one on the first. We can get you to the latter one and then you can return to the ballroom. I will go down the back staircase and cut through the kitchens."

"All right."

He opened the bedchamber door and stuck his head out, glancing in both directions.

"The coast is clear. Come on."

He threaded his fingers through hers and she regretted

having to place the gloves on her hands again because she enjoyed the feel of his skin against hers so much.

They went down the staircase and he paused. "Go from here. I will meet you in the ballroom for our final dance. Then we must talk, Larissa. There are things to be said between us."

She slipped down the remaining stairs and continued down the corridor, seeing a pair of women stepping from a room.

"Is this where the retiring room is?" she asked, trying to appear confused. "The one downstairs was so crowded. A footman directed me to this floor."

"In there," one of the women said, eyeing her. "That is a lovely gown."

"Thank you. It was designed by Madame Floseau. She does excellent work."

The second one nodded. "I do like her work. Good evening."

The two women left and Larissa hurried inside, eager to find a chamber pot.

As she headed toward the ballroom, she made up her mind. She was not going to dance with Aidan a third and final time, causing the gossips to notice. He was a good man, not like his roguish brothers. He would eventually wed. The last person he needed to marry would be her. Her family's reputation challenged even that of the Sinning Flynns. He deserved a woman with a spotless reputation, one he could proudly to escort to various social affairs. A woman from a good family with an unblemished reputation would go a long way in curbing talk of him being a Sinning Flynn. Especially with two of his brothers now wed and walking the straight and narrow, talk would finally begin to die down regarding the Sinning Flynns.

Aidan was kindhearted and might believe he owed offering her marriage because of what had just passed between them. She would not let him throw his life away on someone such as her, whose family was an embarrassment. She couldn't listen to him apologizing for taking advantage of her—when she believed it had been the other way around. She had wanted to experience a bit of fun and romance before she departed London for her new life. He owed her nothing. She had been the one who had gained sweet memories, which she would take to her grave.

It was funny. She had not wanted to wed a rogue. She had wished to marry a man who would pledge his fidelity to her. A good, kind man who would treat her respectfully and love their children.

Aidan would be that man for some other woman, despite being lumped together with the Sinning Flynns. No, she was the one whose reputation would taint him.

Larissa refused to let that happen.

She made her way to the card room and stood at its edge, scanning it until she spotted Lord Silverton. He must have felt her gaze upon him because he glanced up.

Tugging on her right ear, she gave him the sign that she would be at his carriage.

The viscount nodded slightly and returned his gaze to the cards he held in his hand.

Satisfied that she now had a way out of being forced to wed Lord Langdon, Larissa made her way to the ballroom. She would not enter it because she couldn't face Aidan. If she saw him, her resolve would weaken.

She spied him, walking slowly, his head turning from side to side as he searched for her. She stepped back, out of view, and heard the music begin. She remained where she was until the last notes sounded from the orchestra. Then the Duke of Savernake's guests began exiting the ballroom, a trickle at first, and then streaming in large groups that blended together.

She caught sight of her mother and fought her way against the crowd like a fish trying to swim upstream. Reaching Mama, she linked arms with her.

"There you are, dear. Did you enjoy the Stag Ball? I saw you dancing quite a bit. Oh, the bonfire was even more enormous than I recalled. And I heard of three separate engagements that were announced this evening." Mama's face fell. "I am sorry, Larissa, that you were not one of them. I had hoped with Savernake's grandson dancing with you that he might offer for you."

"Please, do not worry about it, Mama. I had a lovely evening. I hope you did, as well."

They continued down the staircase, the swell taking them to the foyer. Just before they reached the front door, Larissa turned and looked over her shoulder.

She spied Aidan a great distance away, at the top of the stairs. She saw his mouth move, forming her name, but the sound was lost in the sea of voices.

"I'm sorry," she mouthed, hoping he could see what she said—and forgive her.

They reached outside and turned to their left. She hurried Mama along, doubting Aidan could ever catch up to them but wanting to be out of sight by the time he made it to the street. She could smell the last of the bonfire as she spied their carriage.

As usual, Campton was already inside. He detested crowds and always left the card room before the last dance commenced in order to avoid them.

She and Mama settled themselves across from him and then her gaze met his.

"Well?" he asked.

Knowing what he meant, she said, "I am not betrothed."

He snorted. "You will be by noon tomorrow," he promised. "From what I gather, Lord Langdon will not wish to wait long. I would say you will be gone by the end of the week."

No. He was wrong.

Larissa would be gone in hopefully an hour's time.

CHAPTER THIRTEEN

FRUSTRATED, AIDAN MUMBLED, "Excuse me," a good thousand times as he nudged and turned and slipped through the throng leaving his grandfather's ballroom.

Larissa had not shown for the final dance. He had searched the room carefully, worried at first, then angry. Something was not right. How that could be when merely a few minutes ago everything was absolutely right was an enigma.

Why would she stand him up?

He thought back to everything they had said to one another and hadn't a clue as to what had scared her off. Surely, it couldn't be the Sinning Flynn reputation. Aidan had tried his best tonight to show Larissa the kind of man he was, apart from his brothers and the nasty moniker that he believed Lord Exford had placed about their necks. The time they had spent together in his bedchamber brought a sweet longing to his loins. He could still feel the smooth, satin skin. Smell the heady vanilla scent that clung to her. Taste her essence.

Had he ventured too far? Was she upset about the liberties he took? He didn't think so. In fact, she seemed to encourage him. Her natural curiosity had been apparent and Aidan knew she had wanted to explore her sensual side. With him.

Then where the bloody hell had she gone?

He finally fought his way out of the ballroom and found himself being moved along the corridor to the stairs. At the top of the stairs, he had a splendid view and scanned the staircase and entire foyer below. Catching sight of her ice blue gown, he willed her to look at him.

She turned and even from this great distance, their gazes met and held.

"Larissa!" he shouted, the sound lost in the crowd.

He saw sorrow in her eyes and read her lips.

I'm sorry.

She was sorry? She was bloody sorry? Hell and damnation, the woman had turned his world upside down. He had started this day with only the vague idea of knowing he would need to wed someday. That had changed with Doo informing him of his illness and the inheritance that would be Aidan's if he found a bride at tonight's Stag Ball.

Meeting Larissa, he now knew, was Fate stepping in and guiding his hand. While he appreciated her looks and lush figure, it was the woman herself he wished to spend the rest of his life with. Her goodness, her graciousness, her intelligence— all made Larissa Warren the perfect woman for him.

Aidan gave up good manners and began elbowing his way through the crowd, finally reaching the door and spilling out of it. He took a few steps on the pavement, the smell of the bonfire permeating the air. Looking left and right and then left again, he saw no sight of her.

He had to get to her. She had revealed that Lord Campton had arranged for that bastard Langdon to come in a few hours and draw up the marriage contracts. Knowing how Campton felt about Larissa, it wouldn't surprise him if once those were signed, he shoved her out the door with the doddering earl.

He needed to find out where the Campton townhouse was and convince Larissa to leave with him. She wouldn't be safe until he slipped his grandmother's wedding band upon her fingers. Aidan berated himself, thinking he should have offered for her before they even left his bedchamber and given her the diamond earrings to show he was serious. Hell, they were in his pocket.

But the necklace and wedding ring weren't. He started back, fighting his way against the crowd coming forward.

Suddenly, Aidan came face to face with Lord and Lady Silverton.

He had met Silverton a few years ago and thought the man genial. Up close—and knowing what he did now—he noticed the striking resemblance between the viscount and Larissa. Every time Campton saw Silverton, he must cringe.

"My lord, I must speak to you," he said, breathing heavily.

"Here?" the viscount questioned.

"Yes. Or somewhere quiet. It is about Lady Larissa."

Silverton and his wife exchanged a glance. Aidan assumed the viscountess must know about her husband's previous indiscretion since most of Polite Society was aware of it.

"Come to our carriage," Silverton said.

Aidan nodded and turned, accompanying the pair to their carriage several blocks away. Lord Silverton handed his wife up.

Thinking their conversation might be better outside the viscountess' hearing, Aidan said, "What I must speak to you about—"

"Inside the carriage, Mr. Flynn. Don't worry. My wife knows I am Larissa's natural father."

"Very well," he agreed, allowing the viscount to enter the vehicle and following him.

Aidan settled himself on the cushions opposite the couple and the coach began to move.

"I saw you dancing with my daughter this evening," Lord Silverton began. "Twice. Exactly what are your intentions with her, Mr. Flynn?"

"I intend to marry her, my lord."

Silverton beamed. "You do?"

"We noticed you danced with Lady Larissa twice this evening," Lady Silverton said, obviously not bothered by discussing her husband's child by another woman. "Twice! I told Silverton you were interested in her. And with His Grace dancing with her mother, that all but declared that an announcement would be forthcoming."

"We were to have danced the final number of the evening together but Larissa did not appear in the ballroom," Aidan shared. "I did see her leaving at the ball's conclusion with her mother."

Lady Silverton sniffed. "That woman has been no mother to her children. She gallivants through Polite Society almost as much as her husband and son do." Looking sympathetically at Aidan, she added, "But I think Lady Larissa is nothing like her family, Mr. Flynn."

"Just as I am nothing like mine, my lady. Don't let me give you a false impression. I love my parents and brothers very much. I simply am cut from different cloth than the Sinning Flynns."

Lady Silverton smiled graciously. "They do say reformed rogues make for excellent husbands. I see where two of your brothers have wed in the past few years. How are their marriages?"

"Strong," he shared. "Love matches for the both of them."

"Are you a love match with my daughter?" Lord Silverton asked, his gaze boring into Aidan.

He swallowed and said aloud what he had yet to admit to himself, much less Larissa.

"Yes. We are. I know about Campton's plans to wed her to Lord Langdon."

"Yes, Langdon is supposed to get with Campton tomorrow morning—or I suppose this morning—and work out the marriage contracts. Oh, dear." The viscount paused. "You haven't yet asked for Larissa's hand in marriage, have you?"

"How do you know that?" he aside, suspicious.

"Because she gave me a sign just before the ball ended. If no one had offered for her, she was tug her right ear—which she did. We are on our way to get her now."

"You are going to Campton's townhouse?" Aidan asked eagerly.

"Not exactly. We arranged for her and her maid to meet us a block away. She is to go home now and get a valise with a few of her things and sneak out through the gardens. We had thought she would go to our country house, at least until Campton's temper cooled."

"He could call you out for this," Aidan warned.

"He won't," Lord Silverton said. "Campton's a coward at heart. All bluster, with nothing to back up his words. If he truly cared about his wife—or daughter—he would have challenged me to a duel years ago."

Aidan took a deep breath and expelled it. "At least this way I don't have to go pounding upon Campton's door. I was going to ask you where he lived and go straight there in order to claim

Larissa."

"This will be much easier, Mr. Flynn," Lady Silverton said. "I think after you have had a chance to offer for Lady Larissa, she should come back to our townhouse and stay while you arrange for a special license. It wouldn't be appropriate for you to take her to His Grace's residence. No matter how large it is, she would be under his roof—with you—and no chaperone. No, it is better this way."

Her words surprised Aidan. "You are certainly gracious about this entire matter, my lady."

Lord Silverton took his wife's hand and kissed it. "I am fortunate to have found such an understanding woman, Mr. Flynn. She has been very supportive."

"Would you care to come to the wedding?" he asked. "It will be held at my grandfather's townhouse. He is ill and we need to wed quickly."

"We would be delighted to do so," the viscount said. "You and Larissa tell us the day and time and we will be happy to be in attendance."

The carriage slowed and came to a halt.

"Do you mind if I wait outside?" Aidan asked. "It would give me a few minutes to speak to Larissa alone."

"Be my guest," Lord Silverton said.

Aidan climbed from the carriage and paced the pavement as he waited.

For the woman he loved.

☙

LARISSA KEPT HER hands folded in her lap, her gaze down, the entire way home. She did not want anyone to guess she had plans and would soon vacate the townhouse, leaving no note behind. Campton would be upset because it would ruin his plans with Lord Langdon. Mama would worry, not knowing where Larissa was. She suspected her mother did love her but never showed it, too hurt by the events surrounding her own life and reminded of the man she loved and lost every time she looked upon her daughter.

They arrived and the footman handed them down.

"I am tired," Mama told their butler. "Do not send up my breakfast until noon at the earliest."

"The same for me," Larissa suggested, buying herself as much time as possible. "The Stag Ball has worn me out."

"No," Campton said. "Lord Langdon will be here at eleven o'clock. I am hoping the settlements will be finished by noon. Present yourself to me then in my study. Is that understood?"

Larissa looked him squarely in the face. "Yes." Turning to the butler, she said, "Have my breakfast sent up at eleven. I will have Lizzy awaken me at ten so that I might dress."

Campton hurried up the stairs and she linked arms with Mama and they followed at a slower pace. At her mother's chamber door, she paused, saying goodnight and kissing Mama upon the cheek.

"I am sorry Silverton is not able to prevent this marriage," Mama said, her face full of sadness. "I hate that you are following in my steps, repeating my own history so that it has become your unhappy story."

"At least I am not leaving behind a man I love," she said, her throat thick, thinking of Aidan.

She didn't love him. She had only known him for a day. Oh, but she could have loved him.

Turning, she wiped away a falling tear as she continued to her own bedchamber. Inside, Lizzy was waiting for her.

"I have a valise packed for us, my lady. I've even hidden it in your mother's sitting room so that we don't even have to carry it downstairs now."

"That was clever thinking," Larissa praised.

"You can't leave in a ball gown. Pity you'll have to leave it behind. His lordship will probably be in such a rage that he'll have it ripped to shreds."

"You are probably right," she agreed.

Lizzy dressed Larissa in a simple day gown. "Let's leave your hair up for now. I used plenty of pins in it and didn't pack any others. This should be enough for you to use."

"What did you pack?" she asked as Lizzy pulled off the dainty slippers and replaced them with sturdy boots.

"Two gowns, an extra shift, and a night rail," the maid replied. "I also slipped in a dress for me. Your hairbrush and a sachet. Your locket and the poem Lady Cressida wrote. That's all we had room for."

Larissa took the servant's hands. "You are certain you wish to come with me? After spending some time in the country, I may be entering service myself."

"I go where you go, my lady. I think that nice Lord Silverton would be kind enough to write me a reference I could use when I look for a new position."

"He would. He has been a blessing."

Larissa took a seat on the bed and Lizzy the chair and they sat silently, waiting. After a quarter-hour, she rose.

"It's time."

They moved to the door and she took one last look at her bedchamber, tonight's ball gown draped across a chair. Then she turned, knowing it was important to look forward instead of backward.

She wouldn't think of Aidan. She couldn't—else she might fall apart.

They slipped down the servants' staircase and to her mother's sitting room without seeing a soul. Lizzy retrieved the valise and insisted upon carrying it. Larissa opened one of the French doors and they stepped into the early morning light. The sun was already rising as they entered the small gardens at the back of the townhouse and weaved their way along the path, coming to a gate.

She swallowed, calming herself, and then opened it. Lizzy stepped through and Larissa followed, closing the gate and hearing the latch catch.

Lord Silverton's carriage was waiting exactly where he said it would be—except someone else was there.

Aidan.

Her heart slammed violently against her ribs as she froze. Lizzy looked ahead and then back at her mistress.

"It's that man. The one who was at the dress shop."

Tears sprang to her eyes. "It is. Mr. Flynn," she managed to get out as she watched Aidan running toward her.

He reached her, slamming into her, almost knocking her off-balance. Then his arms were around her and he was kissing her, kissing her, kissing her.

He broke the kiss. "I'll never let you go."

Tears flooded her eyes, blinding her just as they had the first time she had met Aidan.

"Go to Lord Silverton's carriage," Aidan instructed Lizzy. "He is expecting you. We will be along in a moment."

Lizzy beamed. "Yes, my lord."

"It's Flynn. Mr. Flynn," he corrected.

Lizzy merely waved a hand, her back already to them.

Aidan turned back to her. "I wanted to ask you to marry me before we returned to the ballroom, my love. I should have done so. Foolishly, I didn't."

She shook her head, the tears now falling against her bodice. "I cannot marry you, Aidan. You are trying to be your own man, apart from your family. I believe you will escape the Sinning Flynn reputation and go on to do great things. You do not need my reputation to drag you back into the mire."

He cradled her face. "I don't give a fig what the *ton* says. All I know is that I love you, Larissa Warren, and refuse to live another day without you as my wife. You are to stay with Lord and Lady Silverton while I go to Doctors' Commons and purchase a special license for us this morning. If you wish, we can be married later today."

Aidan paused. "Please tell me this is what you want, Larissa. That you want me as much as I want you. That we can spend a lifetime together as we fall deeper in love every day."

He wanted her. Aidan wanted her. He didn't care about her family. He cared about her.

"I do love you, Aidan," she said through her tears.

"That is all I needed to hear."

His mouth seized hers in a fierce, possessive kiss, branding her for all time as his.

She didn't know how much time had passed when he finally broke the kiss and grinned at her.

"I believe we have kept Lord and Lady Silverton waiting long enough. And your overbearing maid has probably been watching us out the window the entire time."

"I adore Lizzy," Larissa said. "You will, too. She is my fiercest protector."

"She *was* your fiercest protector. That is my job now." Aidan kissed her tenderly. "I love you so much, Larissa. My heart told me you were the one from the beginning."

He swept her into his arms and carried her to the coach, up the steps and deposited her on the bench inside.

"How romantic!" exclaimed Lady Silverton.

Larissa blinked away her tears, even as Aidan handed her his handkerchief to wipe away the ones still on her cheeks.

"We have not met, my lady. I am Larissa Warren."

"Soon to be Larissa Flynn," Aidan interjected. "She said yes."

"Jolly good," declared Lord Silverton.

"The wedding is this afternoon," Aidan continued. "Can you have Larissa at my grandfather's home by two o'clock?"

"We will be there at one o'clock," Lizzy said, taking charge. "It is easier to dress a bride at the site of the ceremony. That way, her gown won't wrinkle in the carriage."

Aidan grinned. "I think I am going to like you, after all, Lizzy."

CHAPTER FOURTEEN

"WAKE UP, MY lady."

Someone gently shook her shoulder. Larissa opened her eyes and found Lizzy hovering over her, smiling.

"It's your wedding day, my lady," the maid said.

"What time is it?" she asked.

"It is eleven o'clock. A bath has been prepared for you."

Larissa rose, sleep still in her eyes. She had not gotten to bed until well after dawn but slept soundly. A smile touched her lips.

Her wedding day . . .

She allowed Lizzy to help her slip into a dressing gown provided by Lady Silverton. The viscountess had truly been wonderful to her, making certain Larissa was settled. Her father was a fortunate man. She would think of Lord Silverton in the future as her father.

Lizzy led her down the hall to the viscountess' suite of rooms, where the bath awaited her, as did Lady Silverton.

"Your maid told me you were found of vanilla and so I have had that added to your bath water," Lady Silverton said. "May I assist you in your bath?"

"Of course," Larissa replied.

Assisting actually consisted of Lady Silverton sitting in a chair talking with Larissa as Lizzy bathed her. What the viscountess had to say, though, touched Larissa beyond words.

"You will have a suitable gown for your wedding," Lady Silverton began. "Lizzy unpacked the two day gowns you had brought and you may wear one of them to His Grace's residence today. Your wedding gown will be waiting at Savernake's."

Confusion filled her. "How is that possible?"

Lady Silverton smiled. "I spoke to your father and explained to him your need of a wardrobe since you'd left yours behind. While you were falling asleep, Silverton went to Madame Floseau's dress shop and got her out of bed. He explained you needed a suitable gown for today's ceremony, as well as a new wardrobe. Which he will pay for."

Larissa shook her head. "I don't think Aidan would agree to that, my lady. He is a proud man and would wish to do so himself."

Lady Silverton smiled. "Not if you tell him otherwise. You are the woman, which means you are in charge of your marriage. Yes, you are to be obedient to your husband and make certain that he is happy. You also subtly make sure he dances to your tune. All you have to tell Mr. Flynn is that your father is supplying a new wardrobe for you and that it is his wedding gift to you. Surely, Mr. Flynn would not reject such a gift."

"This was all your idea, wasn't it, my lady?"

The viscountess nodded. "I care deeply for Silverton and know how unhappy he has been by not being able to acknowledge you as his offspring. I also know of the tender feelings he will always carry for your mother. I am wise enough to understand that what makes him happy will make me happy. You, my lady, were caught up in a situation not of your own making. I know you have suffered because of it. The actions of your family have only made things worse, keeping you from making a suitable match."

She paused. "Until now." Smiling, she added, "I believe Fate stepped in and had you wait until she brought your Mr. Flynn to you."

"It must have been Fate, my lady. I have only known Aidan for a day."

Lady Silverton laughed merrily. "Well, no one would ever have guessed that. You seem to know each other quite well and are perfectly matched. I am happy for you, Larissa. I know Mr. Flynn lives in Cornwall and you will be moving there with him. I also hope you will come to London and try to see Silverton—and me—whenever you are in town."

Tears misted her eyes. "We will do so, my lady. If not for your help, along with my father's, I would be marrying Lord Langdon."

A servant entered the room. "This came for Lady Larissa," the maid said, handing a small package to Lady Silverton and leaving the room.

"What could it be?" Larissa asked. "Is there a note?"

The viscountess pulled a folded sheet from under the string. "There is. Shall I read it to you?"

"Please," she said.

Opening the note, Lady Silverton began to smile.

My dearest Larissa –

I am counting the minutes until I see you today. Please

wear these for our wedding today. They are my engagement and wedding gifts to you.

All my love,
Aidan

"You are marrying a romantic, my dear," murmured the viscountess.

She handed the package to Larissa, who pulled at the string and discarded it before tearing into the brown paper. Inside was a black, velvet box.

"Dry your hands, my lady," ordered Lizzy. "You don't want what's inside to get wet."

She accepted the towel the maid offered and wiped her hands dry before opening the box.

"Oh, my!" she exclaimed, finding a pair of diamond earrings and matching necklace within.

Larissa held them up so that Lady Silverton and Lizzy could see.

"I am liking Mr. Flynn more and more," declared Lizzy.

Lady Silverton said, "I agree. That is a very thoughtful—and expensive—gift."

She didn't care about the cost, only that Aidan had thought to give her something to mark this day. She would wear the set with pride in the years to come.

"I'll take it for you, my lady," her maid said.

Lizzy then dried off Larissa and dressed her in one of the day gowns, leaving her hair down.

"I will style your hair after we get to the duke's and you are dressed," the maid promised. "Let me help you put on your new necklace."

Lizzy fastened the necklace about Larissa's neck and she

placed the earrings on her lobes.

"Mr. Flynn will think you make the diamonds shine bright," the servant declared.

Larissa and Lizzy left her bedchamber and as they started down the staircase, she heard shouts. Her blood ran cold when she recognized the voice.

It was Lord Campton.

Lizzy clutched Larissa's arm. "We should return upstairs, my lady. Lord Silverton will work this out."

"No, I am not retreating from that man ever again."

Breaking away from Lizzy, Larissa hurried down the stairs. In the foyer, she saw her father and the man her mother had married all those years ago.

The earl turned to her and growled, "There you are. I knew you had to be here. That Silverton was lying. You had no one else who would even consider taking you in. You are to come with me. Now. Lord Langdon is waiting for you. He has a special license already. You will wed him today."

Larissa did not cower as she knew he would expect her to. Instead, she boldly said, "Then have him rip up the special license. It is worthless. Yes, my lord, I am getting married today—but not to your choice. It is *my* choice."

Campton appeared baffled. "But you told me in the carriage last night that you were not betrothed."

"I wasn't at that time. I am now."

"Who would wed the likes of you?" he snarled. "A girl passed off as mine when all of Polite Society knows you are *his*."

"I am marrying a man who wishes to marry me and accepts me for who I am. A good man. A grandson of the Duke of Savernake. Mr. Aidan Flynn."

Campton looked at her and then burst out in laughter. "*You* are marrying a *Sinning Flynn*?"

Larissa rose to Aidan's defense. "He might be labeled a Sinning Flynn but he is far from that. He is everything you are not. Loyal. Honorable. And he loves me."

"He is only after your dowry, Girl."

This time, it was Larissa who laughed. "My dowry? The amount is miniscule. Besides, Mr. Flynn and his family are incredibly wealthy. More than you ever dreamed of being."

Larissa actually had no idea if Aidan had much money or not. She did know he worked for Flynn Fleet, which was the largest shipping enterprise in England, so she didn't believe they would want for anything.

She looked at the earl with disdain. "Now, get out! You are not welcomed here, much less at the ceremony. You yourself have said as much—you are and never have been a father to me."

She crossed to Lord Silverton and slipped her arm through his. "My true father will give me away to the man I love."

"You are a fool," the earl declared. "As much of one as that featherheaded mother of yours."

This time, it was Lord Silverton who spoke up. "She is no featherhead and you know that, Campton. She was a young girl, in love, forced to wed the likes of you. If you would have given her but half a chance, she would have made a good wife to you. But your black heart and selfishness would not allow it. Get out of my house."

Lord Campton whirled, stomping through the foyer and out the door like a toddler throwing a tantrum.

The moment the door closed behind the earl, Lord Silverton turned to her. "Are you all right, my dear?"

"I am—thanks to you, Father."

It was the first time she had addressed him thus and Larissa saw tears spring to his eyes. He embraced her and she felt loved and protected.

After he released her, she said, "I hear I have you to thank for the wedding gown I shall wear today and a new wardrobe, as well."

"I have been made aware of how important these things are to a woman. Lady Silverton emphasized to me what must be done. I did go to see your modiste and she will deliver a suitable gown for your wedding to Savernake's residence. She will then be working on creating other gowns for the next few weeks."

"I may only need a handful. Frankly, I don't know what our plans are." She paused. "The Duke of Savernake is ill, however, so I am sure we will be in town until he passes."

"Then I will leave it up to you to discuss with Madame Floseau what your needs are."

"Thank you," she said, kissing his cheek. "You and Lady Silverton have been lovely."

"I am happy I was finally able to help you in some small way, Larissa." He cleared his throat and looked up. "Ah, my dear, there you are. The carriage is waiting for us. Are we ready?"

The three of them went to the carriage, Lizzy accompanying them, and soon arrived at the duke's townhouse.

The moment they entered the foyer, Aidan greeted them, already dressed for the wedding, looking so handsome that Larissa had to keep from throwing herself into his arms and kissing him at length.

"Larissa," he said, her name sounding like a caress from his lips. "You are a little late."

"We had a visitor who delayed us a bit," she said lightly.

"But we are here now."

"Who?" he demanded. "Tell me it wasn't Campton."

"It was, Mr. Flynn," Lord Silverton said. "Your fiancée read him the riot act, kicking him to the curb." Her father smiled at her. "You would have been quite proud of her."

Aidan gazed into Larissa's eyes. "I will always be proud of her." He brushed his fingers against her cheek in a caress. "You are wearing the diamonds. Do you like them?"

"They are remarkable, Aidan. I have never owned anything so grand."

"They are the first of the many ways I will spoil you, my love."

Lizzy took charge. "Enough of this, Mr. Flynn. If you want the ceremony to start on time, then I suggest you allow Lady Larissa and me to go upstairs and see that she is properly turned out for her wedding."

Aidan laughed. "I see who will be running our household," he commented. "Madame Floseau is upstairs, ready to help you dress for the ceremony." He turned to Lord Silverton. "I gather you were involved in seeing that Larissa had a proper wedding gown today."

The viscount bowed his head in acknowledgement.

"Come, my lady," Lizzy urged, tugging on Larissa.

"May I accompany you upstairs?" asked Lady Silverton.

"Of course," Larissa told her.

"One request," Aidan said. "Would you leave your hair down? For me?"

She smiled brightly at him. "If you wish."

The three of them went upstairs and, much to her surprise, Larissa found a gown waiting for her which rivaled the ice blue one of last night.

"Madame, you have outdone yourself. I don't know how you managed with so little time."

The modiste sniffed. "It wasn't easy, my lady, but I am nothing if not dependable in a crisis. My assistants have already started on your new wardrobe." Madame smiled. "You will be glad to know it has already been paid for in full by Lord Silverton."

Larissa returned her smile. "Thank you for letting me know, Madame. I suppose I should dress now."

With so many helping her, it did not take long to prepare herself. Madame had thoughtfully brought along new under-garments for her, ones much finer than any she had ever worn before. Lizzy then brushed Larissa's hair until it shone, falling about her shoulders and cascading past her waist.

"Are you sure you don't want me to put it up, my lady?"

"My groom wants me to wear it unbound." Glancing to Lady Silverton, she added, "I know it is important to please him in small ways."

The viscountess smiled and nodded.

"I also included a night rail for your wedding night," the modiste said. "At no charge. My gift to you, my lady."

"Thank you," she said graciously. "You are the only modiste in London that I will ever patronize."

"I was counting on that, my lady," Madame said.

Lady Silverton looked at Lizzy. "We should go ahead and make our way downstairs for the ceremony."

Lizzy looked blankly at the viscountess. "Me? You want me to attend the wedding?"

Lady Silverton nodded. "You have been not only a loyal servant but a good friend to Lady Larissa. She would want to have you present. Besides, if something goes wrong, I have a feeling you would be the one to step up and fix things."

The room of women laughed and they began filing out the door.

Lady Silverton paused, saying, "I will send your father up to escort you to your wedding."

Larissa took the viscountess' hands. "Again, thank you for being so gracious in what is a most unusual and awkward set of circumstances."

"I am happy to do so. Besides, when you have children, I will look upon them as my grandchildren as much as Silverton's."

She went and looked at herself in the mirror a final time. It was a bit odd seeing her hair spilling about her shoulders but she wanted to please Aidan on this day of all days.

A light tap sounded at the door and her father entered. "I hear my daughter needs an escort to her wedding."

She joined him, slipping her arm through his. "I am happy to have your escort, Father."

He led her downstairs to the drawing room, where Aidan and his grandfather awaited. His Grace sat in a chair but signaled for Aidan to help him up when Larissa appeared.

Crossing the room, she came to stand before him.

The duke looked upon her with great affection. "I told you I had hoped to see you soon," he said, a glint of mischief in his eyes. "I am pleased that my grandson had the sense to offer for you. He could not have chosen a better woman for him."

"I love him with all my heart, Your Grace. I hope I will make him happy."

"You will, my dear," the duke said. "The pair of you have had to live down your families' reputations. But you will start a family of your own and I know you will teach them to be kind, honorable people. Thank you for having the wedding so quickly. Aidan told me that he shared with you I am in poor health and have only a short time to live. It means the world to me to see my favorite grandson marry the love of his life. For that is what you are to him."

The duke turned and said to a man Larissa had not noticed, "Begin the ceremony now."

The clergyman had them gather in a semi-circle. Aidan laced his fingers through hers. They spoke their vows, ones Larissa knew they would honor for a lifetime—and beyond.

EPILOGUE

Larkhaven—September 1814

A IDAN FINISHED UP at the stables and returned to the main house. As he approached it, he took in the beauty of the house itself and the land around it, thankful that Doo had seen fit to make him Larkhaven's custodian.

His grandfather had only lived another two weeks after Aidan and Larissa wed. He insisted on being given a week to spend with them before Dr. Lawford began administering the powerful laudanum. They had eaten every meal with Doo and spent hours in his company, listening to stories that went all the way back to his childhood. Aidan had learned things about his grandfather he had never known, appreciating the gift of the time they were able to share with him.

Doo and Larissa got along famously, with Doo telling her that he felt she was like a granddaughter to him. It was Larissa who sat beside Aidan as they watched Doo slip further away. Finally, he passed peacefully. His new wife had kissed Doo's hand and brow in goodbye, thanking the duke for everything he had done to make Aidan the man he was today.

He had sent word to Cornwall and his entire family met

them at Summerwood, where the Duke of Savernake was laid to rest. Uncle Martin, who hadn't bothered to visit Doo during his final weeks, actually came to the funeral. When Doo's will was read, Uncle Martin was furious that Larkhaven had been awarded to Aidan. He had already told his family about the bequest and Da convinced Uncle Martin to stand down when he threatened to bring in solicitors and judges, telling the new duke that Larkhaven had been unentailed and it was Doo's last wish for Aidan and Larissa to make it their new home.

Grudgingly, Uncle Martin had agreed—but he had never spoken to them since.

Aidan arrived at the house and went straight to the nursery. Larissa sat rocking little Tiernan. The babe's eyes drooped and finally closed. She stood, placing him in his crib. He joined her, his arm sliding around her waist, and they looked down on their little miracle, who had turned four months today.

"He will sleep a good while," she said, leaning her head against his shoulder. "We actually have a few hours to ourselves."

"It's a glorious day in Dorset, my love. How about a picnic?"

His wife beamed. "I would like that."

They left the nursery and stopped in the kitchens, where the nursery governess was finishing a cup of tea. She went upstairs to sit with Tiernan in case he awoke so that she might soothe him back to sleep.

Cook quickly packed them some Cornish pasties and pilchards, along with fairings for something sweet to finish their meal. Cook add a jar of pear cider, something Larissa had grown fond of during her time in Dorset.

Aidan had a servant fetch a blanket and soon they were off,

heading down to the seashore. He inhaled the scent of salt, which always meant home to him.

He spread out the blanket and they sat upon it, Larissa removing the items Cook had packed from the hamper and placing them on plates, while he opened the jar of cider and took a swallow, offering her some.

They talked about the new racehorse he had recently purchased. Aidan had taken Doo's final advice and had given up his smuggling operation. With Larissa in his life, he no longer wished to take the risks he previously had. Da had bought the three ships and hired on all the men on Aidan's crews who wished for a job.

He no longer worked for Flynn Fleet. Though they visited his family upon occasion in Falmouth, his life was with his wife, here at Larkhaven. Aidan had built a huge stable to house his racehorses and he continued to have tenants farm the rest of the land. Their tenants adored Larissa and several of them had made baby clothes for little Tiernan upon his arrival.

Full now, they stretched out beside one another and began kissing, glad to have private time to themselves. The beach was deserted and so Aidan made sweet, leisurely love to his beautiful wife, knowing he would never get enough of this woman.

As she lay nestled in his arms, she asked, "Do you think we made another babe just now?"

He stroked her belly. "I hope so. I want the next one to be a girl, as sweet and lovely as her mother." He kissed her. "And hopefully, she will have your auburn hair."

Larissa often wore it freely about her shoulders or in a single plait down her back, simply to please him. He thought her hair, which fell to her waist, one of the most beautiful things about her.

As they lay together and watched the clouds drift across the sky, Aidan felt that their life was perfect.

"Each day will be better," Larissa said. "Doo told me that. He said the days will blend into months and those into years, more quickly than we could ever imagine."

Aidan cradled her cheek tenderly. "Doo was always right. Today is better than yesterday. Tomorrow, my love for you will be stronger than it is today. I love you, Larissa. Now and always."

Aidan kissed his wife and smiled. They would live for today, for each other and their son. Tomorrow would take care of itself. And when it came, it would also be lived in love.

☾ THE END ☽

ADDITIONAL DRAGONBLADE BOOKS BY AUTHOR ALEXA ASTON

Second Sons of London Series
Educated By The Earl
Debating With The Duke
Empowered By The Earl

Dukes Done Wrong Series
Discouraging the Duke
Deflecting the Duke
Disrupting the Duke
Delighting the Duke
Destiny with a Duke

Dukes of Distinction Series
Duke of Renown
Duke of Charm
Duke of Disrepute
Duke of Arrogance
Duke of Honor

The St. Clairs Series
Devoted to the Duke
Midnight with the Marquess
Embracing the Earl
Defending the Duke
Suddenly a St. Clair

Starlight Night

Soldiers & Soulmates Series
To Heal an Earl
To Tame a Rogue
To Trust a Duke
To Save a Love
To Win a Widow

The Lyon's Den Connected World
The Lyon's Lady Love

King's Cousins Series
The Pawn
The Heir
The Bastard

Medieval Runaway Wives
Song of the Heart
A Promise of Tomorrow
Destined for Love

Knights of Honor Series
Word of Honor
Marked by Honor
Code of Honor
Journey to Honor
Heart of Honor
Bold in Honor
Love and Honor
Gift of Honor
Path to Honor

Return to Honor

Pirates of Britannia Series
God of the Seas

De Wolfe Pack: The Series
Rise of de Wolfe

The de Wolfes of Esterley Castle
Diana
Derek
Thea

ABOUT THE AUTHOR

Award-winning and internationally bestselling author Alexa Aston's historical romances use history as a backdrop to place her characters in extraordinary circumstances, where their intense desire for one another grows into the treasured gift of love.

She is the author of Regency and Medieval romance, including: Dukes of Distinction; Soldiers & Soulmates; The St. Clairs; The King's Cousins; and The Knights of Honor.

A native Texan, Alexa lives with her husband in a Dallas suburb, where she eats her fair share of dark chocolate and plots out stories while she walks every morning. She enjoys a good Netflix binge; travel; seafood; and can't get enough of *Survivor* or *The Crown*.

THE SIN
COMMANDMENTS

A REGENCY HISTORICAL ROMANCE

BY KATHRYN LE VEQUE

A SIN LIKE FLYNN NOVELLA

Not content to follow the family business, Rory Flynn is embittered by the Sinning Flynns' reputation as a wildly wealthy family from Irish stock, hated by the *ton* but accepted because of their links to the crown.

The worst offender against his family is none other than the man Rory's mother jilted those years ago, the Earl of Exford. He's never forgiven Lady Amy for her offense against him even though he managed to marry well. Knowing the earl and his daughters will be at the Stag Ball, Rory is determined to compromise one of them so they will be forced to wed. But what he didn't count on was a chance encounter with a sweet, beautiful woman who pulls him off his quest.

As he goes in pursuit of Lady Edith "Edie" Rhodes, Rory finds himself entrenched in a world where secrets are darker than his own and sins are something that can never be forgotten… but can be forgiven.

Will Edie forgive him his family's past – or can Rory forgive her for withholding hers?

The Sin Commandments isn't just a title…

It's the code that Rory Flynn lives by, a code that has taken a lifetime to compile. Rory has built his life on the backbone of his family, becoming a greater smuggler, a bigger rake, and the most notorious brother. The code of conduct he lives by is something that shapes his life and on the night of the Duke of Savernake's Stag Ball, it's a code he intends to use.

Every word of it.

But codes change.

And so do men.

Welcome to Rory and Edie's story.

PROLOGUE

May 1811
Behind The Hungry Horse Tavern

HE'D SAID HE loved her and that made this encounter a holy thing, because if God was love, then Myles Forrester was possessed by the holy trinity.

When he'd said he loved her, she had believed him.

Now, it was time for her to prove her love to him.

It had been soft and dark and quiet in the livery behind The Hungry Horse, an ancient tavern near her home and easy for her to reach. That's where he'd told her to meet him and meet him she did.

For a goodly dose of the holy trinity.

It hadn't been easy, however. Her parents were aware when it came to her adoration for the older, married man who had taken such a fancy to her. He had wealth, so he wasn't after her money. He simply wanted a young, nubile body in his bed and that's exactly what he was pursuing.

Her young and nubile body.

His wife didn't understand him. Myles had told her that a thousand times. She was the mothering type who, after having children, ignored her husband completely.

At least, that's what he'd said…

He needed what only the young and nubile could provide. All he could speak of was his longing for her and she'd declared her longing for him. He'd come for her now and would make everything right between them, as he'd promised. He'd divorce his wife, just for her. Divorces were practically unheard of, but for her, he would risk the shame and expense of it.

He'd sworn this.

But first, he needed a demonstration of her love for him so he knew that he was doing the right thing.

So, she met him in the livery behind The Hungry Horse Tavern. It had been very late at night, when her entire family had been asleep, and it had been a simple thing to slip out and come into town. He'd come to her in the livery, smelling of wine because he'd been drinking all evening.

At first, he had been gentle, and their embraces had been innocent. But that innocence was short-lived when he pinned her against the stable wall and his mouth began to wander, his tongue tasting every bit of flesh from the shoulders up. She'd resisted at first, but he had ignored her resistance as he continued to speak of his love for her. Of her love for him.

If you love me, you will prove it, he'd said.

His tenderness soon turned rough.

Now that he had her where he wanted her, he wasn't going to waste any time.

With the idea that she needed to prove her love for him, her uncertainty faded. If she loved him so much, then surely they were doing the right thing. As the horses around them shifted and snorted, he grasped her by both arms and pulled her down onto the cold, dirty straw at their feet.

Forcing her onto her back, he began fumbling with the bottom of her cotton gown. The cloak was in the way and he tossed it aside. He was a big man and his old, sweaty body was heavy atop her, squeezing the breath from her, and her hesitation returned. Her eyes remained open, darting around frantically, as he kissed her with a sloppy mouth.

The skirt of her dress was pushed up, past her knees as he tried to expose her soft, white body beneath him. He grunted and gasped and sweated on her as his hands continued to yank up the fabric He couldn't pull it any further, so his hand came in from the top of her bodice.

Once he touched her bosom, she realized exactly what he was intending.

That's where the progression stopped.

"Myles," she finally hissed, pushing his hand away and pulling her clothing back down. "We cannot do... *this*."

"Why not, my dearest?"

With the last shred of willpower, she pushed him away and sat up. "Must I explain this to you, truly?" she said. "Because if we continue along this path, it will be my ruin and the ruin of my family. You cannot expect me to participate in my own destruction this way."

He was panting. "But if you love me..."

"If you love *me* you would not demand such a thing."

He looked at her as if she'd gravely wounded him with her words. "I do, Edie," he breathed. "You know I love you."

"Then we will pursue a respectable relationship *after* you have divorced your wife."

"But..."

"I trust that you will do the right thing, Myles," she said in a clipped tone. "If you love me, then you will not ask me to do things that respectable ladies don't do."

His eyes glittered in the darkness, reflecting the distant light from the gas lamps in the livery yard. After a moment, she heard him sigh heavily.

"Do you mean I cannot touch you unless I have divorced my wife?" he asked, his tone far different from the breathy tone he'd been using. "Is that fair, Edie?"

"It is not only fair, it is necessary," she said. "Why would you take issue with this? You have told me that you intend to divorce your wife. That is why I met you here tonight. Did I misunderstand you?"

He paused. Perhaps it was because he thought he could get away with something tonight, something to satisfy him and ruin her for life. He was very fond of her, but mostly because she was pretty and compliant.

At least, she used to be.

But tonight, she was taking something of a stand.

"You did not misunderstand me," he said, sounding vastly disappointed. "But I must ask – if you did not intend to demonstrate your love for me, why did you answer my summons?"

Edie could feel the warmth that had been so recent between them drain away. It was a cold question looking for a cold answer. She backed away from him and stood up, brushing the straw from her skirt.

"Because I thought you had something to tell me," she said. "Good news."

"Is the news that I love you not enough?"

"It will mean more when your actions prove it."

Myles wasn't happy in the least. His entire face changed, his features taut and bordering on rage. But he simply nodded, an insincere gesture, and stood up, brushing the chaff off his fine breeches.

"Will you at least let me ply you with wine?" he asked.

Edie shook her head. "No," she said. "There might be someone inside who will recognize me. I will return home, Myles. I will wait for news of your divorce there."

With that, she turned on her heel, making her way back into the cold night, walking away from a man she thought she loved. She truly did. But Myles, so far, had been long on promises and short on action.

But still, Edie held out hope.

Tonight, she left with a wounded heart, but at least her innocence was intact.

And she intended to keep it that way.

God help her, it was the beginning of the downfall of Edie Rhodes.

CHAPTER ONE

*"Thou shalt seek vengeance... in the most satisfying
way possible..."*
Sin Commandment #1

June 1813
London

T HE EVENING SMELLED of dew and dampness from the River
Thames, filling the air with the scent that everyone in
London was privy to in the languid summer months. The day
had been warm and fabric stuck to moist skin, something even
the afternoon bathing and the ritual of powder couldn't
remove.

But he didn't particularly care at the moment.

He was on the hunt.

The great Stag Ball would be his hunting grounds this night.
He'd come for a reason. Oh, they *all* came for a reason and that
reason was mostly to find spouses in the great preying lands of
the ballrooms of London where the heartiest of beasts preyed
upon the weak, the rich, and the beautiful – usually in that
order – but for Rory Flynn, this night was different.

He had a motive in mind.

Revenge.

As the third son of the Earl of Sinbrook, Rory didn't stand a chance of inheritance. He was the most Sinning Flynn brother out of all of them – dashing, daring, and reckless in so many ways. He had glistening blond hair and flashing green eyes, a smile that could melt even the most iced maiden's heart. But most of all, he had the cunning and the ambition and the inherent sense of vengeance.

Anyone who shamed his family shamed him.

The family...

The Sinning Flynns is what Polite Society called his family, a breed descended from an Irish smuggler who had gained favor with King George III and had received an earldom as a result, much to the shock of the *ton*. The new Earl of Sinbrook had been granted a vast estate in Cornwall that was supported by the equally vast wealth the Irish smuggler had accumulated over the years.

Armed with his new title, the smuggler known as Sean Flynn had ingratiated himself to some of those in Polite Society who actually thought a Gaelic pirate added a little flair to the usually tight-lipped, upturned noses of the *ton*. One of those men had been the Duke of Savernake, a man with the mile-long name of Hugh Herbert Marmaduke Algernon Wellesbourne. His family went back centuries, back to the conquest of 1066, and he had a son, Martin, and a daughter, Amy.

It was Amy who had caused the biggest scandal of her debut Season.

Pledged to the prestigious Earl of Exford, a man named Halburton, Amy's future was set. As the most eligible young lady of the entire Season, she was much sought after by earls and viscounts and the relatives of earls and viscounts. Amy's family was wildly wealthy and any man to tame Lady Amy, with her flowing red hair and flashing dark eyes, would participate in that extreme wealth. Men who had never considered marriage before were considering Amy because of the untapped coinage she brought with her. He who controlled Amy would control some of the Savernake coffers.

But Amy had other ideas.

Sean Flynn.

In his youth, he was roguish and handsome in a way few men were. Sean had the Irish spirit in him and he was damned proud of it. In fact, he made sure that everyone around him knew exactly where he'd come from and what he was about, and sometimes that meant the Irish brogue grew stronger and the actions more exaggerated. He'd met Amy, quite by chance, when she was visiting a family friend in Cornwall and one look as they'd passed one another on the street was all it took for Sean to turn around and follow her. That had been in the afternoon. By evening, she couldn't get rid of him, nor did she want to, and by morning, he'd all but proposed marriage to her. A duke's daughter and an Irish pirate with an English title. Amy had been more than agreeable.

But there had been a complication.

And that was why Rory was here, in London.

That aforementioned vengeance.

The Earl of Exford was his target. Rich and arrogant, John Halburton had been engaged to Amy and when Amy broke off their engagement, the man made it his mission in life to ensure Amy was whispered about, spoken of, and gossiped over in the most unsavory ways possible. Men gossiped and women pointed. Rory had been far removed from it as a child. Then as he became older, attending school and finally on to Oxford, he began to have a grasp of just how much his mother had been whispered about.

Exford had a younger brother who had been an instructor at Oxford. Professor Halburton had taught Rhetoric, a class that Rory had detested, but made worse by the fact that Henry Halburton knew who Rory's mother was. He knew what she had done and whom she had married. All of that snobbery and vindictiveness was fired right at the head of Rory, in front of everyone in the class.

That was from the very first day.

At first, Rory was grimly determined to drop out of the class to save the regular punishment. But he realized that if he did that, Halburton and his vile behavior would win. With Rory and his competitive nature, that didn't sit well, so he was determined to sit in class and take every single sling and arrow that was aimed at him. When Halburton insulted him and the class laughed, he laughed right along with them. He was determined to show his classmates that the ridiculous Rhetoric professor couldn't get to him.

That was on the outside.

The inside was much different.

That kind of humiliation buried a seed inside of Rory, a seed that had grown by the day. It was the seed of vengeance. He'd even come up with the Sin Commandments, a doctrine he lived by, listing how and why and when vengeance and retribution should be achieved. Not only against Exford, but against anyone who got in his way.

Anyone who wronged him.

The months and years passed and, still, the seed of vengeance grew. It grew against Exford and his stupid brother and everything they held dear. The Flynns had taken years of abuse from a jilted suitor who had ended up marrying well, anyway. From that marriage had come two daughters.

Rory had known from the beginning how his vengeance would be sated.

Exford's daughters.

But it would be done properly. Rory may have been a smuggler at heart and a wild Irishman in his soul, but there were lines he didn't cross. Children and the weak were out of bounds. When he exacted revenge, he preferred that it be with an adult in his or her right mind, fully capable of making decisions. There would be no physical abuse; certainly, that wasn't something he condoned when it came to a woman and with men, only if he was provoked. Even the most sinningest of the Sinning Flynns had his standards.

So, he waited.

The years passed.

His grandfather, the Duke of Savernake, had a grand ball on the summer solstice every year. The Stag Ball was one of the biggest and most prestigious balls during the Season and Rory had attended every year since his mother allowed that he was old enough. He'd met countless men and women and had made countless friends. Rory was, if nothing else, likeable and personable. He had a disarming way of smiling that endeared him to most. He was generous and witty. But he'd waited year after year for Exford's daughters to come of age and attend their first Season which, of course, meant the Stag Ball. Everyone who was anyone attended.

This was that year.

So many things reflected in his mind, balls and sins and vengeance, as he sat at the gambling table he'd been attached to for the past two days. Breaks came and went, but he always returned to the table in one of the seediest gambling dens London had ever seen. The Lyon's Den, they called it, a miraculous and horrifically sordid place that was as mysterious as it was legendary. He was in the main salon of the hall where the men gambled from mysterious dealers, each with a moniker that suggested sloth or greed or gluttony. No one knew the real names of the dealers, Rory included, but that was of little consequence.

Bored with the gambling dens he owned or had a stake in, he'd only come here to win money and perhaps a winsome courtesan, one of many who prowled the place. That was typical of Rory. He was never satisfied with what he had.

Or perhaps he was simply searching for something more.

He'd know it when he found it.

Two days in this hellish place. Two days of drink and smoke and the sweet scent of perfume from both men and women. Rory had trouble sleeping, so staying up for two days was nothing to him. When he wanted to sleep, he'd force down a measure of laudanum and that would pull the veil over his eyes for a few hours at most. He was coming to think that he needed to sleep today, at least for an hour or two, because the Stag Ball was this evening and this night – this event – was what he'd been waiting for.

The time had come.

And the hunt would begin.

CHAPTER TWO

"Thou shalt keep one's eyes on the prize, for opportunities of value happen only once..."
Sin Commandment #2

"IT LOOKS TERRIBLE," a young woman lamented. "This is positively ghastly the way it looks beneath my gown. Edie, what do you think?"

Edith "Edie" Rhodes eyed the silk gown that her younger sister, Matilda, was wearing. Matilda, or Tilly as she was known to the family, was making her debut this Season and tonight was the night she'd been looking forward to with great enthusiasm – the Stag Ball, given by the Duke of Savernake. It was the ball to see and be seen at this time of year, so Matilda was determined to present the perfect picture of pretty propriety.

Unfortunately, her clothing was not cooperating.

Matilda was roped into her stays within an inch of her life, holding in what her mother so sweetly termed as her "soft rolls". She was delightfully round, but she very much didn't wish to be, so she forced the poor maids to cinch her in very tightly to the point of being unable to breathe. Sausage casing was what she called it. The pale blue silk gown she was wearing showed every bump, bulge, and tie underneath the fabric and Matilda was greatly distressed.

But Edie kissed her on the cheek.

"I think you look lovely," she said, looking at her sister's reflection in the mirror. "The blue is stunning on you."

Matilda frowned as she put her hands on her belly, smoothing out the silk. "Are you certain?" she asked. "I feel as if one can see every line underneath."

Edie turned to look at her, inspecting the folds of the dress. "I think you worry too much," she said. "Silk wrinkles easily and the way you're pressing on it, you're going to damage it. Keep your hands off it and let it fall naturally. That's right. See? No lines."

She had removed her sister's hands to show her how the dress was meant to fall. It wasn't a clingy dress. But Matilda wasn't so certain, wanting to press her hands all over the dress yet trying to keep her hands away. When the maid appeared with feathers for her hair, she stopped fussing and Edie stepped away, standing near the door and smiling at her younger sister.

A more self-conscious woman had never lived.

"Well? How does she look?"

Edie turned to see her mother in the doorway. Dressed in an ivory-embroidered silk with matching slippers on her feet, she wore one of her collections of jewelry around her neck, a pearl and diamond necklace with big drop pearls. With matching earrings and her hair artfully arranged, Henrietta Rhodes looked every inch the wife of a viscount and the daughter of an earl, of which she was both. Daughter of the Earl of Ornsby and wife of Viscount Rossington, Henrietta was a handsome woman with graying, dark hair and blue eyes.

Edie resembled her down to the shape of her mouth.

"Lovely," Edie said, running a practiced eye over her sister. "If she would stop pulling at the fabric, I think we might actually make it through the night unscathed."

Henrietta watched her younger daughter try desperately not to manhandle the dress that was draped against her body.

She sighed heavily.

"Tilly," she said. "Sooner or later, your hands are going to leave prints all over that dress and those attending the ball will think that you are letting every unmarried young man in attendance rub their hands all over you and grab places that are best left unmolested. They will not believe the handprints are your own."

Matilda looked at her, horrified. "But the dress," she said, pinching at her waist. "It is so very tight."

"It is not," Henrietta said. "It is simply that you are so very round. Keep your hands off it or I'll leave you behind."

Rebuked and insulted, Matilda lowered her head. But she side-eyed her sister, standing near the doorway.

Her sister who could do no wrong when it came to presentation.

Edie was, in fact, the beauty of the family.

Willowy but shapely, Edie possessed an ethereal aura that was both strong and fragile. She looked like an angel with her blue eyes, dusky lashes, and dark hair, but it was her inner strength that set her apart from the rest.

Stubbornness, really.

Edie Rhodes did anything she damned well pleased.

As the eldest daughter of Viscount Rossington, she was rich. That was the simple truth. And what wealth – her father was quite rich from the white-faced cattle he bred in the north, not only on the Rossington estate, but on three smaller estates that he owned. One of them, Everton, was deep in the country-side and full of those cows that had made her father so rich. That's where they spent most of their time. There were also horses there, finely bred Thoroughbreds, and Edie was particularly fond of that little slice of heaven out in the wilds of South Yorkshire.

Far from the gilt halls of London's Season.

Matilda and Henrietta were quite fond of the tony London townhome in Belgravia, a gorgeous piece of architecture called Rossington House but lovingly referred to simply as Rossy. It was Matilda's first Season and her first Stag Ball, something she'd heard about for years but had never been permitted to attend.

Tonight, that changed.

Edie watched her little sister primp for her first prestigious ball in a dress that had been made by one of London's finest dressmakers. They'd come to London in late-January because preparation for the coming Season was almost busier than the Season itself. Dressmakers, shoemakers, visiting friends and the like made all of it a whirlwind.

But an exciting whirlwind.

Edie had her own reasons for being excited for this particular ball, however.

"Edie." Henrietta caught her attention. "Come with me, darling. Let Tilly finish dressing, but you and I must speak."

As Henrietta blew past her, out into the corridor, Edie followed.

"What about, Mama?" she asked.

Henrietta descended the stairs that led to the main corridor downstairs, carefully gripping the banister. It would not do to step on the hem of her expensive garment and ruin it.

"The guests tonight," she said, making it down without incident. "You know how big this ball is and there will be many, many people in attendance."

"I know."

Henrietta entered the parlor. "Then you know what I am going to say."

Edie had an idea, but she didn't give herself away. That very reason for her excitement, in fact. "What, Mama?" she said innocently. "Please speak freely."

Henrietta came to a halt and turned to her daughter. "You will stay away from Myles Forrester," she said quietly. "I am not entirely certain he will be there, but he is usually a fixture at these events. If he is in attendance… stay away from him."

Edie knew that was to be the edict. She'd known it all along. This wasn't the first time her mother had brought up Myles Forrester, a taboo subject in her house yet a subject that could be broached on occasions such as this.

Edie stiffened with resistance.

"I do not know why you feel the need to say such a thing," she said. "I've not seen him in quite some time."

It wasn't exactly a lie. She hadn't seen him, but she had received a missive from him. It was why she was so excited for the Stag Ball in the first place. She hoped God wouldn't punish her for trying to mislead her mother.

"Good," Henrietta said, her gaze lingering on her daughter in a way that suggested she more than likely didn't believe her. "He is no good for you and you know that. If he is in attendance and you happen to be seen with him, people will talk and… well, you do not need that kind of gossip, Edie. Promise me that you will stay away from him."

Edie's normally easygoing nature was in danger of fracturing. "I told you I would," she said. "I think you should be more concerned with Tilly throwing herself at one of the handsome DeWolfe brothers or making a fool of herself at the midnight buffet. Truly, Mama, you have no reason to be concerned with me."

Henrietta's eyes glittered in the candlelight. "I hope not," she said. "I've had enough concern for you to last me a lifetime."

Edie didn't want to be lectured. She didn't want to hear her mother speak of things that were better left buried, things from Edie's past that hadn't seen the light of day since they had happened.

Things that didn't need to be set free in the stillness of the parlor.

"Shall I hurry Tilly?" Edie asked, turning away from her mother before she could say anything further. "We do not want to be late."

Edie was heading out of the parlor to the stairs and away from her mother and her concerns. Somewhere in the house, Edie could hear her father speaking, more than likely to his valet. Frederick Rhodes had a booming voice even when he was whispering and as she took the stairs to the second floor, she could hear her father behind her, heading into the parlor and speaking to her mother.

Anything to get away from my mother.

Truth be told, Edie had no intention of staying away from Myles Forrester. Secret messages over the years had been the extent of it, but tonight… tonight would be different. Myles' last message spoke of news, of something he was eager to tell her.

All of that hope she'd been holding on to might actually come to fruition.

If her mother found out, however, there was sure to be trouble.

CHAPTER THREE

"In all things, keep your friends close... and your enemies at a disadvantage."

Sin Commandment #3

"YOU REMEMBER THAT Rhodes girl, don't you?"

"Rhodes?"

"The daughter of Viscount Rossington."

The hackney coach was lurching over the damp road as streetlights lit the way through a marvelous sunset. Rory had left his gambling den much later than he'd expected, but it was a good thing he'd left at all. If he'd had his way, he'd still be there.

His grandfather would simply track him down and drag him out by the neck.

Therefore, he'd taken a cab home. He was looking from the window, up at the townhomes as they neared the Duke of Savernake's resplendent residence, reportedly the largest in London. Rooms and more rooms, chambers, passageways and the like comprised a gargantuan feat of engineering. His chatty companion was his closest friend and most annoying companion, a man he'd known since childhood he couldn't seem to shake, nor could he live without him.

Forbes Dinnington was that man.

"I do not think so," Rory said with disinterest. "Why bring her up? When I was asking about the guest list tonight, I meant men. Perhaps we can pull together a game."

Forbes snorted. "Your grandfather would not look favorably upon you for that," he said. "At least, the type of game you are talking about."

"The duke does not have to know."

"He knows everything."

That was true. Rory leaned back against the cab, bracing a dirty boot on the cab wall in front of him. Though the man had a stable full of his own transportation, he still took a hackney cab from time to time, especially when he knew his own driver would speak on his ungodly hours and, somehow, that would make it back to his grandfather.

Yet one more thing to keep from his all-knowing, all-seeing grandfather.

"You mean Doo?" he said, a hint of sarcasm in his tone. "Only Aidan calls him that, you know. I went through a phase when I was younger and called him Doody. Aidan was young and cried when I stole his name for our grandfather and my own father told me to stop antagonizing my little brother."

"Did you?"

Rory looked at him, smirking. "Never," he said. "That is why God gave me a little brother."

"To torment?"

"Indeed."

"But you love him, anyway."

"I suppose I do." Rory turned his attention to the townhomes moving by as the hackney team trotted down the road. "In fact, he's probably at the duke's home right now, kissing up to him like he aways does. The little bastard. Mark my words, Forbes – when the duke dies, he will find a way to give everything to Aidan that my Uncle Martin doesn't already legally own. Aidan always was the duke's favorite."

Forbes listened to him, a smile playing on his lips. "You sound bitter."

"I am."

"You have plenty, Rory. You do not need ducal funds."

Rory looked at him. "Everything I have, I've had to earn," he pointed out. "Unlike my older brothers who had some money and property given to them by both of my parents, I had nothing. And Aidan has my grandfather under his thumb, but I have no one. I never have."

"Yet you seek revenge tonight for a mother who does not love you?"

Rory lifted an eyebrow. "I never said that," he said. "She loves me. But she loves my brothers more. What I do tonight is for the Flynn name – *my* name. I do it because of that bastard at Oxford who humiliated me every chance he got. I do it for the women who will look at me tonight and whisper *Amy's son* and then look the other way. Because this is my grandfather's ball, I should be the most sought-after man there, but I will not be. Oh, people will be polite. I will dance with women. But that's where it ends."

"Then how do you expect to gain a foothold with Exford's daughters?"

Rory turned his attention to the window again. "Find the eldest one and compromise her," he said simply. "I already live with a shameful reputation. But Exford does not. Let him see how it feels for a change."

Forbes had heard this before. Too many times to count. He knew the stakes and they were high, indeed.

Higher if Rory failed.

But Rory wasn't used to failure.

"My dear Rory," he said. "You know I love you madly, but I think you bring much of this upon yourself."

Rory looked at him again, sharply. "What do you mean?"

Forbes leaned back against the side of the cab. "Because you have no regard for anything," he said simply. "Let me finish before you scold me. You are brilliant; the most brilliant man in any room you choose to enter. You have an Oxford education to prove it. You have made a fortune following in your father's footsteps, but you took it further than he ever did. Sean Flynn was clever and lucky, but you are clever and lucky and unscrupulous. You are richer than God Himself for such a young age and even as you complain that your older brothers have everything, you have even more than they do, yet you spend your life in gambling hells and racetracks and in clubs and dens that even the heartiest man would be fearful of. Yet you do it, day in and day out."

Rory was trying not to look defensive as a tidal wave of criticism and compliments came his way. "And so I do," he said. "It is my life. Let me ruin it if I want to."

"You are the most ruinous man I know," Forbes said. "But if you go after Exford's daughter, you are not only going to ruin yourself, but your entire family. Not even Savernake will be able to save you."

"I do not want to be saved."

"Then I wish you well."

Rory turned away. He knew Forbes meant well, but the man

didn't understand that he *had* to do this. He'd been planning it for so long that it was part of his very fabric.

A fabric of ruin.

After tonight, perhaps there would be no return.

"You mentioned the Rhodes girl," he muttered. "What about her?"

Forbes yawned and settled deeper against the cushioned cab set. "Oh, that," he said. "Don't you remember Edie Rhodes? She had her debut a few years ago, but she had a reputation at the time for keeping company with a married man. In fact, someone actually saw her leaving a tavern near her father's estate with this man and, after that, she disappeared for a year or two while her parents tried to repair her reputation. You don't recall that scandal?"

Rory looked at him. "I don't think so," he said. "But then again, I don't pay attention to gossip like you do. I don't seem to remember Edie Rhodes."

"You would if you had seen her," Forbes said. "She's a stunning creature."

"Truly?"

Forbes nodded. "If she's here tonight, you might have an easy conquest of it if she's as unrestrained as they say she is," he said. "Too bad, too. Her father is Viscount Rossington. There is a good deal of money there, enough to overlook any youthful indiscretions."

"Forgive and forget for a price, eh?"

"Exactly."

Rory pondered a loose woman of some means but only for a couple of moments. He turned his attention back to the street. "There are enough desperate men out there who would be willing to do that," he said. "Who else will be at the ball tonight?"

"Everyone who is anyone," Forbes snorted softly. "Several of our friends."

"Who?"

"The DeWolfe brothers," he said. "Handsome rakes, all of them. Too much competition for the women."

Rory cracked a smile. "And women like men who live dangerously," he said. "Who else?"

"Joshua Wethersfield. Remember him? With the mother that drives herself through Oxford like a madwoman?"

Rory grinned. "Of course I remember him," he said. "Joshua and I have known each other for years. A solicitor."

"A very fine one."

"I know," Rory said. "I've had need of him in the past. Anyone else I should know about?"

"The warlords," Forbes said, affectionately referring to a group of their friends who were from very old nobility. "Delohr and Russe, for example. I think DeWinter will also be there."

"It has been a long time since I've seen that bunch."

"Indeed," Forbes said. He leaned towards Rory. "If I were you, I would ask them about the rumors."

"What rumors?"

"That they have an underground fight club. Much money to be made, Rory."

That perked Rory up. "*Fight* club?" he repeated. "Why have I not heard this?"

Forbes snorted. "Because you come to these events and shut yourself up in a smoking room or in a den of gamblers," he said. "You do not mingle like you should. Dance with a few women tonight and keep your ears open. You might learn something."

Rory chuckled ironically because it was the truth. He spent

so much time pursuing his own endeavors and indulging in his own vices that he didn't keep abreast of things like he should. But tonight wasn't the night to dance with women and keep his ears open.

He had something else to do.

And he was going to do it.

CHAPTER FOUR

"If they cannot see you coming, then they won't know when you arrive.

Be the ghost."

Sin Commandment #4

*T*HE ARRIVAL.

It was always such a moment in the life of a young woman to arrive at the biggest ball of the year. Or her first ball. Or any ball, really. But in this case, it was different for Edie.

She was looking for someone.

He'd promised he'd be here. Myles had told her that he would be in attendance and she was desperate to see him. It had been such a long time. After their encounter in the stable and the rumors that followed in spite of their attempts to be cautious, her parents kept a very close eye on her. She went everywhere with a chaperone and that had been by design. Two years out of the public eye, away from balls and parties, waiting until the scandalous rumors died down before she was allowed to come out again.

And here she was.

Myles was somewhere, waiting.

IT HAD BEEN a dangerous liaison from the start.

Myles was older, a friend of her father's, in fact. That was how Edie had met him. He'd been kind to her and kinder still when she came of age. That was when the trouble started. Myles was married but his wife was a shrew and he made that clear to Edie. He had from the start. Their relationship had consisted almost entirely of secret messages and that was how she knew he would be at the Stag Ball tonight. He'd sent her a message through his valet to Edie's maid, a message that told her to meet him in the garden to the rear of the residence because he had news for her. Edie wasn't exactly sure how to get there, but she was going to find out.

The man had news and that's all she cared about.

The weather had been mild so a barouche had been ordered and Edie sat next to her sister, her gaze upon the great ducal townhome that was the very center of London society on this night. There was a massive square across from the townhome where an enormous bonfire would be lit to end the Stag Ball, and the Savernake footmen were directing traffic in and around the area.

Edie had never seen so many carriages.

There were all manner and sizes of transportation on this night as fine vehicles were directed to the steps leading up to the townhome, and women and men disembarked. Edie's barouche had to get in line to be offloaded because Henrietta didn't want to walk across mud and horse leavings and chance messing her fine silk slippers. Therefore, they had to wait their turn, affording Edie an opportunity to see all of the fashions as the nobility of London made their way up the stone steps and into the duke's townhome.

Silk, velvet, and the like seemed to be the common theme and the color for the Season was anything pale. No vibrant colors that Edie could see, which was good considering she was wearing pink. A gorgeous pink silk frock with a crepe silk overlay that had hundreds of tiny beads embroidered into it. Her long hair was up, fashionably neat upon her head, and she smelled of the jasmine fragrance her father had purchased for her, just for this occasion.

But Myles will be the only one who smells it, she told herself.

Beside her, Matilda and their mother were chatting excitedly about all of the fine houses that were in attendance. Henrietta, in particular, seemed to be singling out all of the eligible men, and there were dozens of them. Young or old, rich or moderately rich, it didn't matter. Henrietta had her eye on them, as she had two daughters that needed husbands and the eldest one in particular.

She made no secret of that.

Though Edie had been out of circulation for a couple of years until the Forrester scandal blew over, Henrietta intended to market her daughter as a viable prospect for any proper gentleman.

Knowing this, Edie couldn't help but feel the rise of irritation in her breast. So far, it was just Henrietta and Matilda discussing the gowns and fashions, but soon it would move to men. Always men.

But Edie only had eyes for one man. "What do you think of that gown, Edie?" Henrietta asked, pointing to a yellow silk confection. "What of that color?"

Distracted from thoughts of Myles, Edie turned to look at the color on a very heavy older woman. "That is the Countess of

Binbrook," she said. "I saw her at the very first ball I ever attended, the ball held in Broughton. The dogs got loose and ran across the ballroom floor."

Matilda giggled. "I remember you telling me about it," she said. "One of the dogs pissed and people were sliding all over the floor."

Edie grinned but Henrietta shushed them both. "You will not speak of such things," she said. "Look – our carriage is next. Are we ready to disembark?"

Edie craned her neck to look ahead, but she wasn't on the right side of the carriage to see the activity. Across from her, Henrietta collected her fan, preparing to step out with her head high, her jewels on display, and her eyes focused on the prize.

She knew other women would be studying her as she had been studying them.

"Then we are off," she said quietly as the carriage moved forward, guided by two footmen. More footmen were waiting to help them disembark. "Come along, ladies. We have arrived."

Henrietta was the first one off the carriage, giving her name and family name to an underbutler who was there for that very purpose. He spoke to a man standing behind him, who was writing everything down. The Stag Ball would be carefully documented, as it was every year, so the society columns would have the correct information. As Henrietta made sure to mention her father's name and title to the man doing the writing, Edie looked around at all of the people, the servants, and the splendor, all of it dazzling.

The Stag Ball was living up to its name.

But her focus was already in the garden. Edie was thinking ahead to the moment she would meet Myles, but the truth was that her date in the garden would have to wait. It wasn't as if she could simply run off. She had to remain with her mother until they entered the residence and she did, although she was quite nervous about it. She could feel herself sweating through the fabric as she followed her mother and Matilda through the entry and towards the crowded corridor that led to the receiving line and, subsequently, the ballroom.

She felt like a sheep. All she'd done for the past two years was follow her mother like a lost and lonely sheep, every place they went. No parties, no social events, but marketing or dressmaking or something else. It had become habit with her to keep her head down and follow her mother and for an independent young woman, that was a fate worse than death. But it had also been necessary to rebuild the reputation she'd shredded when she'd agreed to meet Myles Forrester in the stable.

Such was the penalty of her foolishness.

"Look there," Henrietta said, pointing to the veranda that was near the entry, facing the square. "I see Lady Criswell and her sister. I must greet them."

Henrietta rushed forward with Matilda right behind her. Edie followed, that same silly sheep again, listening to her mother engage in a lively conversation with her friends and following the women all the way to the receiving line.

But Edie couldn't even focus on what they were doing.

She needed to get to that garden.

It was a horrible conflict, knowing she had to stay with her mother, knowing this was her chance to solidify her restored reputation by behaving as a proper young lady would. She also knew that her behavior would reflect on Matilda and that was something that gave her pause. She was willing to be responsible for her own reputation, but damaging her sister's chances was something else altogether.

Therefore, she remained with her mother throughout the introductions and the greetings and everything else that came with an event of this magnitude. She smiled at the old women who had once clucked their tongues about her, the same women who were now in approval that she'd been properly defeated and restrained. The blithe, free spirit that was once Edie Rhodes had been summarily curtailed and forced into submission. No more wandering to a livery in the middle of the night to meet a married man.

Lesson learned.

Edie was on the right side again.

Therefore, Edie knew that she had to plan her escape very carefully. No one could see her or notice that she'd gone. She would have to stay to the shadows and keep out of sight. That moment came when they'd made it past the receiving line and ended up in one of the numerous rooms that was crowded with people in conversation, all of them waiting for the dancing to commence. It was a night to see and be seen and the excitement in the air was palpable. It was, at that moment, that Edie excused herself to the ladies' room with her mother wrapped up in conversation with another gossipy matron. Henrietta gave her approval as Matilda clung to her mother.

Edie could go alone.

And she did.

THE GARDEN TO *the rear*, his message had said. Heart pounding with excitement, Edie lost herself in the crowd, heading for the floor to ceiling doors that opened to the side of the house with the garden to the rear. Once outside in the mild June night, she moved quickly for the garden and into the bushes to make sure she wasn't seen.

CB

HE'D BEEN ROPED into the receiving line.

Unfortunately, Rory didn't have a chance to get a few hours of sleep as he'd hoped. He'd left The Lyon's Den too late and by the time he reached his grandfather's townhome, preparations were in full swing for the evening's event.

Forbes was his guest, so when the cab came to a halt, footmen were waiting. Both Rory and Forbes were hustled into the home to be met by the duke's butler, an older man by the name of Simms. Simms was quiet and efficient as always, directing Forbes to the unmarried male visitor wing, which was down on the lower level, and further directing Rory to the room he always occupied while in London.

Rory took the steps two by two, finally reaching the upper floor of the house that had the faint scent of tobacco. The duke liked to smoke and he did so without closing any doors so, over the years, the smell had permeated the very walls.

Rory found it a comforting smell.

The duke's valet, a somber man named Howard, was on his tail the moment he reached his bedroom. Howard had already helped the duke dress and since Rory's younger brother, Aidan, didn't like nor employ a valet, the man was at Rory's disposal. As Rory began to quickly undress, he eyed the valet in the mirror's reflection.

"Has my brother arrived?" he asked.

Howard nodded, his hawk-like eyes focused on laying out Rory's clothes. "He has, my lord."

"Is he in his room?"

"I am not entirely certain, my lord," Howard said. "Shall I send a servant for him?"

Rory shook his head. "Don't bother," he said. "I shall see him soon enough."

The valet finished laying out his clothing as Rory quickly bathed and shaved, something he wouldn't have normally done except he hadn't bathed in quite some time and he knew he smelled quite rancid. If the duke got a whiff of it, he'd make his displeasure known, so it was better not to stir the pot.

Rory stirred it enough without trying these days.

When he finally finished dressing and smelled like sandalwood, Howard collected his dirty clothing and carted it off, leaving Rory to finish with his hair. It was dark, with a bit of a curl, and he combed it into a fashionable arrangement. Normally, he simply ran his fingers through it and that was enough of a comb but, tonight, he wanted to make some effort so his grandfather might find something pleasing in him.

That was the hope, anyway.

Just as he was finishing, there was a knock on the door.

"Come," he said.

The panel creaked open and Aidan Flynn entered. Rory glanced at his younger brother, a sensitive soul and a man who never quite fit in with his older brothers. But Rory and Aidan were close as brothers went and they'd always gotten on, even when they disagreed.

Rory smiled weakly at his brother.

"Ah," he said. "I was told you were here. Where is Grandfather?"

"Downstairs already," Aidan said.

Rory put the comb down. "Then we had better join him before he comes up here to retrieve us."

He moved for the door but Aidan put up a hand to stop him.

"Wait," he said quietly. "I want to speak with you before you go down."

Rory came to a halt, his brother's hand on his chest. "Why?" he said. "What's amiss?"

Aidan dropped his hand. "When was the last time you saw Grandfather?"

Rory cocked his head thoughtfully. "A few months ago," he said. "Why?"

"So you've not seen him lately?"

"No. Why?"

Aidan shook his head, recalling the conversation he'd had with his grandfather and his grandfather's physician earlier in the day. A cancer, their grandfather had. The physician had confirmed it. It wasn't as if he'd been sworn to secrecy about it but, somehow, he thought their grandfather should tell Rory about his fate. That wasn't something that should come from him. But he'd had no choice and had confirmed the diagnosis when Aidan had visited the good doctor's offices.

But he wasn't sure Rory would even notice.

The man was so wrapped up in himself that he seldom saw beyond his own nose.

"He doesn't look… well," Aidan said. "He's growing older, Rory. Someday, he will die and the Stag Ball… it very well may be that it does not continue. In fact, this may be last glorious ball for all we know and although I know you had plans for Exford and his daughters, I am wondering if you would reconsider."

"Reconsider what?"

"I told you. Your plans for Exford and his daughters."

Rory's jaw tightened. "That's what I thought you meant," he said. "To that, I will say this – what I do is my business, Aidan. You have never interfered with me and I have never interfered with you, so whatever I do will not reflect upon our grandfather. Only me."

Aidan sighed heavily, as if he knew his request had been a foolish one. Rory always did what Rory wanted to do.

His irritation bloomed.

"I am asking you, for once, to think of someone other than yourself," he said. "I am asking you to think of Doo, Rory. Will you at least give the man the dignity of not causing a great scandal at his prestigious ball?"

Rory's pale eyes glittered in the weak light. "His dignity is not at stake," he said. "Exford's is. And no, I will not reconsider. I have been waiting too long for this."

That was as far as Aidan would go in pleading with his brother. The man was so selfish that no amount of begging would cause him to change his mind. Aidan knew that. Years of humiliation and shame had compounded into this night, so there was nothing that could change the direction.

Not even a dying grandfather.

Therefore, Aidan simply turned away, exiting the bedroom as Rory lingered behind. Aidan had irritated him. But the more he thought on it, he realized that there was something more behind that suggestion that this might be the last Stag Ball, at least with their grandfather at the head of it.

Something in Aidan's eyes suggested it.

Bordering on brooding, he remained in his bedroom for a short while, long enough for the receiving line to get started and for him to be a late addition. But something told him this night would be different.

There was something in the air.

A most monumental night, for all of them, was about to begin.

CHAPTER FIVE

*"Time is the only true constant. Vengeance is the only
true path.
At some point, they will converge."*
Sin Commandment #5

T HE BUSHES WERE dark.
And wet. Just a little damp and Edie struggled not to
get the moisture on her gown, which would surely ruin it. How
would she explain it to her mother? Therefore, she'd been
forced to step out of the foliage and stay to the shadows as
much as possible, terrified she would be seen and it would get
back to Henrietta. The evening would be over before it started,
perhaps permanently.

But then, it happened.

Myles came out of the bushes, rushing towards her in a
flutter of wool and blond hair and white gloves, all of them
reaching out to Edie and nearly scaring her to death.

Myles finally made his appearance.

"My darling girl," he whispered, putting his arms around
her and pulling her into the shadows where the gas torchlight

wouldn't reach. "You received my message. I am so glad."

Edie gladly gave herself over to his kisses. The man tasted like wine, the fine drink he consumed more than he should have, but she didn't care.

HE COULD KISS her as much as he wanted to, wine or no wine.

"I do not have much time," she said breathlessly. "Mama and Tilly are here and if I do not rejoin them inside quickly, Mama will come looking for me."

"I know, my dearest."

"She has expressly forbidden me to see you."

"And your father?"

Edie slowed her kisses and looked at him. "He said he will kill you if he ever sees you again."

Myles slowed his kisses as well, reaching up to gently cup her face. He was tall and fair and had a tremulous way about him, as if he were always eager and trembling. It was rather endearing, something that had been useful against the army of women he'd seduced over the years. Edie was just one in a long line of many although he'd managed to keep them all fairly separate. Myles may have been married, but he wasn't reckless or stupid.

He was a man in control.

"It has been so long since I've beheld your beauty," he said, studying her face. "I'd forgotten how lovely you are."

Edie smiled, feeling encouraged by his words. "You said you had news for me," she said. "What news, Myles? What is it?"

He ran his thumbs over her cheeks. "You've been kept from me for far too long," he said. "It simply wasn't right for your parents to do that. They caged you like an animal."

Edie's smile faded somewhat. "They did what they felt was

right," she said. "I cannot say I was happy about it, but they did what they felt was right to help me regain my reputation after that night at The Hungry Horse."

The light in his eyes dimmed. "I still don't know who saw us leaving the livery," he said. "Someone was clearly spying on us."

"Perhaps someone followed me. I've always thought so, though my mother would not confess."

Myles' jaw ticked faintly. "That will happen again if we are seen tonight," he said. "We must do something drastic if we are to be together, Edie."

"What do you mean?"

His features grew intense.

"I've come tonight to ask you to come with me," he said. "We'll go north, where my mother's family has property, and there is a little cottage where you will live and I will come to you when I can. I will support your every need, my dearest. What say you?"

Edie looked at him in surprise. "Go north?" she repeated. "You… you wish for me to go with you?"

He nodded eagerly, that tremulous little-boy manner coming forth. "I do," he said. "I very much do. Mrs. Forrester and the children remain at Mansfield and forever shall. My wife does not like to travel and she certainly hates the north, so we may live there as we please during the times I am able to come."

Something in Edie's expression dimmed. "Then you will not be with me, always?"

"Heavens, no," he said quickly, cupping her face and kissing her lips again. "That is impossible. But if you come with me, you will be away from your mother and father, free of their influence. They shall only know of your location if you tell them and surely you will not tell them. It will be our own paradise, my dearest. Will you come?"

His request gave Edie pause. She had a sickening feeling in the pit of her stomach. "But… but you said that you would divorce your wife," she said. "The message you sent me said that you had news and I thought it was about your divorce. You said we could go to France and be married there, returning to England well after the scandal faded. I do not want to only be a mistress to you. I am more important than that."

"Of course you are," he insisted. "Edie, don't you understand? I choose you. I didn't choose Mrs. Forrester – my father did. But you – I choose *you*."

She dropped her hands from him. "But I want to be your wife," she said, tears stinging her eyes. "You promised, Myles."

She was backing away and he was trying to follow her, his hands on her shoulders. "My dearest darling, there are realities in life that we must face," he said. "I can never have a divorce. We must face that fact."

Edie was growing more upset. "You promised."

He threw up his hands. "I know!" he said. "I should not have. It is impossible. The expense is incredible. And the time – it could take years and years before it is granted and, even then, there is no guarantee it *would* be granted. My wife is inconsequential, Edie. She means nothing to me, to us. You mean everything. Please, my dearest… please, come with me."

More people were starting to wander into the garden now as guests arrived and began to roam the grounds. They were aware of people now within earshot and Edie moved further away from Myles, half-concealed by the bushes, eyeing him in the moonlight.

"You have made promises to me that you have not kept, Myles," she said after a moment. "This is not the first time. For argument's sake, let's say that I agree. There is no guarantee that if I go with you that you will even come to visit me."

His eyes flickered, perhaps with the realization that she was quite right. He'd never been the most dependable of men and even though their one and only encounter had been brief, she'd known him for a few years before that, as he'd been her father's friend. She knew that he'd had difficulty keeping his word. She knew that he was flighty and insincere at times. She knew that he was kind and lively and enjoyable to be around, but beneath that exterior, there was little else.

She knew.

"Do you doubt my word, then?" he said in a tone that suggested it was her problem and not his. "Is this how you treat the man you love? Edie, how can you believe the worst?"

It was simple, in truth. Though Myles was an old friend of her father's, she'd heard her father speak of him enough to know him for what he was. She supposed she'd always known it but it had never been more evident than it was at this moment.

That sick feeling was growing worse.

"I don't wish to be locked up in a cottage in the north by myself, waiting for a glimpse of you and hoping for a sweet word or a touch," she finally said. "That is not fair, Myles."

He looked gravely wounded.

"Please don't tell me that you do not trust me," he said, putting his hand over his heart. "I could not bear it if you did."

"You have broken your word to me."

"It is not my fault!"

HE WAS STARTING to snap at her, a side she'd never seen of him. Gone were the warm feelings, the joy at having seen him again after so long. Now, there was only cold, hard reality between them and it wasn't pleasant. Myles wanted something and he'd beg, borrow, or steal to get it.

But Edie wasn't going to comply. It was the same merry path he'd led her down since they'd first declared their affection for each other, a path that had only turned into near ruin for her.

But he'd come through unscathed.

"No, Myles," she said after a lengthy pause. "Understand that the only reason I came tonight is because you said you had news. And based on our previous conversations, I believed you were to tell me of your impending divorce. That is the *only* reason I came."

"But…"

She wagged a gloved finger in his face, cutting him off. "Understand that in an unguarded moment, I met you in a livery and I've spent two years of my life trying to repair that failing," she said. "Two years of spending time away from Polite Society so the rumors and gossip could recede. Time for other outrageous scandals to take place and cover up the memory of ours. Two long years of my life wasted because I listened to you when I should not have."

Myles, sensing that he was losing her, invoked the wounded expression again. "How can you think that I don't love you?" he asked. "If I am willing to provide handsomely for you and give you anything you wish, does that not profess my love for you strongly enough?"

Edie honestly wasn't sure. She was growing increasingly disillusioned and Myles' begging wasn't helping. It was only serving to inflame her. He always begged to get what he wanted, convincing her that he and his declarations of love were sincere.

But Edie was starting to disbelieve everything that came out of his mouth.

"I deserve a husband and a home and children," she said. "What you are offering is something secretive and shameful. So you will hide me away, will you? A convenience at your whim? I am to pine away in the wilds of the north, living for the very sight of you? Is that what you expect from me?"

Myles' eyes widened. "I said that I will provide most generously for you," he insisted. "You will want for nothing."

Edie sighed heavily, starting to see Myles for the very first time. A man who wanted only what *he* wanted.

To hell with what she wanted.

"You promised me that we would be together as man and wife, but now I discover that you have no intention of divorcing your wife," she said. "I risked *everything* for you, Myles. Am I not worth more than being a simple mistress? Is this what you had intended all along?"

"But you have my love, my dearest. No one can ever take that away."

Edie didn't want to hear that. A man's declaration of love was only valid if he followed through on his promises. Otherwise, it was an empty dream.

Edie was coming to realize that.

The dream was dead.

"No," she finally said. "No, I do not want to be shipped off to the wilds of the north as your convenience."

"But I adore you!"

"I will not ruin my life for you."

Their voices were starting to grow louder and Myles held up his hands, silently begging her to lower her tone. Edie glanced around nervously, hoping no one had heard the outburst, terrified her mother had realized she'd been gone overlong and was out looking for her.

"Go home, Myles," she finally said, tears stinging her eyes. "Go back to your wife and children, for I shall not be a…"

She was cut off when a man suddenly stood in their midst, a tall man with messy hair and messy clothes. He looked rather disheveled, in fact. He reeked of alcohol and body stench and Edie found herself backing away quickly, simply because he'd startled her.

But the man was looking straight at Myles.

"Are you Myles Forrester?" the man asked, his voice trembling.

Myles, unhappy with the interruption, forced a smile. "I am," he said. "How may I be of service?"

The man seemed to study him and Edie studied the man. He was trembling, his hands working into fists.

"I have been looking everywhere for you," the man finally said. "I thought you might be here tonight. The biggest ball of the season. Where else would you be? So many young women to choose from."

The smile on Myles' lips faded. "I'm afraid I do not know what you mean."

The man nodded. "You will," he said. "You see, I've been looking for you. I've followed you from town to village and back again since last summer. You are not an easy man to find, but your description is unmistakable. Tall and fair, with a big mole on your big chin. I ask shopkeepers and clergymen if they've seen you and I've been able to follow you that way."

Myles' hand flew up to his face, fingering the dark mole on the left side of his chin. "So you have found me," he said, less friendly and more suspicious. "What do you want?"

The man leaned closer. "To look you in the eyes," he said,

his voice having gone from moderately friendly to threatening all in a swift breath. "You see, last summer, at a country ball in Willington, you became acquainted with my wife. Her name is Lucy Edwards. I was away on a business venture, but I was told by servants and neighbors, gleefully I might add, that you and my wife were seen together during the ball and for three days afterwards. Months later, my wife gave birth to a baby boy."

Myles' features tightened. "Surely you do not come to…"

"Yes, I do," the man said, cutting him off rudely. "The truth of the matter is that I cannot father children, Mr. Forrester. My wife confessed that she had a liaison with you and that you are the father of her child. That is why I have followed you. A man like you must be stopped. I want to look into your eyes when you beg me for your very life."

Startled when he realized the man meant to do him harm, Myles stepped back. "Get away from me," he commanded weakly. "How did you even get in here? Get away from me or I'll call the duke's men."

But the man didn't move. He was tracking Myles with the intensity of a cat tracking a mouse. "There is a guard at the gate leading from the mews who will have a very bad headache in an hour or two," he said. "It was a matter of hitting him over the head and slipping in. But he will soon be discovered and my time is limited. I must do what I intended to do."

With that, he moved swiftly, hitting Myles in the face with a balled fist. Edie was far enough away that she didn't get caught up in the fight, but she screamed in shock and terror as the confrontation deteriorated into a vicious brawl. Others in the garden were gasping with horror and the footman just inside the door leading into the morning room, which opened onto the garden, began shouting for help.

In little time, the entire garden was in an uproar.

For several long moments, Edie simply stood there in horror, watching Myles being beaten within an inch of his life. The men had rolled close to her and she ended up being kicked in the shin, standing too close for her own good, unable to move. But men that the duke employed to keep the peace and security of his home and affairs began to flood the garden and before Edie realized what had happened, someone had grabbed her from behind and pulled her into the shadows of the foliage.

Away from the fighting and the people who were now coming to watch it.

Now, they wouldn't see her standing there in the middle of it.

When next Edie realized, she was standing in the open doorway of the duke's orangery and someone was pulling her inside. When she looked up, all she could see was a profile against the moonlight coming in through the glass walls. A strong, regal, male profile.

Evidently, her knight in shining armor.

CHAPTER SIX

"Patience is not a virtue. It is a choice."
Sin Commandment #6

R ECEIVING LINES HAD never been something Rory had looked forward to.

They were long and tedious and ridiculous and most of the women simply wanted to speak with his grandfather, who was looking frail and old on this night. He could see Aidan on his grandfather's other side, hovering over the old man, and it occurred to him what Aidan may have been trying to tell him earlier in his bedroom.

Their grandfather was not a well man.

That was obvious.

Rory had only seen the man a few months ago and he'd been his usual, robust self, but over the course of those months, something had changed drastically.

And he hadn't even known.

Aidan was correct when he'd called him selfish. He *was* selfish. When he wasn't wrapped up with his business operations, he was wrapped up in himself and all of the vices that kept him going. Those addictions were like blood through his veins. The gambling, the drinking, the women were all things that kept him alive. Or perhaps not so much alive as an escape. Possibly an escape from the fact that, as he'd told Forbes, he had no one.

He never had.

An escape from himself.

As he mulled over his grandfather's physical state and the disappointment radiating from Aidan's eyes, he caught a glimpse of Forbes as the man moved through the drawing room. He was chatting with a group of other young, unmarried men and Rory identified several of them as his good friends. When he found himself wishing he was standing with them rather than in his grandfather's receiving line, he experienced an emotion that didn't normally suit him.

Guilt.

He was feeling guilty because, once again, he was thinking about himself and not his grandfather or his duty. As far as Rory was concerned, his duty was to himself, but as he watched his fragile grandfather greet his guests, that guilt grabbed at him. Would it kill him to do his duty and make his grandfather proud of him, for once?

He wasn't sure that was even possible.

"Rory?"

A voice caught his attention and he turned to see that his grandfather was now standing next to him, addressing him. But the old man was forced to turn away and greet a family of three women and their elderly father before turning to Rory once again when the group passed by.

"I'm glad that you could join me," the duke said, his eyes twinkling. "I wasn't sure you would. Better late than never, I suppose. I know how you hate these formal affairs and I wasn't sure if the lure of cards was greater."

Rory forced a smile at a man he truly loved. He just wished the feeling was reciprocated. "It's not that I hate them," he said. "It's that I think they are ridiculous. This is simply a parade of beasts, Grandfather."

The old duke laughed softly. "That is true," he said. "But a necessary parade of beasts."

"Why necessary?"

The duke shrugged. "For example, how else are marriageable people supposed to find one another?"

Rory eyed him. "Is that what this is?" he said. "A massive matchmaking event?"

"To some," the duke said. "What else would you suggest for interested and unmarried people?"

"Church," Rory said flatly. "Strolling down the street. I have no idea. But something like this… it is simply not my taste."

"It never has been. You even hated parties as a boy."

"I'm surprised you would remember that."

"I remember everything about you, Rory. I always will."

There was something more intimated in that brief statement. Something touching, almost. Rory looked at the old man more closely, seeing just how pale and gaunt he was.

He couldn't help the next question.

"Grandfather," he said slowly. "Are you feeling well?"

They were cut off when another group approached and the duke was forced to greet them. Frustrated at the interruption, Rory turned to the guests in time to see that they were the guests he'd been waiting for, the very people who had been the bane of his family's existence since the day his mother decided to marry Sean Flynn.

John Halburton in the flesh.

Caught off guard by their appearance, Rory struggled not to appear rattled. He'd hoped to see the man and his daughters before they saw him so he could map out his final plan, but that wasn't to be. Here they were, in front of him, and he watched his grandfather greet the man who had spoken so poorly of his own daughter.

Exford was sickeningly pleasant.

"It is an honor, your grace," he said to the duke. "Once again, I am thrilled and humbled to be invited to your gathering. Surely there is no more prestigious gathering in all of London."

"Thank you," the duke said, his gaze moving to the two young women next to the earl. "And these are your lovely daughters?"

Exford turned to the women. "Indeed," he said. "My daughters, Lady Rose and Lady Sarah. Ladies, this is the Duke of Savernake himself."

Rory found himself looking at the daughters and feeling a sense of disappointment but, in that same breath, he felt a sense of glee. Standing before him were two young women who were probably a little older than they should have been to have just had their debut Season and both of them, to be brutally honest, were not the most attractive of women. Sarah had blemishes on her face, neck, and chest that she'd tried to cover up with powder while Rose had close-set eyes and an enormous nose.

Women like this would be desperate for male attention.

That would work in his favor.

"Welcome, ladies," the duke said, smiling politely. He indicated Rory. "One of my grandsons, Rory Flynn. He is Amy's son, as is the other young man off to my left. That is Aidan, the youngest. Your father surely remembers my Amy."

He said it in a way that dared Exford to even hint at anything negative. Gone was the congenial old man. Before them stood a hardened old boar who suggested in just those few words that he knew exactly what Exford had been doing all these years.

Your father surely remembers my Amy.

Since the man had all but called her a whore, it was a rhetorical question. The duke's tone intimated that he was inviting Exford to say such things to his face, but Exford sensed it because he plastered a phony smile on his face and visibly demurred.

"Of course I do," he said. "I trust Lady Sinbrook is well?"

"Quite."

"Excellent."

"Good evening to you."

The conversation was over. That was Exford's cue to depart and he did, quickly, pulling his two daughters with him, but not before the eldest daughter gave Rory a rather coy expression. He smiled at her, that sly smile that had endeared him to many a maiden, before she turned away completely.

But in that gesture, Rory knew who his target would be.

His eye was on the prize.

"Imbecile," the duke muttered as Exford walked away with a tight grip on his daughters. "I wonder where his wife is."

Rory didn't know and he surely didn't care. "I would not know," he said. Then he looked at the groups that continued to filter in through the front door, resplendent in their finery. "How much longer must we stand here like baboons on display and shake the hand of every man and woman who comes in the door?"

The duke glanced at him, grinning. "Until the last one enters," he said. "The dancing cannot start until I open the ball."

"Then is there anything you wish from me before the festivities start?"

The duke was still looking off towards the ballroom. "No," he said, almost casually. "But you and your brother may assist me when I light the bonfire to end the ball."

That wasn't a hugely important task, at least in Rory's mind, but it was better than nothing. He didn't care much about this social event, as he'd indicated, but the truth was that he did care, just a little. He wanted to be included but he'd let on as much as he intended to.

"If you wish," he said, trying to sound disinterested at that point.

"I do," the duke said. But then he turned to Rory and looked the man in the face. "Until then, you have other things to do tonight, do you not?"

"Other things? Like what?"

"Like a little matter of vengeance?"

Rory's brow furrowed. "Vengeance?" he repeated. "What vengeance?"

The duke sighed heavily. "I have ears, Rory," he said. "You've made no secret of the fact that you wish to seek revenge for your mother against Exford and, truth be told, I am glad it is you. You are the wildest brother, the boldest, and the bravest. You are what I wish I could have been in my youth. You fly in the face of caution, do as you please, and have the strongest sense of family honor of all of us. Exford has been shaming your mother for more than thirty years and, in that time, you are the only Flynn brother who has had made the decision to avenge her. You are the only one courageous enough to do it. Of course

I know what your plans are. Why do you think I invited Exford this year?"

Rory tried not to look entirely shocked as he gazed at his grandfather, but when he realized the old man was on his side in all things, he couldn't help the smile that tugged at his lips. For the first time in Rory's life, he and his grandfather agreed on something.

Somehow, their relationship had unexpectedly changed.

"Then I have your permission?" he said, surprise in his voice.

The duke simply cocked an eyebrow. "I have opened the door," he said. "All you must do is step through it, if you are genuine about your intentions. Will you?"

Rory thought on his answer. It was clear that he was doing what the duke had always wanted to do but by virtue of his station, had refrained. With his daughter marrying Sean Flynn, the Savernake name had already taken a licking. It wouldn't do for the distinguished duke to seek revenge against the man Amy had jilted. In a delicate situation, the duke had taken the high road.

But that didn't mean Rory had to.

And the old duke was glad.

Glad!

"I do not intend to merely step through it," Rory said. "I intend to charge through with all my might."

A smile licked at the duke's lips. "My brave Rory," he murmured. "I shall miss you when I am gone."

"Are you going somewhere?"

The duke nodded. "Somewhere," he said vaguely. "We shall discuss it later. But in the meantime… you know what they say."

"What do they say?"

"That revenge is a dish best served cold," he said quietly. "For Amy's sake, be cold, Rory."

Rory put his hand on the old man's arm and fixed him in the eyes. He'd never felt closer to the old man than he did at this moment, as if they finally had a connection.

Even if it was a connection over revenge.

"Like ice," he whispered.

CHAPTER SEVEN

"Emotions will be your death. Feel nothing and live."
Sin Commandments #7

R ORY KNEW HIS grandfather's townhome like the back of his hand.

Having spent a good deal of his later childhood here, he'd learned all of the pathways, doorways, corridors, secret passages and the like, so once he left the reception line – or, more correctly, was *allowed* to leave it – he immediately headed outside.

It was a balmy night with the gardens and grounds of the townhome lit with expensive gas lighting, fixtures with the Savernake crest on them, and it made for lovely pathways and seating areas for those who wished to venture out into the night to flirt or converse. He'd slipped out through the leather-scented library and onto a pathway that led out to the garden where it was mostly empty at this time of night because people were inside, mingling and waiting for the dancing to begin.

The scent of summer flowers filled the air like a heady wine as he made his way down the dim path. Rory wanted to single out Rose Halburton before he approached her for a dance and he didn't want to do his spying from inside the townhome. The entire south side of the structure had windows from floor to ceiling, designed to catch the sun for most of the day, and he could see every major room from the pathway.

He could also see his friends.

Along with Forbes, he could see a few of the DeWolfe brothers. There were so many of that great northern family that it wasn't unusual to see four or five at a time. They bred prolifically. He could also see Daulton DeWinter and Augustus Lara, two of the men he and Forbes had been talking about, very old families with roots deep in England's past and politics. The very men that evidently had some kind of underground fight club and the mere thought of it almost pulled Rory off of his hunt.

But not quite.

He'd get to them later.

Rory ended up on the path again with the main part of the garden straight ahead. It connected to the morning room, which wasn't usually part of a gala event, but the room was quite large and next to the library and it was being used for refreshments at the moment. He could see people inside, milling around, and thought he might have even caught a glimpse of the elusive Rose.

But something off to his right distracted him.

He could hear whispers. Ducking back into the carefully cultivated foliage, he could see a couple in the shadows. They seemed very happy to be together, holding one another as the man kissed the woman gently. At that point, they didn't have all of his attention because, from where he was standing, he could see the library and the morning room quite clearly. He was about to move positions when Rose and her willowy sister entered the morning room without their father's presence.

Rory didn't know where the earl was but he didn't care. He was on the hunt now with his prey defenseless. Rose was with her sister and he didn't exactly want an audience for what he needed to do. His only hope was if he could get the sister away from Rose so he could work his seductive magic on her.

Perhaps he needed to enlist the help of one of his friends to do that.

As he debated that possibility, he watched the young women as they met up with other young women, all of them chatting amiably from the looks of it. Now, instead of a sister to worry about, he had four more young women.

Rose was gaining a pack.

Not exactly pleased with the setback, Rory remained in the foliage and calculated his next move. But off to his right, that same loving couple was now beginning to argue. At least, the raised voices and body language suggested that. People were beginning to wander out into the moonlit garden, a breath of fresh air before the festivities began in earnest, but the couple in the shadows was becoming rather animated.

It was enough to cause Rory to look at the pair and as he did, a man came up the garden path, walked right past him, and interrupted the fighting couple. With the voices quieted down, Rory turned his attention back to the morning room and Lady Rose.

But that was only temporary.

The man who had interrupted the fighting couple abruptly threw a closed fist at the other man and the two of them went down. Shocked, Rory watched the fists fly and the legs thrash as the woman stood there and gasped. Rory's first thought was to stop the fight, but he watched the woman get kicked again, hard this time, and she stumbled back. Footmen inside the house began shouting for help and people began to swarm. The man who had thrown the first punch was now on top of his victim, his hands wrapped around the man's throat to choke him to death.

Perhaps the woman was next.

Rory had no idea why he pushed through the bushes and pulled the woman away from the fight. If two men wanted to beat each other's brains in, that was their affair, but the woman needed to be protected. In an uncharacteristic show of chivalry, he swept the woman away, through the shadowed foliage, away from the shouts that were now coming because his grandfather's men were rushing out to stop the fight. The duke had hired men on a night like this, especially with so many of the wealthy in attendance and Savernake didn't want to be blamed if anything went missing, so he always had men of protection watching out for his guests.

It was those men rushing out to stop the fight.

But Rory was halfway down the path, heading towards the front of the house. Off to his left, shrouded in the trees, was his grandfather's orangery. It was quiet and private, so he pulled the woman inside and shut the door. When she realized they were alone, she began to resist.

"Stop pulling on me," she demanded, trying to yank herself from his grip. "Unhand me at once."

Rory let go with one hand but not with the other. He had her by the wrist as she leaned towards the door of the orangery.

"Stop," he commanded quietly. "Do not go out there unless you wish to be part of a scandal that will see your family banished from the Stag Ball for generations to come. If that is what you wish, however, then by all means, go outside. I'll not stop you."

She had one hand on the door, now frozen in indecision. They could all hear the shouts as the fight was broken up, but there were more people coming out of the house to watch a completely shameful situation. She watched the people moving down the path towards the commotion, entertainment as far as they were concerned, and she took a deep breath to try and regain her composure.

The man was right.

"You… you pulled me away so I would not be caught up in it?" she finally asked.

"Yes," he said. "If two men are going to act like fools, then let them. But you should not be part of it."

She finally turned to look at him, her features partially illuminated from the distant light. "Then I should thank you," she said. "May I go now?"

He shook his head. "Wait a few moments longer," he said. "I am afraid someone may have seen you out there and they will recognize you as having been part of that mêlée. They may even think you started the fight. It is best if you stay out of sight for a little while."

"How long?"

"A half-hour or so," he said. Then he tilted his head curiously. "What happened?"

Her expression took on some uncertainty and she took another deep breath before disengaging her hand from his. "Foolishness, as you said," she said quietly, tugging at her gloves to remove them. "I've never even seen the man who started it."

"Did he say anything before he threw his fist?"

She shrugged in confusion. But then she nodded. "Something about his wife named Lucy," she said. Then her brow furrowed and as Rory watched, she sank down onto the stone bench behind her, one glove off and one glove on. "Good Christ, what have I gotten myself into? Lucy was *pregnant*?"

"Lucy the wife?"

She nodded, growing increasingly despondent. "The man said that his wife was pregnant and he could not be the father, so he accused Myles of…"

She suddenly trailed off, looking at Rory with some horror. He sat down on the bench opposite her. "Who is Myles?" he said. "Your lover?"

The woman looked as if she were about to burst into tears. In fact, after a moment, she did. "He has been promising me that we would be married," she sniffed. "All the while, he would not leave his wife. He would not even try to divorce her. He said it was too expensive."

"It is," Rory said. "He actually told you that he would divorce his wife?"

She nodded, opening the purse around her wrist and pulling forth a handkerchief. "I simply do not understand why men lie," she said, handkerchief to her nose. "No… that isn't exactly true. I think the question is why I believed him, not why he lied. Two years of being fed lies like a bird is fed breadcrumbs, little by little, leading me along a merry path and now… now, here we are. I suppose I simply never believed it until now."

"Believed what?"

She sniffled. "That his promises were as weak as his honor," she said. "That became abundantly clear tonight when he…"

She looked at Rory as if just realizing she were pouring out her entire heart to a perfect stranger. A stranger who had saved her, but a stranger nonetheless. She'd already said far more than she should have, but her emotions were running high at the moment.

She was coming to see just how big of a fool she'd really been when it came to Myles Forrester.

"Go on," Rory encouraged gently. "What happened tonight?"

The woman looked at him before smiling weakly and shaking her head. "You must think me quite ridiculous," she said. "We've not even been properly introduced."

"My name is Rory," he said without hesitation. "And you?"

She resisted for a moment but quickly gave up. She'd already told the man her damnable life story; what was left but putting her name to it?

"Edith Rhodes," she said. "I am known as Edie."

He cocked his head curiously. "Rhodes," he said, realizing he'd heard that name today when Forbes had been indulging in some gossip. "Of course. Your father is the… the…"

"Viscount Rossington."

"Of course he is," Rory said quickly, as if he'd known it all along. "I've heard the name but I am ashamed to admit we have never met. I feel as if I should have known you well before now."

For the first time that night, she smiled. "England is a big place."

"London is a small place."

She snorted. "Not so small," she said. "But the social circles are small."

He nodded. "That is quite true," he said, looking her over and remembering what Forbes had said about her. "Small and snobbish and gossipy."

Edie sighed with agreement. "Completely," she said. "What

is your family name?"

Now she had him cornered. If he'd heard about her, undoubtedly, she'd heard about him. She was a lovely woman; quite lovely, in fact, with dark hair and an angelic face. He was coming to feel a little regretful that his reputation had more than likely preceded him because he rather liked talking to her.

He'd never experienced that before.

"Flynn," he said quietly. "My grandfather is the Duke of Savernake."

As he feared, her eyes widened with surprise and she quickly stood up. "I am very sorry to have troubled you, Mr. Flynn," she said. "Please... you said that my family could be disinvited from future Stag Balls if it were known that I was involved with the brawl in the garden, but I pray you keep this to yourself and..."

Rory realized she wasn't stammering because of his reputation, but because of who he was. His family name. Therefore, he cut her off gently.

"I would not dream of telling anyone," he said, hoping to ease her. "I certainly cannot cast the first stone in the event of a scandal, so your secret is safe with me."

Edie visibly relaxed, but she was still on edge. "Everything I told you," she said with some hesitation. "I did not mean to. It simply came out."

"It sounds as if you have experienced some trouble with this Forrester man."

She nodded. "Trouble, indeed."

"Perhaps you need to speak with someone about it," Rory said. "Someone who will not judge you because he is in no position to judge."

Her gaze lingered on him for a moment. "You?"

"Me," he confirmed firmly. "Have you not heard about me?"

Her expression turned thoughtful. "I don't think so," she said. "But I remember hearing that Savernake had an Irish pirate for a relative."

"My father."

"I see," she said, her focus lingering on him as if appraising him. "Are you a pirate, too?"

He was. More than his father or brothers, Rory was a pirate and then some. His smuggling, however, was high-value merchandise – antiquities and rare jewels, mostly, things the *ton* adored but wouldn't let anyone know just how much they adored them. Even when these items were in their homes, they would make excuses... *Grandfather bought it on a trip...* or *this has been in my family for hundreds of years.* He'd smuggled ancient Greek frescos for an earl's dining room wall and artwork and stones from Baghdad for a duke's drawing room. The jewels he'd smuggled from Ceylon and Brazil were worn by the richest women in England.

Was he a pirate?

It was in his blood.

"I am many things," he said evasively, though it was the truth. "The point is that I have seen and done my share of questionable things. I do not judge people because I do not like to be judged, and if I promise not to repeat a word of our conversation, you can be assured that I will take it to my grave. Honestly, Miss Edith, you could not find a better Father Confessor. Now, what has this Forrester man done to you to upset you so?"

He was pointing to the bench that she'd been sitting on. Edie eyed the bench before lowering herself back onto it. But her gaze returned swiftly to Rory. She couldn't believe that she was actually considering answering his question, but there was a part of her that needed answers. She'd spent several years of her life pining for a man who had only lied to her and there was great confusion in that.

Great confusion in herself.

If she'd had any sense of self-worth, she would have kept her mouth shut.

But she didn't.

"I suppose he's done nothing that thousands of men haven't done before him," she said with a sigh. "Tell me something, Mr. Flynn – why do men lie to women so brazenly? Is it because they are fearful that the truth will not achieve the desired results? Or is it the mere fact that they feel powerful when manipulating a woman?"

Rory sat forward, elbows on his knees and his chin on his folded hands. "That is a question that has been asked for centuries," he said. "I do not think there is an easy answer."

"Have *you* lied to a woman?"

He snorted softly, averting his gaze. "I would be lying if I said I had not."

"Why did you do it?"

He shrugged, feeling the slightest bit uncomfortable. "Who knows?" he said. "Perhaps it seemed like a good idea at the time."

"Were you trying to control them?"

"Was Forrester trying to control you?"

She nodded, looking rather sickened. "He was," she said. Then she sighed heavily. "Of course, he was. He was a friend of my father's, you see. I say 'was' because their friendship has since ended because of me."

"How did he try to control you? What did he want you to do?"

"Become his mistress," she said, both ashamed and outraged. "As if I am not worthy enough to be someone's wife. I have never been married, you see, and he wants me to be his mistress. If he cannot marry me, then he wants to keep me tucked away in the wilds of the north so that he may come to me at his convenience. That is all I will ever be to him – a convenience."

Rory was studying her. "But there is some feeling involved."

She hung her head. "I thought there was," she said. "To be perfectly honest, when I came to the Stag Ball, I thought I loved him. I thought I'd loved him since I'd met him, but now… it is so strange. Whatever I felt for him has vanished. His empty promises have drained it all away."

"That is because it was not real love," Rory said quietly.

"Are you certain?"

He nodded. "We have all had those moments with people we thought we loved but, in the end, what we thought was love vanished quite easily," he said. "You did not really love him, Miss Edith. You loved the idea of loving him and nothing more. It sounds as if he never did anything to earn your love."

She looked at him as if startled by the entire analysis. "That is the most appropriate thing I have ever heard," she said. "You are absolutely right – he never earned my love. He told me that I needed to prove *my* love for him, but he never did anything to prove his love for me. Not ever."

"Then you have your answer," Rory said.

It was true. She did. Edie looked at him as that realization settled but the truth was that she wasn't all that surprised.

Disappointed, but not surprised.

It took a stranger to help her figure that out.

"Good heavens," she muttered. "I suppose I always knew that. I suppose I wanted it to be true so badly that I tried to wish it so."

"There is no crime in that."

"I suppose," she said with some sadness. "I was young when I met him and simply believed what he told me."

"But now you are older and wiser."

"Older, anyway. I am not sure about wiser."

He smiled in the darkness. "But you have been counseled by me and that *will* make you wiser," he said. "Tell me, Miss Edith – what do you do when you are not in London, spending time at an unbearably formal ball?"

He was diverting the subject a little, which was a welcome relief. Edie could only talk about her failure so much.

"Ah, that is the great mystery," she said, smiling weakly. "What does a young woman do with all of her time when she has no home or husband to tend to?"

"Surely you must do great and creative things."

She laughed softly. "Perhaps only in my own mind," she said. "But surely you don't wish to speak about such things. You have an entire ball going on around you, yet you sit here with me in the orangery."

He shrugged. "I can think of worse things to do."

"Is this how you planned to spend your evening?"

It wasn't. He was reminded of Rose Halburton but, somehow, the lure of sad Edith Rhodes was greater than his lifelong sense of revenge at the moment. She was far and away more beautiful than Rose and perhaps that's why she had his attention, but there was something more to it. A little zing of excitement bolted through him whenever she laughed or smiled. That had his attention more than anything because it had never happened before.

It was quite intriguing.

"My evening was planned long before tonight," he said, which was true. It had been. "I would be honored with a dance if you are so inclined, however."

Edie's focus moved to the house beyond the orangery. "I am certain my mother is frantically searching for me," she said. "I'm sure word of the fight has spread through the ball by now and she is wondering where I am."

Rory nodded with some irony. "Nothing is more welcome than the fire of scandalous gossip," he said. "I can smell the smoke from here."

She grinned. "As can I," she said. "But I suspect I cannot stay here too much longer or else you and I might be caught up in a scandal of our own."

That was quite possibly true. Rory stood up and moved to the orangery doors, trying to get a look down the path at the garden. All he could see were people gathered around, undoubtedly watching the duke's men deal with the combatants.

Too many people made for too many witnesses.

He turned away.

"I would be happy to escort you inside while everyone's focus seems to be elsewhere," he said. "Shall we?"

Edie stood up. "Do you think we can leave now?"

He nodded. "I do," he said, reaching out to grasp her hand in a protective gesture. "Come with me."

She did.

Rory took Edie out of the orangery, through the darkened foliage, and into his grandfather's library. Because it was early in the evening, only a few men were gathered there and they were over by the hearth, undoubtedly partaking of the duke's fine tobacco that he had so generously provided for them. Rory and Edie slipped by, through the connecting door into the dining room, which was still being prepared at this point.

Rory came to a halt.

He stuck his head through the doorway leading into the main corridor to see who was about. The main entrance was off to his left, next to the library entrance, and the main staircase was in the entry. But a servants' staircase was directly in front of him, through a door, so he tugged on Edie's hand and they rushed across the hall and into the servants' corridor.

On the floor above were two massive drawing rooms with a door that connected them. The door, however, was collapsible and could be rolled back to make one giant ballroom. This was where the actual ball of the Stag Ball was taking place and once Rory took Edie up the stairs, she could simply slip into the ballroom as if she'd always been there. But before he let her go, Rory whispered to her.

"They are preparing to dance," he murmured, his eyes flicking over the crowd in the next room. "If you would like to dance with me, then you had better find your mother so that we may be properly introduced. It would not do for me to simply grab you and drag you to the dance floor."

She looked at him. "Who will introduce us?"

Rory gave her a rather sly look. "That is for me to know and you to find out," he said. "Go now, and find your mother. Do not stray from her. I will be along shortly. And try to be somewhere that I may easily find you."

"Where?"

"Near the windows."

It seemed as good a location as any, but Edie seemed hesitant. Rory could see that and he lifted his eyebrows at her. "You *do* wish to dance with me, don't you?"

Edie started to nod, but then she merely chuckled with some irony. "I did not think I would dance at all tonight," she said. "I thought I would be with… it does not matter now. What do you suppose has become of Myles?"

"Mr. Forrester?"

"Yes."

"I suspect he has either been escorted out or carried out, depending on how badly he was beaten." Rory watched her face for a moment before continuing. "Miss Edith, if you do not wish to dance at all, I would understand. Already, you have had a rather harrowing evening. Perhaps you simply wish to sit somewhere and rest."

She looked at him, studying his face, thinking that the man was incredibly handsome. But she couldn't think about him more than that. In fact, she wasn't entirely sure it was a good idea to dance with him because she'd only just discarded the only man she'd ever loved in a romantic sense or, perhaps more accurately, she'd only just freed herself.

But she knew she wasn't completely free. She and Myles had a history that couldn't be replaced. Somehow, she knew that Rory Flynn might make her forget all about Myles and then she'd be back where she started, only with another man. She simply didn't have the strength to fight off Rory's charm should he decide to overwhelm her with it.

"If I do, it will be alone," she said softly. "Mr. Flynn, you have been kind and chivalrous in a circumstance where you did not have to be. You could have just as easily left me to my own stupidity. But you did not and, for that, I am forever grateful. But I do believe it would be better if we were to part ways now."

He let go of her hand, which he had been holding the entire time. "I see," he said. "I've been quite clumsy, haven't I? I do apologize."

She shook her head. "Not at all," she said. "As I said, you've been kind and charming, but I think it would be best if we part friends."

"If I've not done something wrong, then why must we?"

"Because I don't think I want to be around any charming man right now and you, Mr. Flynn, have the capacity to disarm and enchant," she said, watching him grin. "You've given me so much to think about regarding Myles and I cannot thank you enough. But if I am to think clearly at all, it must be alone."

"For how long?"

"Beg pardon?"

"For how long?" he repeated, more firmly. "An hour? An evening? A day? How long?"

"I don't know," she said. "Does it matter?"

He scratched his ear, a nervous gesture. "Perhaps not," he said. "But if I want to call upon you to see how you are faring, how long must I wait?"

Her brow furrowed. "Why on earth would you want to call upon me again?"

"I told you. To see how you are."

"I am fine."

"Clearly not if you must go off and become a hermit, away from all men."

She started to giggle. "It will not be forever."

"Good," he said. "Will you be able to entertain male friends by tomorrow? You see, there is always a garden party after the Stag Ball at my father's estate in London near Teddington. I should like to invite you and your family to attend."

"Your *father's* home?"

He nodded. "My father does not attend the Stag Ball, but he allows my grandfather to use the property for his garden party," he said. "My grandfather only invites close friends and their families. I would like to invite you."

She didn't give him any indication that she would accept the invitation. "Why does your father not attend the ball?" she asked. "And where is your mother? Is she here?"

Rory shook his head. "She does not attend, either."

"Why not?"

He peered at her strangely. "Miss Edith, if you know of my family and have heard the rumors, you need not pretend to be ignorant of it all," he said. "I thought we were more honest with each other than that."

She genuinely had no idea what he meant. "I know nothing of your family," she said. "Should I?"

His eyebrows lifted. "You mean that you are the only person in London who does not know of the Sinning Flynns?"

She looked at him with surprise. "The Sinning Flynns?" she said. Then she chuckled. "Is *that* who you are?"

"Ah," he said with something that sounded like satisfaction. "You see? You have heard of us."

"I think so," she said. "We live a life at Everton in South Yorkshire that is far removed from London, so my trips here are not terribly frequent. I've heard of the Sinning Flynns, but I do not recall if I was told they are related to Savernake."

"We are," he said. "My father was an Irish pirate who was granted an earldom from a grateful king. My father kept many a supply line open in the West Indies and the English Channel and he was amply rewarded by King George. He became the Earl of Sinbrook and married my mother, who was betrothed to another man. Our sinning days started before I was even born."

Edie was listening with a surprising amount of interest. "I suspect there is a good deal more to your story," she said. "Much more than you can tell me in one night."

Rory grinned. "I can tell you tomorrow at the garden party."

"You will have to speak with my mother."

"Go and find her. I will be along shortly."

With that, the conversation seemed to come to an end, but it wasn't awkward. In truth, there was some anticipation in the air, at least as far as Rory was concerned. He hadn't felt like that in a very long time, as misplaced and unexpected as it was. Edie was easy to talk to and they seemed to have an excellent rapport, which was quite unusual for him. He wasn't easy to talk to, nor did he ever have a good rapport, with anyone. He wasn't quite sure what made Edie special, but something did.

Something, indeed.

CHAPTER EIGHT

"Thou shalt not shun a beautiful lady... or leave her to someone else for the picking..."
Sin Commandment #8

"Ⓦ ＨＡＴ DID HE say his name was?"

Edie had never seen her mother look quite so shocked. Near the windows of the grand ballroom, on the side of the house that overlooked the infamous garden, she had just told her mother a lie. Well, not all of it was a lie. She had just told her mother that although she had failed to find her friends, she'd met a very polite young man who had helped her when she'd become lost. The only part that was truthful was the part about meeting a polite young man.

It was the man's name that had her mother up in arms.

"Rory Flynn," Edie repeated patiently. "He is the grandson of the Duke of Savernake. You wanted me to meet a young man and I have, Mother. He's utterly wonderful."

Henrietta stared at her daughter. "Rory Flynn," she said. "Good heavens, Child... a Flynn?"

"He's the duke's grandson," Edie said with a hint of sarcasm. "The man is going to be at his grandfather's event. Why is that so shocking?"

Henrietta took a deep breath. "It is not shocking in and of itself," she said. Then, she rolled her eyes in frustration. "When I brought you here to meet a young man, that directive did not include a Sinning Flynn."

"Why does everyone call them the Sinning Flynns?" Edie asked, sounding as if the entire thing were ridiculous. "I've heard that name mentioned, but why do people say that?"

Henrietta looked around to make sure they weren't being heard. She spied Matilda in a group of other young people, laughing and chatting, before continuing. Thank God they weren't present to hear what she had to say.

"Because they are nothing but Irish scum," she muttered. "Sean Flynn stole Savernake's daughter away from Lord Exford many years ago and married her. She had four children, all boys, and all just as dark and reckless as their father. They are notorious, Edie, and Rory most of all. The man is a legend in London and Cornwall and he's not even seen his thirtieth year."

Edie was listening with great interest. "Notorious?" she repeated, aghast. "How would you know that?"

Henrietta's eyes narrowed. "Don't be stupid," she hissed. "I have been around the *ton* enough to know the gossip. And… and years ago, I knew Amy Wellesbourne. She was such a sweet girl and so very pretty. If you must know, she was far too good for John Halburton, but he was a smart match. She would have had everything had she married him. Instead, she fell for that… that *pirate*."

Edie didn't much care about Sean Flynn or even Amy Wellesbourne. But she did care about Rory Flynn.

"But what about Rory?" she said. "You said he is a legend in

London. I've never even heard of him."

"Good," Henrietta said firmly. "But so you know why you must stay away from him, I will tell you – they say that Rory Flynn is a smuggler and not just any smuggler. No! The man smuggles rare antiquities and jewels for those who can pay him. He also owns gambling dens in London, one he won from the owner, and those who know about it say the place is called Gomorrah. A man can bet on anything at all at Gomorrah."

Edie was enthralled. She wasn't going to deny it. "Gomorrah?" she said. "Like the wicked city in the bible?"

"That is why they call the place Gomorrah!"

Edie had to fight off a smile. She thought it all sounded incredibly scandalous and, truthfully, incredibly exciting, but if her mother knew she was thinking such things, the woman would lock her up in a closet and throw away the key. Therefore, she kept her enthusiasm to herself.

For the moment.

"He seemed quite nice to me," she said. "He didn't seem wicked at all."

"That is how they seduce you," Henrietta said. "Silken tongues breed silken words until a woman is hypnotized by them. Don't be hypnotized, Edie. The man is trouble and he is far and away an unsuitable match. I did not spend the last two years hiding you from Polite Society for you to ruin your life again and possibly Tilly's as well. If Myles Forrester was bad, Rory Flynn is worse. You don't seem to have the best judgment when it comes to men, Edie."

Edie wasn't happy to hear those words. They were insulting even if they were true. But she'd hoped her mother would have been impressed by her informal acquaintance with Rory Flynn, but that wasn't to be. If anything, she was downright averse to the entire suggestion that a duke's grandson should be a suitable prospect.

"Who *is* suitable, Mother?" she asked, her gaze moving over the ballroom with its finely dressed women and dashing men. "You've been quite free to tell me who is not suitable, but who is? Keeping in mind that I am damaged goods, who is to your taste, Mother?"

Henrietta looked at her sharply. "You'll not take that tone with me," she said in a low voice. "Do as I say, Edie, and you shall have a happy and fulfilling life. Follow your childish and irresponsible instincts and you shall only know ruin. Which choice will it be?"

Edie was growing weary of her mother's constant demands. She was so rigid that it made Edie feel as if she were choking somehow, unable to breathe, unable to simply live her life the way she wanted to live it… and with whom.

It wasn't fair.

She felt as if she should have a say in her own happiness.

"He's a duke's grandson," she finally said. "And from what you've said, he's wildly rich. What more could you ask for in a husband for your eldest daughter?"

Henrietta sighed heavily. "I will not discuss this with you."

"He has invited us to the garden party the duke is giving tomorrow," she said, glancing around the ballroom in the hope of locating the elusive Flynn son. "His father has a townhome near Teddington and we have all been invited."

Henrietta looked at her as if she'd just announced her decision to murder the pope. "He *what*?" she hissed. "He invited you – *us* – to Sean Flynn's home?"

By the time Edie looked at her mother, the woman was fanning herself furiously because she'd grown lightheaded at the mere suggestion of attending an event at the home of the notorious pirate. Forcing herself to show some concern, Edie reached out to grasp her mother's arm.

"Let us find you a chair so you do not fall down and embarrass us all," she said. "Breathe, Mother. You needn't be so dramatic."

Henrietta wouldn't move in spite of her daughter trying to force her towards the nearest chair. "If it is ever known that one of the Sinning Flynns has invited us to a social event, it will be our ruin," she said. "You must never tell anyone that, Edie. Not even your silly friends."

Edie couldn't help but feel disappointment. "Then we will not go?"

"Most assuredly not," Henrietta said with more force than she should have. "In fact, I… good heavens. What is *he* doing here?"

She was looking off into the ballroom. Edie had no idea what her mother meant until she turned to see what had the woman so shocked. Coming in through one of the doors to the ballroom was none other than Myles himself, holding a handkerchief up to a swelling lip.

Normally, she would have been thrilled to see him and already plotting to have a dance or two with the man. Or slipping away with him. That kind of behavior had been infused into her heart and soul since she'd met the man. But as she looked at him, all she could manage to feel was enormous disappointment. The conversation in the garden rolled around in her head, emphasizing just how foolish she'd been.

She was finished making the biggest mistake of her young life.

Quickly, she turned away.

"Let us go into another room," she said. "Surely there are refreshments, somewhere."

In her grip, Henrietta seemed to come to life. All around them were the sights and smells of an opulent ball – the smell of the candles as they burned heavily in the stale air, the smell of perfume and powder, even the smell of the walls that had been freshly painted for the occasion. Lights were blazing, jewels were glistening, and women were trying their best to show off their expensive and custom gowns.

But Henrietta didn't seem to notice any of that at the moment.

She grabbed Edie by the hand.

"Come," she hissed, moving swiftly through the crowd as she dragged her daughter. When she came to Matilda in a group of young adults, she nearly broke Matilda's wrist when she grabbed her. "Come, Tilly. Come now, quickly."

Matilda was yanked away, back through the ballroom, down the stairs, and out the front of the townhome.

Across the road in the square, the bonfire was still in the process of being prepared. Henrietta approached one of the footmen and demanded their carriage be brought around. As the footman went running, Edie finally managed to break her mother's grip.

"What on earth are you doing?" she said. "Why did you order the carriage?"

Henrietta was rattled. She focused on her eldest daughter with a wild look in her eyes.

"Because we are leaving," she said, almost in tears. "First, you make an acquaintance with one of the Flynn brothers, enough so that he invites you to a garden party on the morrow. Then, Myles Forrester coincidentally makes an appearance. I am not stupid, Edith. Not a decent man in sight, but you are gathering rogues and rakes of the worst kind and I will not stand for it. I do not know what it is about you, but you attract the undesirables. I'll not have it tonight and I'll not have you ruining Tilly's reputation before she even has a chance to earn one. Even if you are a lost cause, she is not. We are *leaving!*"

Matilda, realizing that they were departing, broke down in tears. Her accusing eyes turned to Edie, who was greatly ashamed by her mother's accusations. She couldn't even look her sister in the eyes.

Mostly because Henrietta was right.

She did attract the worst kind.

Edie stood off to the side until the carriage was brought around, hurt and ashamed. Perhaps leaving was best. She didn't want to see Myles and even if Rory Flynn had a horrible reputation, she still wasn't worthy of him. Her mother had made that clear. Duke's grandson or not, smuggler or saint, she wasn't worthy of any of them.

It was time to go home.

For Edie Rhodes, the Stag Ball had come to an end.

CHAPTER NINE

"Ambition is never wasted on a ruthless man."
Sin Commandment #9

H E NEVER SAW her again.

Rory spent the rest of the evening looking for Edie and the more he looked, the more confused he became. Women just didn't vanish into thin air, but Edie had apparently done just that.

She'd gone off to find her mother and that was the last time he saw her, so there was some concern with that. He searched the entire bottom floor of the townhome looking for her and when he reached the ballroom, dancing had already commenced. He caught sight of his brother and had a few words with him because in his search for Edie, he'd heard something about a lady his brother had been seen dancing with. A lady whose family reputation seemed to be tarnished. After teasing his brother about it, which Aidan wasn't so keen on, he continued on in his quest.

But there was no sign of her.

He might have thought her abducted by the man he saw her

with earlier in the evening, but Forrester was dancing. He saw him, bloodied lip and all, dancing with a young woman who seemed quite enamored with him. He wondered why the duke's men had allowed him to stay, but he couldn't give it much thought beyond that.

He was on the hunt.

Rose Halburton caught his attention as he passed from one side of the ballroom to the other. She was standing with her sister and father, watching the dancing, perhaps hoping that someone would ask her to dance. Rory knew it should be him; that's what he'd planned. For years and years, he'd planned this moment with Exford's daughter, and now that the timing was perfect, he simply couldn't bring himself to do it.

What in the hell is the matter with me?

Everything had fallen into place. Exford's daughter was available, with no male attention, and it would have been so easy for him to slide in and charm her. Perhaps have a dance or two before stealing her away from her father, out into the orangery, where he would proceed to seduce her. While the earl would be frantically looking for her, he would be compromising her. *That was the plan, damn it all!* A kiss, a touch, and she would be his but he had to make that move. Years of humiliation to his mother and those degrading years at Oxford demanded it.

Yet… he was distracted.

Edie.

As he watched, one of the duke's men walked up to Exford and introduced a tall, pale, and homely young man to Rose. She smiled. A dance was offered.

And Rory didn't particularly care.

Was it possible his sense of vengeance could be so easily

forgotten?

Evidently so because he turned away from the ballroom and continued his search for Edie. He'd known the woman all of an hour and, already, he was attracted to her as he'd never been attracted to a woman in his life. She was exquisite and she smelled of blossoms, but there were other women who were exquisite and smelled of flowers. He simply couldn't figure out what made Edie so different.

Perhaps there was a kindred spirit there.

That brought him pause.

He remembered what Forbes had told him, how rumors suggested that Edie had been seen in a tavern's stable with an older man, and Rory would have thought that only to be vicious gossip except for the fact that he saw her in the arms of the man who evidently *was* her love. Or at least, had been. A married man who had promised to leave his wife for her but who had lied about it.

Edie had known scandal and betrayal.

She wasn't alone in that shame.

That's where Rory felt that she was a kindred spirit. So many women at the ball this evening had impeccable reputations, something their families worked hard for. Rory wasn't worthy of any of them and he truly didn't care. But Edie…

She was different.

If what he'd heard was true, then he'd found a woman who was as flawed as he was.

Rory ended up outside in the front of the townhome, with the bonfire being set up in the square across the street and the night above still and cold. He asked one of the footmen if he'd seen a pretty woman in a lavender gown and the footman answered that he had. He told Rory that the lady had left not an hour before but he could tell him no more than that.

It was time to find his grandfather.

After meeting Edie, he'd planned to have his grandfather introduce him to her formally since he wanted to dance with her, but now that she was gone, he wanted to pick the old duke's brain. Savernake knew everyone who was anyone and surely the man would know who Viscount Rossington was. He wanted to find out where the man lived.

Where Rossington was, Edie more than likely would be.

Unfortunately, it was hours before he was able to speak with his grandfather. For such a frail, old man, he'd held up admirably for the ball. It wasn't until after the midnight buffet had been spread out that Rory was able to speak with the man as he wearily retired to his bedroom.

When he did, Rory was waiting for him.

"Why aren't you feasting with the rest of them?" the duke asked as he shuffled into his room.

Rory had been sitting in a chair in the duke's big chamber, half-asleep at the late hour.

"Because I wanted to speak with you," he said. "This might be my only opportunity."

The duke's valet had been following him but when the old man heard Rory's statement, he paused and looked at his grandson with some trepidation. In spite of the fact that he'd all but told Rory bluntly that he supported any act of vengeance against Exford, he was still leery to hear about it. He shooed his valet out of the room and had the man close the door. Only then did he dare to speak.

"Very well," he said. "You may speak. What have you done?"

Rory scratched his head. "Nothing," he said. "If you are

referring to Exford, I did… nothing."

"Why not?"

Rory shrugged. "Tonight was not the night," he said, somewhat lying about it because he was feeling such confusion. "Too many people, I suppose. And perhaps… perhaps it's best not to shame the man in your home. That would reflect badly upon you and the more I think about it, the more I don't want to do that to you. Let my vengeance on Exford happen somewhere else, away from you. I'd not thought much of you and how my actions affect you and, for that, I apologize. I'm a selfish man, Doody."

The duke looked at him in surprise at the mention of a very old nickname, the very name Rory would use to taunt Aidan with. Then, he started to chuckle.

"Do my ears deceive me?" he said. "Is it possible that Rory the Rogue is actually growing up? Maturing? Because that is something a mature man would say, my boy."

Rory was uncomfortable with the suggestion that he had changed. "Rory the Rogue is alive and well," he said. "I may go down, but I do not want to drag you with me. Yet, have no doubt that I will exact vengeance against Exford. But not here. It is not the right place nor the right time."

The duke nodded his head as if accepting that. "If that is the way you feel," he said. "You've waited a very long time only to back away from your victory."

"I've not backed away. I've simply decided tonight was not the night."

"Is that what you've come to tell me?"

Rory nodded. "That," he said. "And I want to ask you something."

"What is it?"

"Do you know Viscount Rossington?"

The duke sighed wearily as he made his way over to the bed. "Frederick Rhodes," he said. "I know him. Why?"

"Where does he live?"

The duke sat down heavily. "Over in Belgravia," he said. "As I recall, it's called Rossington House. The largest home on Belgravia Square, if I recall correctly."

"*What* do you know about him?" Rory asked carefully. "About his family?"

The duke yawned. "They have property near Doncaster, as I recall," he said. "The viscount's family is rich in cattle. They're quite wealthy."

"And he has children?"

"Daughters, I believe," the duke said. Then he eyed his grandson strangely. "Why so many questions? What's on your mind?"

Rory shrugged. "I met the eldest daughter this evening," he said. "Quite by accident, really, but I was going to have you properly introduce us when she suddenly disappeared."

"What do you mean?"

"Precisely that," Rory said. "She went to find her mother and I never saw her again after that. The footmen told me that she had left with her family. Before the dancing even started, they went home."

The duke shrugged. "Perhaps she fell ill," he said. "Why is it of such import to you?"

Rory didn't want to tell him why. If he did, the duke might figure out why he hadn't gone after Exford's daughter.

He'd been distracted by another woman.

God, that made him sound so shallow.

"Because I saved her from a rather unsavory situation and I

feel some responsibility for her," he finally ventured. "Perhaps I should go to Belgravia tonight to make sure she is well."

The duke put up a hand. "Rory, if you want to go to Belgravia to pluck the viscount's daughter from her bed, that is your business," he said. "But do not lie about it. I still do not know what you've come to tell me other than you decided not to take your revenge on Exford tonight and there's a viscount's daughter you wish to ravage."

Rory shook his head. "It's not like that," he said. "I do not wish to ravage her."

"Then what?"

Rory was closer to a personal confession than he'd ever been in his life, but his interaction with the duke this night had made him feel closer to the man than he ever had. It would be so easy to confess everything to a man he'd always adored.

Still...

"I always wished I'd had the relationship with you that Aidan has," he muttered in an unguarded moment. "Growing up, I always envied Aidan. He is your favorite."

The duke gazed at him in the dim chamber light. "He is the only one out of all of your brothers, including you, who took the time to form a relationship with me," he said, his tone softer. "Carmack and Kellen were always off forging their own way and you... you simply didn't need me. You didn't need anyone."

"I don't think that's true," Rory said quietly. "I didn't think anyone cared, so I pretended that I did not need anyone. A self-fulfilling prophesy, I'm afraid."

The duke nodded his head slowly. "You were the stubborn one," he said. "A sullen and determined child."

"And lonely."

The duke stared at him a moment before smiling. "That is the first time I've ever heard you give a hint of human emotion," he said. "I am seeing more of that mature man."

Rory smirked. "Then here is much more from that mature man," he said. "I have asked you about Rossington's daughter because I am attracted to her. Not in the usual way. I have no desire to sneak into her bedchamber while her parents sleep in the next room. She… she's different somehow. She left just as I was coming to know her."

The duke sensed something quite different from his grandson and that caused him to stand up and move in Rory's direction.

"Is she the reason you failed to move forward with your plans for Exford?" he asked.

Rory couldn't look him in the eyes but, after a moment, he sighed heavily and hung his head. "There is no use lying," he said. "I don't know what happened. All I know is that I met a woman who made me feel as I've never felt in my life and just when I was coming to know her, she left. I had a perfect opportunity with Rose Halburton and I did not take it because I was too preoccupied with Edie."

"Edie?"

"Rossington's daughter."

The old duke looked down upon Amy's third-born son. In today's society, the third-born sons were usually meant for the clergy, but that had never been an option for Rory. He'd been born with fire in him and, until today, the duke wondered if that was all Rory would ever be – full of fire and recklessness. But at this moment, he saw something from Rory he never thought he would.

Feeling.

"You came to me today as a boy," he said, putting a hand on Rory's shoulder. "But for the first time in my eyes, you have actually become a man. I cannot tell you how pleased I am, Rory. I am glad I lived to see it."

Rory was torn between embarrassment and warmth. His grandfather had never said such things to him before so it was difficult to know how to react.

"I suppose we must all grow up sometime, although I'm not exactly sure I've changed all that much," he said. "We were only speaking of a woman, after all."

"A special woman, evidently," the duke said. Then he dropped his hand from Rory's shoulder and went to the table against the wall, the one he'd had imported all the way from Italy with its leather-bound top and legs of gold leaf. There was a crystal decanter on top of the table, filled with dark red liquid, and he poured a measure into a small, crystal glass. "Rory, there is something you should know."

"What is it?"

The duke looked at him. "I'm dying," he said quietly. "I have a cancer that is slowly killing me. It has been going on for some time, but now I am at the end. My physician feels that in a week or two, I will be bed bound. Death will not be far behind. I wasn't going to tell you, but given our exchange tonight, I am comfortable to confide such things in you."

Rory was trying to keep the expression of horror off his face. "But… but that's not possible," he said. Even as he said it, he was looking at a man who was far from the robust grandfather he had known all his life. His grandfather had even alluded to his health earlier in the evening, so his confession shouldn't have come as a surprise. "Surely it cannot be. Surely there is…"

The duke put up a hand to silence him. "Denial will not

make it so," he said. "The diagnosis has been confirmed. But I want to tell you personally a few things, now that we have this time together. As you know, your Uncle Martin will inherit the title and properties, although I do have an unentailed property that I have offered to Aidan."

Rory's eyebrows lifted. "Aidan?"

"If he marries before I die."

Rory's mouth popped open in surprise. "And he agreed?"

The duke fought off a grin. "I am not certain if he actually agreed," he said. "But let us not speak of Aidan right now. I want to speak of you. Are you serious about this Rhodes woman?"

Rory still wasn't over the fact that not only was his grandfather dying, the man was offering property to his youngest brother. "I don't know," he said. "All I know is that one conversation has made me feel as I've never felt in my life. One simple conversation with a woman who knew my family name and she didn't run away. It was *one* conversation, Grandfather, but a conversation that I could have quite happily engaged in forever."

The duke sipped the brandy in the little glass before speaking. "When I met your grandmother, she made me feel like that," he said. "How odd that you and I should have such similarities, Rory. It seems to me that you may be serious about her, indeed."

"Possibly."

"What of Exford's daughter?"

Rory sighed. "Somehow, it seems oddly unimportant," he said. "It makes no sense because I have been planning this for years. How can I forget about something so important?"

"Simple," the duke said. "It involves another woman. You

cannot think of another woman when your focus, and possibly your heart, lies elsewhere. Vengeance pales by comparison to love."

Rory eyed him. "I *don't* love her."

"Not now," the duke said. "But she has your attention enough that she has made you forget your vengeance. Do not diminish the significance of that."

"Aye," Rory sighed softly. "She has my attention."

"Do you want my advice? You have never wanted it before."

"I may not now, but what is it?"

The duke laughed softly. That reply sounded much more like the Rory he knew. "If she makes you feel like the sun is rising on a new day, then find her," he said. "If she makes you feel as if you cannot breathe or you cannot remember your own name when you look into her eyes, then find her. Even if you don't know how, exactly, you feel about her, find out. Life is too short not to take an opportunity when it comes. I wish I had more time for more opportunities. For me, Rory... take this opportunity."

Rory looked at him seriously. "But what if her father will not receive me?" he asked, genuinely fearful. "That has never mattered to me until this very moment. What do I do?"

The duke set his glass down and turned to him. "I have two weeks or less before this poison inside of me weakens me too much," he said. "Find your lady. If she is all you imagine her to be, you will tell me and I will send word to her father. I cannot offer you lands or properties. I cannot even offer you money. There is nothing I have that you do not already have more of. But I can offer you my support. Let me do this for you, Rory. If it is what you truly want."

Rory stood up, feeling closer to his grandfather than he ever had. It was joy he'd never known. "It is," he said. "I am sure it is. And I am sorry that we were never closer, Grandfather."

"We are now. Go and find her."

Rory didn't have to be told twice.

CHAPTER TEN

"Women are always, invariably, hiding something."
Sin Commandment #10

"MAMA SAYS WE are leaving for home tomorrow," Matilda said sadly. "Why, Edie? Why are we leaving?"

Edie knew why but it would not have made sense to Matilda if she told her the truth. She'd had all night to think about it and she'd come to the conclusion that perhaps her mother was right. Matilda was young and untouched by scandal and all Edie seemed to be doing was trying to ruin her sister's chances by bleeding her questionable reputation onto her. Guilt by association, as it were.

Edie simply couldn't give her a straight answer.

"Perhaps she misses home," she finally said. "We did enjoy the Stag Ball for the short time we were there, didn't we?"

Matilda nodded, though she was becoming tearful. "I don't want to leave," she said. "We have been planning for this all year. I don't understand why we must leave."

They were sitting in the mews alleyway of Rossington House, back behind the house where the conveyances and horses were kept. There was peace here, away from their parents. Around them, the usual collection of dogs and cats roamed about and that included Matilda's little dog. Edie put her arm around Matilda's shoulders to comfort the confused and sad young woman, while keeping an eye on the brown and white dog.

"Did you ask Mama why?" Edie asked quietly.

Matilda nodded, sniffling. "She told me that it was none of my affair," she said. "Did I do something wrong, Edie?"

Edie shook her head. "No," she sighed. "I did."

"What did you do?"

"I spoke to the wrong man."

"What man?"

Edie wasn't sure what, or how, to tell her. Matilda was growing up, that was true, but she didn't know about her older sister's escapes with Myles Forrester. Edie was still pure and virtuous in Matilda's eyes and Edie wanted to keep it that way.

"A man with a bad reputation," she said. "I didn't know it at the time, however, so I will tell you that he was very kind to me. Kinder than… well, it does not matter, but suffice it to say that he was extremely kind and he invited us to a garden party, but when I told Mama, she thought the man's reputation was a questionable one and we could not accept. And that is why we left the ball last night. Mama was afraid that the man would lure us into his seedy world with his invitation. She did it to protect us."

Matilda actually understood that explanation and it didn't put Edie too much in a bad light. "Oh," Matilda said, her tears fading. "Why didn't she tell us?"

Edie gave her a squeeze. "Because you were upset enough," she said. "Mama was upset, too. Did you not notice? She didn't want you to beg her to remain because it was a difficult decision for her to make. No one runs from the Stag Ball."

Matilda thought on the situation with surprising clarity for a girl on the cusp of womanhood. "The man," she said. "What was his name?"

"The one who invited us to the garden party?"

"Yes."

"Rory Flynn," Edie said, thinking on the man with the dark hair and flashing eyes. "The Honorable Rory Flynn. His father is the Earl of Sinbrook."

"An earl's son?" Matilda said with some excitement in her voice. "Why would Mama not want us to attend his party?"

"Because the Earl of Sinbrook is Irish," Edie said. "He is not of the best reputation, nor is his son, though I did not realize the extent of it. He seemed so… perfect."

Matilda was watching her face. "You like him."

It wasn't a question. Edie didn't have to think very much about it. "I do," she said. "He didn't speak to me like Mama and Papa do, as if I were a wayward child, or even like Myles, who speaks to me as if I only have half a brain in my head. He spoke to me as if I were a responsible and respectable woman. As if my thoughts and actions mattered."

Matilda, though she was young, could still understand that it had meant something to her sister. But she also recognized a name that was taboo in her house – *Myles*.

"You still speak of Myles?" she said. "Mama shushes you when you do."

Edie sighed faintly and looked away, back to the dog that was now finding a place in the sun to lie down. "I will speak of him no more," she said. "Remember something, Tilly – remember that men will often say things to trick a woman into doing something she does not want to do. You've not had experience with men yet, but when you do… be cautious. They only mean to bring you to ruin."

"Not always."

It wasn't Matilda who replied. Startled, Edie turned to see the very reason for fleeing the Stag Ball the night before.

Rory Flynn in the flesh.

CB

"YOU'RE SURE SHE'LL be here?" Forbes asked. "Then why have I come? I have no desire to see the woman."

Rory grinned. Seated next to Forbes in his fashionable barouche, the one he called *Darling Libby* because, in his words, "like a woman, a coach needs to be handled". He watched the scenery go by as they headed south towards Belgravia.

"But I do," he said. "You're here in case I need a decoy. I was thinking about it all morning, Forbes. I know why she left the Stag Ball."

"Why?"

"Because I chased her out," Rory said with some disgust. "Think about it – I saved her from disgrace only to invite her to dance with me which, for a woman of her stature, would be as bad as if I had molested her in public. I'm not a man women want to be seen with. At least, not respectable women."

Forbes yawned. He'd gone to bed at dawn, like everyone else who had attended the Stag Ball, only to have Rory pounding on his door a few hours later and demanding he bring around his barouche because they had a journey to make to Belgravia. It bumped down the avenue, avoiding pedestrians who were going about their business on this breezy day.

"You have enough women that want to be seen with you

that you should never be lonely a day in your life," Forbes said. "What makes this one so special?"

"Because she is."

He sounded final, as if he didn't want further questions about her. Forbes knew that tone well.

"As you say," he grumbled. "But why am I to be a decoy?"

"In case I need you to call upon the family and distract them so I can prowl around looking for Miss Edith," Rory said. "If she's there, I will find her."

Forbes simply shook his head. "It all seems like a great deal of trouble for just one woman."

"I told you. She's not just any woman."

"I'm coming to suspect that."

They entered the area of Belgravia Square, with the verdant lawns attracting an array of people on this fine day. While Forbes was watching the women, Rory was watching the townhomes. *The largest home on the square*, his grandfather had told him. They made their way around the square, avoiding people and other conveyances, until Rory spied what he thought was, indeed, the largest home on the square.

All of the homes were built from sand-colored stone, four stories tall and sometimes five. The architecture was strong, with pillars guarding doorways and thick, solid walls. Rory had Forbes pull his barouche to a halt just past the largest home on the square and he climbed out onto the sidewalk.

"Well?" Forbes said. "Where are you going?"

Rory was looking at the enormous structure that had his attention. "There," he said, pointing. "Grandfather said it was the largest home on the square and that looks like the largest to me. Doesn't it?"

Forbes craned his neck back to study it. "It's big," he agreed.

"Why would a mere viscount have such a large place?"

Rory shrugged. "Grandfather says the family is obscenely wealthy," he said. "Cattle, evidently."

Forbes yawned again. "Now that we're here, what do you want me to do?"

Rory's gaze glittered with the prospect of seeing Edie. "I am not certain," he said. "Drive around the square a few times and if I don't come running out and jump in for a fast departure, park somewhere within sight of this place and I will find you. Whatever you do, don't leave."

Forbes wasn't so sure this was a good idea, but he didn't argue. "I won't," he said. "But when you're finished with this, I want to return to The Lyon's Den. I lost a small fortune there over the past couple of days that I need to reclaim."

Rory held up a hand, essentially agreeing with him, but his focus was on the house. As Forbes pulled away, mingling with some traffic, Rory headed towards the townhome that had a big balcony on the second floor, projecting over the walkway like a masthead. But as he approached, he began to think of a plan. Now that he was here, what was he going to do? It wasn't as if he could walk up to the door and announce himself.

That brought him to a stop.

No, he couldn't go to the front door. But perhaps he could go to the back door. Perhaps there was a servant back in the mews that he could pay for information.

Perhaps that was the place to start.

Turning in the opposite direction, he walked quickly down the street and rounded the corner. There was less foot traffic on the side street as he hunted for the mews, which he found quickly. There was a massive arch over the entry to the long, narrow alleyway and he headed into the area where horses and carriages were stored for the entire block.

There were both men and women working back here, tending horses or cleaning carriages. It was a busy world, with dogs barking and cats darting across his path. As he neared the house he'd targeted for Rossington House, he noticed a dog running about and a few cats.

And then, he saw her.

He couldn't believe the luck.

Even at a distance, he could see Edie with her sister, sitting on a wooden bench. A smile crossed his lips at the sight of her, realizing he'd been right all along. This *was* Rossington House and he'd been fortunate enough to locate the exact person he wished to see. No paying servants, no sneaking around.

He'd found her.

Moving closer to the mews themselves, he came up on Edie's left side. She'd been talking to her sister, focused on their conversation, and hadn't noticed him. As he came to within a few feet of her, he heard her say something about men driving women to ruin.

He couldn't help his answer.

"Not always," he said quietly.

The young woman next to Edie was startled by his answer and gasped as she turned to him. Edie was a little slower to react, but not by much. When their eyes met, she bolted up from the bench, her eyes wide at him.

"Mr. Flynn," she gasped. "How… what are you doing here?"

He smiled. The woman had been beautiful in the moonlight, but it hadn't done her justice. In the daylight, she was positively radiant.

"I was traveling through Belgravia and thought I might take a chance that you would be in residence," he said. "You left the ball last night before we were properly introduced and I feared for your health and safety. Are you well, Miss Edith?"

Edie nodded, still in disbelief that Rory was standing in front of her. "I'm quite well," she said. She could feel her sister pressing against her and she indicated the young woman. "This is my sister, Matilda."

Rory acknowledged the pale, younger woman. "I see that beauty runs in the family," he said, smiling. "It is an honor, Miss Matilda. Did you enjoy the ball last night?"

Matilda flushed furiously. "We left early," she said. "But… but I liked it while I was there."

"Good," he said. "I am sure there will be many more that you will be invited to."

"I hope so."

The silence that followed was slightly awkward. Rory wanted to speak to Edie, but her sister seemed permanently attached to her hip. He wasn't sure how to ask the girl to leave, so he cleared his throat softly and went to the point.

"May I have a word with you, Miss Edith?" he asked. "Without an audience, preferably."

Edie had no idea what he meant until she saw him look at Matilda. Being that she was thrilled to see him, and didn't mind a private word with him, she turned to her sister.

But there could be… complications.

Her heart began to race.

"Tilly, I want you to keep an eye out for Mama," she instructed quietly. "Go to the garden gate and watch for her. If you see her coming, you will tell me quickly. Please?"

"But do not go too far," Rory said, a twinkle in his eyes. "Your sister must be chaperoned when speaking to an unmarried man."

Matilda's eyes widened. "Me?" she said. "I'm the chaperone?"

Rory nodded, grinning, and Matilda's gaze lingered on him for a moment before she sauntered over to the gate that led towards the garden of Rossington House and, subsequently, the house itself. When she was far enough away but still close enough to bear witness, Edie turned to Rory.

"How on earth did you find me?" she asked, incredulous.

Rory's grin was back. "I asked my grandfather what he knew of your father and he told me about Rossington House," he said. "I assumed you would be here, so I took a chance. I wanted to know why you left before the ball ended last night. Was it something I did?"

Edie wasn't sure how to reply. Was it something he did? Of course it was, but it was a lifelong string of actions and not simply one. She wasn't sure how she could tell him without insulting him.

"My… my mother wasn't feeling well so we had no choice but to leave," she said. "I am sorry I wasn't able to bid you a farewell and thank you for what you did for me."

He waved her off. "It was nothing, but you are welcome," he said. "I wanted to tell you that I very much enjoyed speaking to you and I was wondering… wondering if I could speak with you again sometime. I should like to call on you, Miss Edith. My grandfather is more than happy to make the proper introduction to your parents."

Edie was more than thrilled to hear his intentions. Under normal circumstances, she would have been positively giddy, but it simply wouldn't do. After what her mother had said about him and his family last night, she was quite certain her mother would not receive Rory Flynn. Perhaps it was best that he know it at the start, as disappointing as it was for her to tell him.

She couldn't let the man make a fool of himself.

"I am not certain that is possible," she said with regret. "Mr. Flynn, I…"

"Rory. Please call me Rory."

She eyed him a moment. Calling the man by his first name was quite forward but, then again, the entire association with him had been unconventional.

"Very well," she said hesitantly. "Rory, I'm not certain that would be possible. You see… oh, blast it all. You may as well know the truth. My mother wasn't ill last night. I told her you had invited us to a garden party and she proceeded to tell me that I was to have nothing to do with you. That was why we left. For that reason and also for the fact that she saw Myles in the ballroom. She panicked. She thinks that I am going down the merry path to ruin. Perhaps she's right."

Rory wasn't surprised to hear that. He'd known it all along. But he was disappointed. "I see," he said. "Thank you for being honest. What did she say about me?"

Edie sighed heavily and averted her gaze. "That you were a smuggler, like your father."

"I am."

"I asked you and you did not give me a direct answer."

"I told you that I was many things – and I am. Importing goods is one of my business ventures."

She cocked her head, studying him intently as the breeze blew her dark hair across her face. Perhaps there was a hint of surrender in her expression.

Truth had a way of breaking down those barriers.

"I want you to know that I do not care that you are a smuggler or a pirate or whatever people say you are," she said quietly. "Men must make their living somehow and you are making yours. Perhaps it is not the most honorable profession, but at least you are not a thief or a beggar. It could be worse."

He smiled, but it was without humor. "You may as well know all of it so there are no illusions of grandeur," he said. "I gamble. I own gambling establishments. If there is a money-making venture to be had, I usually participate. I am not a saint, Miss Edith. You may as well know that now because I am quite certain your mother filled your head with the rumors that abound about me, rumors that are more than likely true. But my character is not all damage and ruin. I have my good points. I am loyal to the bone. I would kill or die for my family and friends. And I never, ever lie. My word is my bond."

Edie smiled, but hers was genuine. "I find that all rather exciting," she said. "Perhaps it would bother some, but it does not bother me."

"You *do* understand that Polite Society does not speak fondly of me."

"Nor do they speak fondly of me," Edie said, her smile fading. "At least, that used to be the case. You already know that I was in love with another man. *Was.* He was married and I did not care, so you probably suspect that I am not a saint, either. I have not made wise choices in my life and I suppose that was what my mother was fearful of when we left the ball. Another questionable choice."

"With me?"

"With you."

"She would not have been wrong."

But Edie shook her head. "You come from a fine family, Rory, and your grandfather can smooth over any imperfections you may have," she said. "You will find a wife that is worthy of the grandson of a duke, but do not have any false impressions that I would be such a candidate."

"Why not?"

Those words hung in the air between them. Suddenly, his goal was revealed. The very reason for his presence was now laid bare and, for a moment, they looked at one another in shock – Rory because he'd said it and Edie because she'd heard it.

There was romance in the air.

"Can this be true?" Edie finally breathed. "Did you truly come with such intentions?"

Rory almost shook his head, as if he'd misspoken, but he couldn't bring himself to do it. Indeed, he'd come with such intentions. His attraction to Edie had been so strong from the beginning that he'd never entertained anything else. This beautiful, intelligent woman who found his lifestyle and reputation exciting.

Exciting!

God, maybe there *was* a woman meant just for him and her name was Edie Rhodes.

"I did," he said. "Miss Edith… Edie… may I call you Edie? I don't know why I ask because that is what I am going to call you whether or not you approve. I am a greatly flawed man, but you don't seem to mind. Am I misunderstanding you?"

Edie shook her head, but she was becoming edgy. Uncertain, even. Rory had appeared and declared his intentions and she simply didn't know what to make of it. It was all happening so quickly but, in the same breath, nothing had ever felt so right. With Myles, everything had been an uphill battle and, truth be told, she'd never felt her path with him was clear. She'd never felt that it was the right thing because she'd constantly had to fight for it.

But with Rory…

She wasn't fighting.

Everything was happening intuitively and easily.

God, maybe there *was* a man meant just for her and his name was Rory Flynn.

Except for one thing.

"No," she said, feeling her throat tighten with emotion. "You are not misunderstanding me. Perhaps you think I am a foolish creature because last night I was declaring my love for another man, but as you pointed out, it was not love. I am stubborn – terribly stubborn – so perhaps it was more a matter of refusing to surrender something I wanted. *Thought* I wanted. In any case, it was stupid of me. But what I said earlier is true – I am not meant for you, Rory. You must have someone virtuous and…"

He cut her off. "Virtuous?" he repeated. "Are you mad? You are the most virtuous woman. I *know* you are. You are from a good family with a mother who clearly watches out for you. How could I find someone more virtuous than you?"

Edie was willing to be truthful with him only so far. She simply couldn't confess her darkest sin to a man who thought she was pure and virtuous. Perhaps he was a gambler and a rake of the worst sort, but for a man, that could be acceptable to a certain extent, at least by some. A man could redeem himself in the eyes of the *ton*, but a woman… if Rory married her, it would do little to help his reputation. The poor man didn't need any assistance from her to be even more scorned than he already was.

It was a heartbreaking realization.

Unable to reply, the tears came before she could stop them. Humiliated that she'd started to cry, Edie whirled on her heel and ran off, dashing inside the garden gate and fleeing back to the house. Concerned, Rory followed her to the gate but would go no further. In fact, he sank back against the mews, watching her disappear into the house.

Baffled, he shook his head.

"What did I say?" he muttered to himself.

But it wasn't just to himself. Matilda was still standing there, watching. She'd been watching and listening to everything said. She may have been young, but she knew her sister well. She understood things that no one thought she was old enough to understand.

And she wasn't as naïve as her parents assumed.

"You called her virtuous," she said softly.

Rory looked at her, surprised. "You heard that?"

"I did."

"But why should that upset her so?"

Matilda gazed up at him with her big, dark eyes. "She wants to be," she said. "But Edie… she loved Myles. He promised her that he would divorce his wife and marry her. He told her that quite a lot. Edie used to write him letters every night and send them out with the maid to a tavern in town where Myles had a man who lived there, just to take her messages to him."

Rory had known about Forrester. But what he didn't know was how deeply involved Edie had been with him.

"I see," he said. "How long was this going on?"

"Two years," Matilda said. "But Myles was a friend of my father's, so she has known him a long time. We all have."

Rory digested that bit of information. "She told me about him," he said. "She told me that he lied to her."

Matilda nodded sadly. "My parents think I don't know what happened," she said. "But I know. Edie and I share a bedroom. I know everything that happens with her. I know she believed him when he told her that he loved her. I know she believed him when he told her that he would leave his wife and marry her. One night, he sent her a message asking her to meet him at The Hungry Horse."

"What's that?"

"A tavern near our home," Matilda said quietly. "She slipped out one night and met him there. One of the maids saw her go and followed her. She saw Myles and Edie go into the livery behind the tavern and then come out a short time later. She threatened to tell everyone but my father gave her money and sent her away. She still told people what she knew."

"And your sister knows this?"

Matilda shook her head. "Papa never told her," she said. "I only knew because I heard my parents arguing about it. It threatened to be a terrible scandal so Edie was restricted for at least two years, watched constantly, chaperoned everywhere, until Mama felt the scandal had faded. Until her friends no longer asked about it and went on to other gossip. But Edie... she does not feel as though she's virtuous because of it when the truth was that she only kissed Myles. There was nothing more."

"She told you that?"

"She did."

Rory thought on the truth of the matter, the shame that Edie had been forced to endure as the result of one ill-advised decision. His head turned in the direction of the house as if he could see Edie through the walls, realizing why she'd run from him. Why she'd told him he needed to find a virtuous wife. And then, stupidly, he'd called her virtuous when she knew damned well that she wasn't. She may have been honest with him about many things, but the one thing she'd hidden from him – her scandalous meeting with Forrester in a livery – remained buried.

A shame her parents had struggled to put behind her.

"Now I understand," he said, a hand to his forehead as he tried to think his way through this. "That's why she told me that she wasn't meant for me."

Matilda nodded. "Please don't tell her that I told you," she said, her eyes starting to well. "I love my sister. She is good and kind. But she believed Myles when he told her that he loved her. You cannot become angry that she believed him, can you?"

Rory looked at the girl, seeing the emotion. "Of course not," he said, reaching out to take her hand. "I am not angry at all, at least not with her. Now all of this makes so much sense."

Matilda nodded. "She was so afraid it would ruin her," she said. "It is difficult to be in love with a man who lies to you. My parents treated her like a prisoner for the past two years. This was supposed to be the Season that she entered into Polite Society again and then she met you."

He eyed her. "And your parents told her I would be her ruin just like Myles was, I would imagine."

"I'm sure my mother did."

Rory couldn't help but feel the disgust building in his chest. A beautiful woman who had been manipulated by a silver-tongued lover suffered the additional blow of being hidden away by her parents when the potentially devastating scandal surfaced. Not that he didn't understand why they did it, because he did. Her parents had been forced to take steps to salvage her reputation. It certainly wasn't the first time something like that had happened and Edie certainly wouldn't be the last girl it happened to, but it was a tragedy all around.

Still… Rory considered her virtuous. Compared to the women he knew, she was a veritable saint. He thought her father should know that in this world, someone thought Edie was wonderful and honorable.

Even if that someone was Rory Flynn.

"Miss Matilda," he said after a moment. "Where is your father?"

Matilda pointed to the house. "Inside."

"Will you take me to him?"

Matilda hesitated. Realizing he'd put her in an awkward position, at least in the eyes of her parents, for letting Rory Flynn in the house, he apologized. But he also thanked her.

A few moments with Matilda had made all the difference when it came to Edie.

Leaving the mews, Rory headed around to the front of the house and knocked firmly on the front door.

Frederick Rhodes was in for a big surprise.

CHAPTER ELEVEN

"Thou shalt not be denied by anyone.
Anyone who wants to live a long and healthy life,
that is."

Sin Commandment #11

"I STILL HAVE business in London," Frederick said. "If you want to go home and take the children, that is your decision, but I must remain for the time being."

In the study of Rossington House, Henrietta stood in front of her husband's desk, wringing her hands with worry.

"Then we will go," Henrietta said. "Last night was a disaster in the making, Frederick. First the contact with Rory Flynn and then the appearance of Myles. I am seriously considering disallowing Edie to attend any further balls or social events. All she seems to do is attract the worst kind of man and we must protect Tilly."

Frederick sighed heavily. His wife was a good woman, but she could be extreme at times. "If we disallow Edie to attend anything social, where is she to find a husband?" he asked. "She must find one somewhere, Henny."

"Then you find her a husband," Henrietta implored. "She cannot do it on her own. She hasn't the judgment you have."

Frederick didn't want to argue about his firstborn. He put up a hand to silence his wife. "I will think on it," he said. "It would not be fair to Edie to treat her like a prisoner, however."

"What do you mean a prisoner?" Henrietta said, incensed. "She is *not* a prisoner."

"Maybe not, but you are preparing to isolate her. Don't you think that's a bit severe?"

Henrietta appeared uncertain. "For her own protection."

"Is it?"

Before Henrietta could reply, they heard voices in the front of the house. Since Frederick's study was near the front door, he could hear something that sounded like an argument. He could hear his butler raising his voice to someone. Frederick looked at Henrietta curiously, as if she knew more than he did, but she simply shook her head. She was as puzzled as he was.

"*Stop, sir!*"

It was Frederick's butler. As Frederick rose to his feet, his curiosity turning to concern, a man he didn't recognize suddenly appeared in the doorway of the study.

"Lord Rossington, my name is Rory Flynn."

As Henrietta gasped, Frederick came around the side of his desk, looking at Rory with genuine bewilderment. Considering they'd just been speaking on the man, his appearance was as surprising as it was unexpected.

… or was it?

"Mr. Flynn," he said steadily. "I've heard the name."

Rory nodded, eyeing Lady Rossington as he entered. "I am certain that you have," he said. "My grandfather is the Duke of Savernake. I've come on a most personal matter, my lord. I beg only a moment of your time."

Henrietta looked at her husband in a panic, but Frederick seemed most interested in the appearance of the very man they'd been speaking of. Unlike his wife, he seemed to have a little more tolerance.

"This is most irregular," he said. "We've not formally met, though I know your grandfather."

"I realize that, my lord," Rory said. "But this is quite important. I would say critical in nature, even. It will only take a moment."

"I am afraid I am busy at this time," Frederick said. "Perhaps later…"

"It cannot wait, my lord. I am sorry." When Frederick opened his mouth to protest, Rory held up a hand. "I realize that I am an uninvited guest, but if you will only give me a moment of your time, I will make sure my grandfather knows that you were most generous and accommodating."

He was invoking his grandfather's name and for good reason. Of course Frederick should want the Duke of Savernake to know that he'd been kind to a wayward grandson. That would make him at least tolerant in the old man's eyes. Perhaps even forgivable since Henrietta had fled the ball the night before without so much as a farewell.

Therefore, his protests died.

Frederick could see the tall, dark, and handsome young man before him. He knew the rumors; everyone of import in London and perhaps even England did. The Sinning Flynns had been notorious for years. He'd heard the story of the previous evening from his wife, though she tended to dramatize things, and he'd not yet spoken to his daughter. Now, the very man at the center of the controversy had appeared at his home, which made the situation even more mysterious.

He *was* curious.

"Out of respect for your grandfather, you may proceed," he said. "But make it brief. What is your concern?"

Rory took a deep breath. "Your daughter," he said. "Edith. My lord, there seems to be an issue that I wish to discuss. It has come to my attention that Edith and the rest of your family left the Stag Ball last evening because of me. I have come to take issue with that and declare that nothing untoward happened between your daughter and me. In fact, just the opposite. I saved her."

Frederick's brow furrowed. "Saved her from what?"

"A man named Myles Forrester."

Henrietta gasped again and Frederick's brow furrowed with concern. "Forrester?" he said quite unhappily. "I was not aware that Edie had any contact with him last night."

"She did, my lord. I witnessed it."

"What happened?"

Rory couldn't help but notice the man had not asked him to sit down, which wasn't surprising considering he'd barged in uninvited. It was an utter breach of protocol and he knew it. But the subject was extremely important to him and he suspected he only had a few minutes before the viscount would chase him away.

Therefore, he spoke quickly and to the point.

"I found your daughter in the garden with the man," he said. "I do believe Edie was telling him she no longer wanted to see him again but he would not listen. Another man came upon them and assaulted Forrester. I pulled Edie away and hid her so that your family would be protected from any involvement in a common brawl at the Stag Ball. Such a thing would have been…

scandalous. For your daughter's involvement, your family would have been banned from future gatherings, at the very least."

Frederick was still in shock at what he'd been told. "But my wife saw Forrester at the ball," he said. "Was he not banned for his involvement?"

Rory shrugged. "I do not know, but I suspect he will never return," he said. "Perhaps the decision was made not to remove him for fear of causing a scene. In any case, I had a glorious conversation with your daughter. I discovered her to be kind and bright and compassionate. Her impression on me was lasting, my lord, and if that is any indication what kind of woman she is, I suspect glorious is just the beginning. It is an impression that will last a lifetime."

Frederick wasn't quite sure what to say. "I will thank you for your kind words," he said. "But it was imperative you tell me this?"

Rory shook his head. "Not that," he said. "I was prefacing what I am about to say. My lord, I realize my reputation isn't as perfect as it should be. It is not perfect at all. I live my life the way I want to live it and you should know that I have no regrets except for in this moment. I was told that your wife removed your family from the ball after I invited them to the garden party at my father's home and that your wife did not wish for your family, and more specifically Edie, to be associated with me. Under normal circumstances, I would not take issue with this but, in this case, I must."

Frederick was looking the least bit uncomfortable. "So you've come to scold us?"

"No," Rory said. "I've come to tell you that in spite of my reputation and my dealings, the core of my soul is loyalty to my family and friends. I would kill or die for them. I may not have many virtues, but those that I do have are true. I am a responsible man. I am also an honest one. Perhaps those are qualities you would consider over everything else you've heard because I would like to court your daughter. As the grandson of a duke, I would ask for the consideration."

Henrietta had to put her hand over her mouth so she didn't speak out, a gut response to something she considered unsuitable and horrific. But her place in the home was not as the decision maker. That role was Frederick's. Her eyes went to him, wide and beseeching, but he wasn't looking at her.

He was looking at Rory.

"It seems to me that this is a discussion that must be given more time and thought than I have to give at the moment," he said. "As you said, you have come into my home, uninvited. I have given you time to state whatever it was that compelled you to do so. But when speaking of my daughter and her future, we must go through appropriate channels."

Rory wasn't sure what that meant. This entire situation was uncharted territory for him. "Are you saying that I am invited to return at another time?" he asked.

Frederick didn't reply right away. It was clear that he was thinking it over.

"I will speak with your grandfather first," he said. "At this time, I will not have this conversation with you."

That wasn't good enough for Rory. From what he had just heard, he had a suspicion that he would be cast aside and Edie would end up in a convent somewhere.

It was just a hunch he had.

"Forgive me, my lord," he said. "I have never done things the way they should be done, but a bold man takes risks and, in this case, I must be bold. I must tell you that Edie's failings mean far less to me than they do to you."

Frederick frowned. "What failings?"

Rory fixed on him. "I know of the scandal in the livery," he said, lowering his voice. "I know of her clandestine meeting with Forrester. I know that you are trying to reintroduce her back into Polite Society and keep this part of her past buried, but it seems to me that she is not being given a fair chance in any of this. The moment she met a man whose reputation is questionable, she was whisked away like a naughty child who should be punished."

Frederick stiffened. "Mr. Flynn, I fail to see…"

"It matters," Rory said, cutting him off perhaps a bit too sharply so he forced himself to calm. "I, myself, am a man with faults. That is difficult to admit for a Flynn, but I have my faults. Loyalty, compassion, and the love for my family have never been any of them, however. I understand that Edie was manipulated. She made a mistake. In many ways, she is as flawed as I am, but she is also far more perfect. I only ask that you consider allowing me to court her because you will not find anyone more willing to devote his time and his life to her."

"But…"

Rory wouldn't let him finish. "What if the man you are trying to match her with asks about the livery rumors?" he asked. "Will you tell him the truth? Or will you lie and say that it was nothing at all? If you seek to lie about it, then you will be establishing a relationship for Edie based on a lie. And what if he finds out that you have, in fact, lied to him? Lies never remain buried, my lord. They always surface."

Frederick looked at him, uncomfortable, realizing that Rory had figured out their entire scheme. "Until you find yourself in this position, Mr. Flynn," he said, "with a daughter who chose poorly, you will not understand the lengths a parent will go to in order to save a child."

Rory snorted softly. "My lord, I know what lengths a parent will go through," he said. "I have been watching my parents deal with scandal my entire life. But consider this – how do you think your lies will affect your younger daughter? If your deception is discovered, she will be ruined. I am telling you now that I know of Edie's past and it does not matter to me. Give me this opportunity to make her happy and you will not regret it, I swear it."

It was an impassioned plea. By the time he was finished, Frederick wasn't looking so shocked or so uncomfortable. In fact, he glanced at his wife as he turned away, making his way over to a sideboard that held fine imported brandy.

"Henrietta," he said quietly. "Leave us, my dear."

Henrietta was terribly reluctant. "But you cannot…"

"*Leave.* Please."

She couldn't argue with him. Slipping out of the study, she shut the door as Frederick busied himself at the sideboard. When he turned around, it was with two small crystal glasses of sherry.

"Here," he said. "I think you need this more than I do."

Hesitantly, Rory took the glass and downed the contents in one gulp. The liquid burned down his throat, but Rossington was right. He needed it.

"I did not mean to speak disrespectfully, my lord," he said. "Merely honestly. You view your daughter as a shame and I view her as a salvation."

Frederick glanced at him as he took a seat. "Yours?"

"Mine."

"But shouldn't salvation come from within?"

"Sometimes it needs a catalyst."

"True," Frederick said. His gaze lingered on Rory for a moment. "If it helps, I do not doubt your sincerity. I can see that you mean what you've said. But a man who has lived a life as you have lived yours… sometimes it is difficult to change."

"Not always, my lord," Rory said. "I've never had a reason to change."

"And you feel that Edie is that reason?"

"Will you at least let me prove it to you?"

"How?"

Rory didn't ask for permission for more sherry. He simply went to the table and poured himself more.

"You do understand that my wealth is greater than anyone in my family, including my grandfather?" he said.

Frederick shook his head. "I don't know that much about you other than your womanizing and gambling reputation."

Rory downed the sherry. "Your daughter would live like a queen," he said, smacking his lips. "There is nothing I cannot buy her. Nothing I would not give her were she to become my wife."

"But the gambling and womanizing?"

"Merely something to fill the emptiness, I suppose," Rory said. "I had no reason not to gamble or spend time with questionable women."

"And you think you can give all that up, just like that?"

"May I ask you a question, my lord?"

"What is it?"

"Did you have women before you married Lady Rossington?"

Frederick prepared to tell him that it was none of his affair, but he stopped short. He ended up snorting, handing his glass to Rory, who filled it for him and handed it back.

"All men have women before they marry," he muttered. "I was no different. If you want to know the truth, I did not live like a saint."

"Then you understand my position."

Frederick sipped his sherry as Rory pounded down another glass. "I understand what it is to be a young man who lives as he chooses," he said. "But if you truly wish to court my daughter, that will end."

"It will."

"Because of your eloquence when presenting your case, I am willing to overlook much of your reputation and even defend you if necessary, but not if you break your word to me."

"I am a man of my word, Lord Rossington."

Frederick merely acknowledged that he understood him, not that he believed him. He took another sip of sherry.

"The truth is that as much as Polite Society likes to turn their noses up at men like you, I can promise you that most of the men who comprise that group have lived freely and wildly at some point in their lives," he said. "The *ton* is full of hypocrites, Mr. Flynn. They love to point fingers and whisper about those who live their lives in a less conventional way while all the time, the men have mistresses and the women have affairs. They're just not as bold about it as you are."

Rory could see, in that instant, that Frederick had the capacity for understanding a man like him. He was right about the *ton* – they were hypocrites. They knew it and everyone else knew it but, still, they judged people.

It was simply the way of things.

"They have been weighing and measuring me since the day

I was born," he said quietly. "They weighed and measured my father and tore my mother apart when she married him. Shall I tell you something?"

"Please do."

Drink in hand, Rory moved for a stiff, leather-bound chair. "Last night, I was going to seek revenge upon a man who had been speaking ill of my mother since she broke her engagement with him to marry my father," he said. "I was going to seduce one of his daughters and compromise her, humiliating the entire family. That was the plan, anyway. I will still seek revenge, though it will not be through seduction. Not if you allow me to court your daughter. But the point is that I defend those I love and punish those who hurt them. If you permit me, your daughter will fall into that category, too. I will defend her to the death, Lord Rossington. All other women will cease to exist for me."

"Nothing like a reformed rogue, as it were?"

"Rogues are rogues for a reason, usually," Rory said. "They are lacking something. They are trying to fill or find something. Sometimes they don't know what they need or want, but when they find it… knowing how hard it was to find that peace, they make for good husbands."

Frederick could see the passion, the determination. This was no flighty, ridiculous young man who behaved horribly and didn't care about the consequences. This was a deliberate and intense man, mature and wise beyond his years, who fought for what he believed in.

Frederick could see it in everything about him.

But that brought up something in his mind, a very salient point.

He had an idea.

"A few minutes ago, I asked you to prove your sincerity," he said. "Are you willing to do that?"

"I will do whatever you ask."

That was a terrifying amount of power given who had spoken the words. This was Rory Flynn, a man with a wicked reputation. He could do whatever he said he would do. Frederick inspected his glass for a moment, thoughtfully, before speaking.

"You said you were prepared to seek revenge last night over a man who wronged your mother," he said. Then his eyes flicked up to Rory. "Would you be prepared to do the same against a man who wronged Edie?"

The light of understanding flickered in Rory's eyes. "Let me guess," he said. "Forrester?"

"For what he has done, he deserves no less."

The corners of Rory's mouth twitched with a smile. "I would do this and gladly," he said. "What would you have me do?"

"I do not want to see him again," Frederick said. "Make it so that he never shows himself to Edie again. Ever. The man has done unfathomable damage and I want him to pay. If you feel for her as you say you do, then you will want that, also."

"With pleasure, my lord."

"Return to me when the deed is done and I will let you court my daughter."

Rory didn't have to be asked twice.

CHAPTER TWELVE

*"There comes a time in every man's life when roads lead
to different destinations.
Be sure not to choose the road to ruin."*
Sin Commandment #12

SHE'D HEARD HIM come in the house.
Edie had been standing on the stair landing leading
from the first to the second floor, the one with the enormous
window that overlooked the garden and the mews. On sunny
days, it was like a picture window into heaven because of the
vibrant sky against the lush and colorful garden, but she'd been
standing at the window in tears, not quite ready to run to her
bedroom and shut the door but also not quite ready to return to
Rory and apologize for her behavior.

She simply couldn't help it.

He'd struck a chord with her in calling her virtuous. She
could have taken any other word – lovely, kind, or even silly –
but virtuous had sent her fleeing. Because she knew that she
wasn't virtuous and he didn't. He didn't know anything about
her.

He was attracted to an illusion.

An illusion of her parents' creation.

Her parents had tried very hard to present her as a normal, honorable young lady after the events of two years ago. It was a dark period in her past that would remain dark and buried as her parents tried to convince the *ton* that the eldest daughter of Viscount Rossington was an eligible marital prospect by bringing her to the Stag Ball.

Every eligible young woman at the ball was looking for a husband and Edie had been no exception, at least in the eyes of the *ton*. They whispered about her – she knew that – but because her father had an excellent reputation and the family in general was well respected, Edie wasn't shunned. She was still whispered about, but she wasn't shunned.

She was an illusion.

She'd been honest with Rory about everything else so it was probably best if she was honest about this, too. If Rory was appalled and talked about it, then her chances of a good marriage were gone. Even if the news was coming from a Sinning Flynn, it would be believed. She was taking a great chance in telling him that, but for her own sake, she felt she had to. Her parents had tried so hard to bury a scandal that she was about to openly admit.

She had been standing on the landing, trying to summon the courage, when she saw Rory depart and Matilda head into the house.

Greatly curious, she went downstairs, trying to catch a glimpse of Rory through the widows facing the side avenue. Rossington House was right on a corner, so she could see people and carriages passing by. She could also see Rory. She followed him right up until he ended up on the main avenue and she though that would be her last look at him.

But it wasn't.

Rory went right to the front door and pounded.

Her father's butler, a big man with a deep voice, answered. As Edie cowered around a corner, trying to hear what was said, she could hear Rory's voice and the butler's voice, but not the actual words. Those came a few seconds later when voices were raised and Rory demanded to see Lord Rossington.

Rory finally pushed past the butler and went straight into her father's study.

Startled, Edie tried to hear what was being said but they were too far away. When the door shut and the butler was finally sent away in a flustered mess, Edie slipped closer until she was able to get near the door.

And what she heard shocked her to the bone.

So much came out in that brief conversation between Rory and her father, not the least of which was the fact that Rory knew about the scandal in the livery at The Hungry Horse. Edie had no idea how he could know such a thing, *truly* know such a thing, and she resisted the urge to run and hide until she heard more.

But Rory didn't seem to care about any of that.

He wanted to court her.

Overwhelmed with what she was hearing, Edie had to scrambled to hide when Henrietta was asked to leave. The study door opened and slammed shut with her mother scurrying away with as much frustration as the butler had. Rory seemed to have that effect on them. Once her mother walked away, heading up the stairs, Edie returned to her position with her ear against the door, but the voices were so low that she couldn't hear much more. The removal of her mother had the men speaking in softer tones and, anxious, she moved away from the door and went to sit near the door leading to the garden, a sunny corner that her mother sometimes used for her sewing but with a clear view of the study door.

And she waited.

It was less than an hour when Rory finally emerged from her father's study and headed for the rear door. He would have walked right past Edie had she not called out to him, quietly.

"Rory?"

He froze, turning in the direction of the voice and spying her through the doorway of the small room. She was sitting at the window, illuminated by the light that danced around her like a halo. He quickly moved in her direction as she stood up from the seat.

"I was contemplating apologizing to you for my silly behavior when I heard you knock at the door," she said before he could speak. "I will not ask you what you said to my father, but I wanted to tell you that I am sorry I ran from you. It was inexcusable."

Rory smiled faintly. "I hardly noticed," he said. "Perhaps you had something very important to tend to inside and you did not have time to tell me."

It was her turn to smile. "You are kind," she said. "But, then again, you have been kind since I met you. For two people who met by chance and have yet to be formally introduced, I would say that we have had more than our share of interaction."

Rory couldn't disagree. He indicated for her to regain her seat at the window bench as he pulled up a small chair against the wall.

"Even if you will not ask me what business I had with your father, I will tell you," he said. "The business had to do with you."

She nodded faintly. "I know," she said. "Although I told you that I will not ask you what your business was with my father, the truth is that I heard some of it. May I ask a question?"

"Certainly."

"Who told you?"

"Told me what?"

"About me. Who told you?"

Rory understood. "It wasn't rumor or gossip if that is what you mean," he said, thinking she seemed quite calm about such an explosive subject. "It was a reliable source, told to me in the strictest confidence. I will never repeat it. Are you angry?"

Edie shook her head. "No," she said, leaning back against the wall in a resigned gesture. "In fact, I had made the decision to tell you myself before I heard what you and my father were discussing. I cannot imagine what impression I ever made on you that you would want to court me, even after knowing everything. It would not be fair to you not to tell you."

He folded his arms across his broad chest, leaning against the wall behind him, adopting a casual stance because she was. Though Edie's manner seemed to suggest defeat more than anything, Rory wasn't going to give in to it.

He'd never been more elated about anything in his life.

This flawed woman who might actually accept his suit.

"If you know half the things about me that are said, then you know I am in no position to judge," he said. "I look at you and I don't see a fallen woman or whatever your parents would have you believe. You're not fallen, Edie. And you're still virtuous to me."

"How can you even say that?"

"Virtue means many things but, in this case, it means honor," he said. "You were going to tell me of your deepest secret yourself which means you are a woman of honor. That kind of honor and honesty must be respected and celebrated."

"What do you mean?"

He shrugged, averting his gaze. But he ended up looking at her hands. She had such lovely hands. Covered by the gloves the previous night, he'd never noticed.

"I have spent my entire life trying to satisfy something within me that I simply couldn't satisfy," he said. "Not money nor women nor gambling could satisfy me. I feel as if I've spent my entire life searching for something that would bring me happiness but I never knew what that was until I met you. An honest and vulnerable woman who is like me in many ways. Does it seem strange for me to say that?"

Edie had heard him speaking to her father, so she wasn't completely surprised by his declaration, but even so, hearing it from his lips brought her a sense of awe.

"Yes," she said honestly. "Because I've never had anyone say such things to me. How can you possibly know such things about me? We've only spoken a few times. You have seen me at my very worst. How can you know I am someone you would like to court?"

He unfolded his arms and sat forward, closer to her. "If you have grace and dignity at your worst, imagine what you will have at your best," he said, his eyes glimmering warmly. "Edie... I cannot tell you what has drawn me to you, only that something has. Something great and glorious. Meeting you made me forget a life that I thought was set, a path that I thought was clear."

"What path was that?"

He debated about telling her. But since she had been honest

with him, he thought it only right to be honest with her. He'd told her father, after all.

Perhaps it was time to start trusting people a little.

"I was at the Stag Ball last night because I had sworn revenge upon a man who has slandered my mother for years," he said. "I told you that I have a strong sense of loyalty to my family. I suppose it is the Irish in me. But I attended the ball with the sole purpose of seeking this man, and his daughters, and making sure they left the ball in humiliation. I'd been waiting years for this, Edie, and last night was my chance. But I met you and it was as if the moon and stars aligned somehow. Though I've not forgotten my vow, you had my attention, all of it, from nearly the moment I met you. Needless to say, my plans for revenge did not come to fruition."

Edie was serious as she looked at him. "But why revenge?" she said. "Why must you do this?"

"Because it is time the Flynns fought for their honor a little," he said, sounding grim. "The man I speak of was once my mother's betrothed. When my mother left him for my father, this man spoke ill of my mother and continued to do so for years. His own brother was my instructor at Oxford and the brother spent a good deal of time humiliating me in front of my peers. It was time for me to pay them back for so much hurt and shame."

"Oxford," she repeated. "I did not know you attended Oxford."

He smiled faintly. "There is much you do not know about me," he said. "All I ask is that you give me the chance to teach you."

The expression on her face was full of hope, something she'd not had in a very long time.

"Are you *certain*?" she asked softly.

He nodded, moving his chair closer to her. "Very much," he said. "You make me want to be a better man, Edie. I've never wanted that before. I've never cared."

Edie gazed back at him, feeling a myriad of emotions. The last time she'd had a man this close to her, it was Myles as he lied to her yet again. She could always tell when he was lying to her, or trying to, because he began to tremble. His voice trembled. She used to find it endearing but as she listened to Rory's impassioned plea, she realized that it had all been ridiculous and tiresome. Rory had been correct; she hadn't loved Myles. She had been in love with the idea of love and nothing more. She hadn't known the difference.

Until now.

Now, gazing into Rory's handsome face, she could see so many possibilities. She could see a man who understood her sins and forgave them. She could see a man who was imperfect but who wanted to do better.

And he wanted to do it with her by his side.

It was difficult to know how people fell in love. Sometimes it took years. Sometimes days. Sometimes hours. It was simply a matter of knowing when the situation and the person were right. A man with so many flaws understood flaws. He understood her failings. Edie knew, as long as she lived, that she could never ask for anything better. As he reached out to take her fingers, she lifted both hands and gently cupped his face.

"Swear to me that this is what you truly want," she whispered.

Rory closed his eyes to her soft, gentle touch. "It is what I truly want."

"And swear to me that from this day forward, I will be the

only woman you ever think about."

"I swear it."

"The only woman you will ever love."

"I cannot swear that."

"*What*?"

His eyes opened, twinkling with humor. "I love my mother," he said. "And if we have a daughter, I will love her, also."

She fought off a grin. "Very well," she said. "You may love your mother and our girl children. But any other woman…"

"There will never *be* any other woman," he murmured. "Our path may not be easy, but it is our path and we will stay the course. We will fight for our right to be happy. I will never leave your side, Edie. Not even after the stars fall from the heavens and the moon is but ashes. Even then, I shall remain by your side, for always."

Edie believed him. There was nothing about the man that didn't scream sincerity and she believed him without question.

Without reserve.

Forever.

Reaching out, Rory put his arms around her, gently, and pulled her to him, slanting his mouth over hers and kissing her gently. She tasted so delicious that he pulled her closer, feasting on lips that belonged to him. Tasting the woman he would taste for the rest of his life. Her scent was intoxicating, filling his nostrils, making his heart race. That kiss, that moment, was seared into his brain.

For eternity.

When Frederick came out of his study a few minutes later, he happened to catch sight of Rory and Edie in an amorous embrace. They were lost in each other's arms and although Frederick should have separated them and thrown Rory into the street, he didn't have the heart to. Well did he remember what it was like to kiss the woman he was going to marry.

With a grin, he looked the other way and went about his business.

CHAPTER THIRTEEN

*"Like a fine wine, the taste of revenge changes as it
grows older..."*
Sin Commandment #13

The Pox Tavern
London

"**Y**OU TRACKED HIM here?" Rory asked.

Gabriel DeWolfe, an old friend, nodded grimly. "Inside," he said. "You told me who you were looking for and I put my men on it. Forrester wasn't difficult to find. The man doesn't cover his tracks in the least."

Rory nodded, peering inside the dirty panes of glass, into the most notorious tavern in all of London. The Pox had been around for centuries, with different owners, but always the same clientele – people with no names, or those who wanted to forget, or those who simply wanted a good time with no commitment. The bad, the ugly, and the incorrigible were regular patrons. There were a thousand reasons for frequenting a place like that and not one of them was honorable.

There was still gambling at The Pox, infamous for that

particular feature because a man could bet on anything and everything, making it a dangerous place, indeed. Rory had once tried to buy a stake in The Pox, but the risks were great. The current owner ran a ring of thugs who roughed up business owners and merchants near the River Thames who refused to pay a protection fee. As Rory had said many times, he was many things, but being an extortionist wasn't one of them.

Even a Flynn had his standards.

That didn't mean he didn't enjoy a game at The Pox now and again, which ran in direct competition with his own gambling enterprise, another ancient establishment called Gomorrah. Gomorrah was more of a combination gambling den and brothel while The Pox was everything else.

It was a wild place.

But they'd found Myles Forrester here.

"Where are your men now, Gabe?" he asked.

Gabriel, a tall and handsome man, tilted his head back towards the livery behind The Pox. "In the alley," he said. "They can move in and collect Forrester if you want them to. I wasn't sure if you wanted to do this yourself."

DeWolfe had a private security service, men hired by the wealthy for a variety of protection and security reasons, but Rory had called upon him for assistance with Myles Forrester, who was particularly squirrely.

It had been an interesting hunt.

After his encounter with Rossington, Rory had set off to find Forrester. That's when he called upon Gabriel, who did this kind of thing for a living. After the Stag Ball, Forrester had retreated to a London hotel he frequented and, as Rory found out, had tried to make contact with Edie by sending her a message through his valet. Edie had returned the message unopened, unaware that Rory had been tasked with removing Forrester from her life permanently, but that rejected message was enough to give Rory a direction.

Forrester was staying at Grenier's.

It was a fashionable hotel for the *ton*, but by the time Rory got there, Forrester had left and it had been a chase ever since. Frederick thought he might have even come to Rossington House to contact Edie directly because a servant recognized him on the street in front of the home, but he never came to the house. DeWolfe's men trailed him to The Pox, a seedy establishment for a man who was part of Polite Society, but it didn't matter why he was here, only that he was.

The hunt was over.

"I do not need to go into The Pox myself," Rory said after a moment of deliberation. "Have your men bring him out here. My men from Cornwall are across the way with a wagon. See them?"

He was pointing to the road that paralleled the river. There were at least five men standing around an old cart, filled with straw and barrels. There was also a coffin on the cart, a plain pine box, just waiting to be filled.

Gabriel could see it in the light of the torches.

"Is *that* what you intend to transport him in?" He grinned.

Rory showed little emotion. "I have been tasked with making sure the man never returns to London," he said. "Outright murder isn't something I would indulge in, so I will remove Forrester, who will more than likely wish I'd killed him before this is over with."

Gabriel was trying not to laugh. "What do you intend to do?"

"You'll see," Rory said with a glimmer in his eyes. "But

before I depart, I want to speak to you about something else I'll need your help with."

"What is that?"

"I've a score to settle with the Earl of Exford," Rory said. "As, it turns out, I can no longer settle it the way I'd intended. My plan was to ruin one of the daughters but, somehow, I don't think ruining an innocent woman's life is the way to go about it. My vengeance is against the father, not the daughters."

Gabriel looked at him curiously. "The Rory Flynn I've known for years would not care whose life he ruins."

"The Rory Flynn you've known for years has grown a conscience when it comes to innocent young women," Rory said, making a face as if such a thing was distasteful. "Do you know of anyone who can ruin the man financially?"

"Perhaps," Gabriel said. "What did you have in mind?"

Rory pondered the question for a moment. "I understand Exford likes to invest his money in speculations," he said. "I heard a rumor that he was interested in purchasing his own vineyard in Burgundy."

"Who told you that?"

"My grandfather's butler, of all people," Rory said. "He heard Exford talking about it at the Stag Ball. In fact, several people heard him talk about it. He made no secret of it, hoping that somehow it might attract a husband for his daughters. What man wouldn't want to marry into a family with its own vineyard?"

"Ah!" Gabriel was beginning to get the picture. "And you want someone to pose as a Burgundian willing to sell a vineyard?"

"Or a Flemish lord with ancient family vineyards looking to offload them because he needs the money."

Gabriel grinned. "I know exactly what you mean."

"Good," Rory said, satisfied that his plan for Exford would still come to completion even though it wasn't the way he had originally intended. But somehow, this way seemed more fulfilling. "Meanwhile... tell your men in the alley to bring Forrester to me."

Gabriel did.

The DeWolfe men entered from the alley, pushing into The Pox and cornering Forrester as he sat with two women he was plying with drink. That tremulous, little boy appeal was abruptly cut short when the men addressed him by name and he responded. Pushing the women aside, they lifted Forrester out of his seat and literally carried the man outside as he struggled and protested.

There, they were met by Rory's men from Cornwall, men who were part of his smuggling fleet. Pirates, some would call them. But they were mostly men of profit and adventure. Rory paid them extremely well for their loyalty and because of that, they would do anything for him.

Even kidnap someone.

They took Myles Forrester, happily.

Gabriel DeWolfe only heard what happened to Forrester quite some time later when he happened to run into Forbes Dinnington. As Forbes told it, Myles Forrester was taken all the way to Mousehole, Cornwall, confined to a coffin, where Rory anchored his fleet of seven fast and sleek ships. They were some of the fastest ships in the world and they had to be for the jobs they undertook. Myles was bundled up onto a ship that was heading for China.

A journey that took several months.

The last anyone saw of Myles Forrester was when he was

taken off the ship at Shanghai, put in a cage, and became part of a caravan heading for Mongolia. Some say he became a prisoner of the Qing dynasty. Others said he ended up becoming a servant in the house of a fine dowager. No one knew for sure. But the truth is that he never came back.

And that was the way Rory had planned it.

For Edie, he would have plucked the moon from the sky and given it to her had she asked for it, but sending the man who had tried to ruin her life into exile was a lot more satisfying.

When Frederick found out, he thought so, too.

EPILOGUE

"Sometimes, life brings the joy of surprising things."
Sin Commandments – last entry

Rossington House
One year later

"DO THESE THINGS always take so long?"

The question came from Rory as he sat in Frederick's study, nursing his fourth brandy of the afternoon and feeling the least bit woozy. But his wooziness wasn't only from the brandy.

The wait for his son was in full swing.

Frederick was sitting behind his desk, brandy within arm's reach. He grinned at his nervous son-in-law, a man he'd become quite fond of.

"My wife has given birth to two children," he said. "With Edie, it took two days, but with Tilly, it took an hour. At least, it felt that way. I suppose every woman is different."

"I suppose," Rory said. "But I've no experience with this kind of thing. How can you remain so calm?"

"Simple," Frederick said. "I drink my brandy and try not to

think about it. Shall we play cards to pass the time?"

Rory eyed him. "No," he said flatly. "I'll be distracted and you'll end up winning a fortune. But that was a nice try."

Frederick laughed softly and turned back to his drink as Rory found himself looking at the ceiling. Edie was up there. She'd been in labor with their first child for about eight hours, since the early morning. They'd been at Rossington House for the past few months because that was where Edie wanted their child to be born, in the very house where she'd been born. But mostly, she very much wanted the comfort of Rossington and the reputable midwives and doctors of London.

It had been Frederick who had paid for the very best midwife he could find, mostly because Edie didn't want a male doctor in her room with her legs spread, as she put it. Now came the waiting game, as Henrietta and Matilda were in the room with Edie while Rory quite gladly waited it out with Frederick, a man he'd become close to over the past year.

Unable to continue sitting, Rory stood up and began to pace.

"Hopefully, it will all be over soon and I shall be holding my son in my arms," he said. "And this midwife is the very best? The very best reputation?"

Frederick had answered that question about twenty times over the past few months. "The very best, I promise," he said. "If you do not believe me, go upstairs and see for yourself."

Rory shook his head. As a man, he was fearless, but as a husband and father, childbirth terrified him.

"I believe you," he said. "I promised my mother that I would send word to her the moment we knew. She wanted to come to London, you know, but she has been ill and my father would not allow her to travel."

Frederick nodded. "I know," he said. "But I look forward to seeing your parents again when they come to see the new baby."

Sean and Amy had been to London for the wedding of Rory and Edie about a year ago, shortly after the death of the Duke of Savernake, but they'd returned to Cornwall a few months later where Amy had contracted an illness in her chest. The death of her father had weakened her spirit and Sean was convinced that it had also affected her health, hence her inability to recover from something as common as a chest cold.

It was something Rory didn't like to think about.

Two deaths of two people he loved in a short amount of time was something he simply couldn't fathom.

The truth was that the death of his grandfather had left a hole in his heart. He was still grieving the man who had passed on just when he was coming to know him, but he was grateful that he'd had the chance to strengthen their relationship towards the end. There was no longer the disinterested disconnect between them but, in the duke's last days, their bond had grown into something more familial and warm. He only wished the duke had lived to see the birth of a great-grandchild.

It was his one regret.

As Rory sat there, musing about his grandfather, one of Rossington's footmen entered the study.

"Mr. Flynn," he said. "There is a man to see you in the mews."

Rory looked over his shoulder at him. "Who is it?"

"He says DeWolfe sent him."

That had Rory on his feet. He quickly made his way out of the house, through the verdant garden, and to the mews where, indeed, one of Gabriel's men was waiting for him. Rory recognized him as having been at The Pox all those months ago.

"You have a message for me?" Rory asked.

The man, older and somewhat grizzled, nodded as he motioned for Rory to follow him. Rory did, away from the mews and the servants who were working on Rossington's fine barouche.

"Well?" Rory said impatiently when they were far enough away. "What is it?"

The man turned to him. "Gabriel wanted me to tell you that, by tonight, it will be all over London that the Earl of Exford will have lost all of his money to a known swindler," he said quietly. "Exford is trying very hard to keep this news quiet, but we've already been whispering it to the servants of some of the most important people in London. By tonight, everyone will know."

Rory's eyebrows lifted. "Finally," he said, pleasure echoing in his voice. "The Scotsman finally came through, did he?"

The man nodded. "A criminal known as Gregor MacGregor convinced Exford to invest the majority of his money in a vineyard in the Loire Valley. He promised Exford that he'd be a rich man. But MacGregor is a known swindler. He gave Exford forged documents and maps, worked the deal, and the man fell right into the trap."

A smile tugged on Rory's lips. "He lost everything?"

The man nodded, seeing the delight in Rory's eyes. "Mostly everything," he said. "According to MacGregor, Exford just returned from France and the lands he does not own. He nearly started another war with France because the French count living on the lands took great offense to Exford attempting to evict him. The man made a damned fool out of himself. Once the news of his folly spreads, his shame will be endless."

Rory couldn't help the smile now. It was exactly what he

wanted to hear. Finally, his revenge against Exford had come to fruition and he couldn't have been more delighted. Better still, he didn't have to ruin an innocent woman's life to do it. Since his marriage to Edie, he was a kinder and gentler man, but that didn't extend to Exford. For all of those years the man tore down Amy, for all of the pain and strife he'd caused, now he was going to know the taste of humiliation and failure.

Rory couldn't have been happier about it.

"I can move the situation along," he said. "I will be delighted to tell Rossington about Exford's failure and I will also send a message to the new Duke of Savernake, Uncle Martin. The Savernake servants will spread the news more quickly than a spark on kindling. Exford will know shame as he's never known before when I am finished with him."

The man nodded in agreement. "Gabriel wants to know if you need anything else."

Rory shook his head. "Tell Gabriel that I am pleased," he said. "Quite pleased. In fact, tell him that I have one hundred bottles of the finest French claret with his name on them. I will have them delivered tomorrow."

The man grinned. "I will tell him."

As the man scurried back down the mews, Rory turned for the house. His vengeance was evidently satisfied, his wife was delivering his first child, and life as he knew it was better than it had ever been. Sometimes, he still couldn't believe it. That terrible rake known as Rory Flynn had found joy and comfort in something he never thought he would.

A wife and family.

He was still surprised to realize that.

He was halfway across the garden when Henrietta suddenly appeared in the garden door, waving frantically at him.

"Rory!" she called.

Rory saw her and bolted, rushing to the house faster than he'd ever moved in his life. "Well?" he demanded. "Is Edie in trouble?"

Henrietta smiled, which was a rare occurrence when it came to Rory. She'd had an entire year to become used to the man and saw, as everyone else did, that he was a sincere, compassionate, and loving husband and father. The transformation had been astonishing, something that softened even Henrietta's hardened heart.

But today was a day for rejoicing. Reaching out, she put a hand on his arm.

"No," she said. "Edie is quite well. The baby has arrived. You have a son, Rory. A fine son who looks just like Edie."

Rory didn't remember running from the garden all the way to the bedroom on the third floor, the one he shared with his wife. The very room she had been born in those years ago. What he did remember was the feeling when the midwife placed his son in his arms for the first time and he found himself looking at a baby that, he thought, looked more like him. He also remembered the feeling when he looked at his exhausted, smiling wife.

Joy.

Unmitigated joy.

Little Wellesbourne Sean Frederick Hugh Flynn, or Welles – Wellie to his mother – had a life ahead of him that he could have never imagined. Rory had it all planned out, but as he looked at that tiny face, all he could see was the culmination of dreams he never even knew he had. From the last Stag Ball where he'd planned to execute his vengeance to the bedside of his wife as he held their son in his arms, the reality that his life had become seemed like a fantasy to him. A fantasy that he would gladly indulge in for the rest of his life. Rory Flynn, the wildest Flynn brother of all, was wild no more.

But Welles grew up with his father's wild streak.

Another story for another time.

○ THE END ○

Kathryn Le Veque Novels

While Angels Slept
Godspeed
Age of Gods and Mortals

Great Lords of le Bec:
Great Protector

House of de Royans:
Lord of Winter
To the Lady Born
The Centurion

Lords of Eire:
Echoes of Ancient Dreams
Blacksword
The Darkland

Ancient Kings of Anglecynn:
The Whispering Night
Netherworld

Battle Lords of de Velt:
The Dark Lord
Devil's Dominion
Bay of Fear
The Dark Lord's First Christmas
The Dark Spawn
The Dark Conqueror
The Dark Angel

Reign of the House of de Winter:
Lespada
Swords and Shields

De Reyne Domination:
Guardian of Darkness
A Cold Wynter's Knight
With Dreams
The Fallen One
Black Storm

House of d'Vant:
Tender is the Knight (House of d'Vant)
The Red Fury (House of d'Vant)

The Dragonblade Series:
Fragments of Grace
Dragonblade
Island of Glass
The Savage Curtain
The Fallen One

Great Marcher Lords of de Lara
Dragonblade

House of St. Hever
Fragments of Grace
Island of Glass
Queen of Lost Stars

Lords of Pembury:
The Savage Curtain

Lords of Thunder: The de Shera Brotherhood Trilogy
The Thunder Lord
The Thunder Warrior
The Thunder Knight

The Great Knights of de Moray:
Shield of Kronos
The Gorgon

The House of De Nerra:
The Promise
The Falls of Erith
Vestiges of Valor
Realm of Angels

Highland Warriors of Munro:
The Red Lion

Deep Into Darkness

The House of de Garr:
Lord of Light
Realm of Angels

Saxon Lords of Hage:
The Crusader
Kingdom Come

High Warriors of Rohan:
High Warrior

The House of Ashbourne:
Upon a Midnight Dream

The House of D'Aurilliac:
Valiant Chaos

The House of De Dere:
Of Love and Legend

St. John and de Gare Clans:
The Warrior Poet

The House of de Bretagne:
The Questing

The House of Summerlin:
The Legend

The Kingdom of Hendocia:
Kingdom by the Sea

Regency Historical Romance:
Sin Like Flynn: A Regency
Historical Romance Duet

Gothic Regency Romance:

Emma

Contemporary Romance:

**Kathlyn Trent/Marcus Burton
Series:**
Valley of the Shadow
The Eden Factor
Canyon of the Sphinx

**The American Heroes Anthology
Series:**
The Lucius Robe
Fires of Autumn
Evenshade
Sea of Dreams
Purgatory

**Other non-connected
Contemporary Romance:**
Lady of Heaven
Darkling, I Listen
In the Dreaming Hour
River's End
The Fountain

Sons of Poseidon:
The Immortal Sea

**Pirates of Britannia Series (with
Eliza Knight):**
Savage of the Sea by Eliza Knight
Leader of Titans by Kathryn Le
Veque
The Sea Devil by Eliza Knight
Sea Wolfe by Kathryn Le Veque

Note: All Kathryn's novels are designed to be read as stand-alones, although many have cross-over characters or cross-over family groups. Novels that are grouped together have related characters or family groups. You will notice that some series have the same books; that is because they are cross-overs. A hero in one book may be the secondary character in another.

There is NO reading order except by chronology, but even in that case, you can still read the books as stand-alones. No novel is connected to another by a cliff hanger, and every book has an HEA.

Series are clearly marked. All series contain the same characters or family groups except the American Heroes Series, which is an anthology with unrelated characters.

For more information, find it in **A Reader's Guide to the Medieval World of Le Veque**.

About Kathryn Le Veque

Bringing the Medieval to Romance

KATHRYN LE VEQUE is a critically acclaimed, multiple USA TODAY Bestselling author, an Indie Reader bestseller, a charter Amazon All-Star author, and a #1 bestselling, award-winning, multi-published author in Medieval Historical Romance with over 100 published novels.

Kathryn is a multiple award nominee and winner, including the winner of Uncaged Book Reviews Magazine 2017 and 2018 "Raven Award" for Favorite Medieval Romance. Kathryn is also a multiple RONE nominee (InD'Tale Magazine), holding a record for the number of nominations. In 2018, her novel WARWOLFE was the winner in the Romance category of the Book Excellence Award and in 2019, her novel A WOLFE AMONG DRAGONS won the prestigious RONE award for best pre-16th century romance.

Kathryn is considered one of the top Indie authors in the world with over 2M copies in circulation, and her novels have been translated into several languages. Kathryn recently signed with Sourcebooks Casablanca for a Medieval Fight Club series, first published in 2020.

In addition to her own published works, Kathryn is also the President/CEO of Dragonblade Publishing, a boutique publishing house specializing in Historical Romance. Dragonblade's success has seen it rise in the ranks to become Amazon's #1 e-book publisher of Historical Romance (K-Lytics report July 2020).

Kathryn loves to hear from her readers. Please find Kathryn on Facebook at Kathryn Le Veque, Author, or join her on Twitter @kathrynleveque. Sign up for Kathryn's blog at www.kathrynleveque.com for the latest news and sales.

.

Lightning Source UK Ltd.
Milton Keynes UK
UKHW020738070722
405516UK00010B/762